SECRETS *of* POWER
PERSUASION *for* SALESPEOPLE

SECRETS *of* POWER PERSUASION *for* SALESPEOPLE

ROGER DAWSON

Author of **Secrets of Power Negotiating**

CAREER PRESS

Franklin Lakes, NJ

Copyright © 2003 by Roger Dawson

SECRETS OF POWER PERSUASION FOR SALESPEOPLE
EDITED AND TYPESET BY JOHN J. O'SULLIVAN
Cover design by Johnson Design
Printed in the U.S.A. by Book-mart Press

To order this title, please call toll-free 1-800-CAREER-1 (NJ and Canada: 201-848-0310) to order using VISA or MasterCard, or for further information on books from Career Press.

The Career Press, Inc., 3 Tice Road, PO Box 687,
Franklin Lakes, NJ 07417
www.careerpress.com

Portions of this book were previously published in *Secrets of Power Persuasion* (published by Prentice-Hall) and are used with the permission of the publisher.

Library of Congress Cataloging-in-Publication Data

Dawson, Roger, 1940-
    Secrets of power persuasion for salespeople / by Roger Dawson.
        p. cm.
    "Portions of this book were previously published in Secrets of power persuasion (published by Prentice-Hall)"—Copyright page.
    Includes index.
    ISBN 1-56414-642-1 (cloth)
    1. Selling. 2. Persuasion (Psychology) 3. Influence (Psychology) 4. Sales personnel—Training of. I. Dawson, Roger, 1940- Secrets of power persuasion. II. Title.

HF5438.25 .D3933 2003
    658.85—dc21   2002031594

Dedication

To all the salespeople who have shared their stories with me over the years.

To my darling wife Gisela, who continues to amaze and delight me!

To my good friend Tom Power, who made this book possible.

To Don Nunley and Suzie Stewart, who let me work on this book at their beautiful beachfront home in Costa Rica.

Contents

Buyers can be sold if they think you can reward them. • Buyers can be sold if you exercise punishment power. • Combine reward and punishment. • Buyers can be sold if you bond with them. • Buyers can be sold, if they think you have more expertise than they do. • Buyers can be sold if you act consistently.

Enthusiasm is *not* excitement. • Enthusiasm comes from a genuine belief in your product and service. • Get positive feedback from your customers. • Improve the quality of your feedback by promising less...and delivering more. • Stimulate your enthusiasm with simulations. • Never let anyone budge you from your belief in your product. • Buyers are not persuaded by logic.

Never assume that the buyer believes you. • Only tell buyers as much as they will believe. • Tell the truth, even if it hurts. • Point out the disadvantages. • Use precise numbers. • Let the buyer know if you're not on commission. • Downplay any benefits to you. • Dress the part of a successful person. • If you do have something to gain, let the buyer know. • Confront problems head-on. • Use the power of the printed word. • Let the buyer know who else says so. • Build and use a portfolio of testimonials. • Get endorsements from people they'd know.

Chapter 4:

Ask for more than you expect to get. • How unions and management get each other's goat. • Sometimes they give you what you want anyway. • Unethical ways of using this concept. • The Oliver Twist syndrome. • Volunteer concessions—but only those that won't hurt you. • Give a small gift. • Use the magic in a gift of flowers. • Give the gift of thoughtfulness. • Make it win-win.

Chapter 5: How Scarcity Motivates Buyers

Even smart buyers can fall for the scarcity yo-yo. • Scarcity drives value and prices sky high. • Buyers and salespeople fight on the battlefield of scarcity.

Chapter 6: Making the Sale With Time Pressure

The faster you can persuade the buyer to decide, the more likely you are to get what you want. • The longer you give the buyer to think about it, the less chance you have of getting what you want. • How children use time pressure. • Moving people with the power of time pressure. • Secrets from inside a timeshare closing room.

Chapter 7: The Zen-like Art of Sharing Secrets

The magical three-step formula for getting cooperation from the buyer: Tell a secret, make a confession, and ask a favor. • Censored information seems more valuable.

Chapter 8: The Power of Association:

It's hard for our mind to break associations. • Celebrity spokespeople are valuable, because we cannot disassociate the product from the celebrity. • Buyers react more favorably to a proposal when they're doing something they enjoy. • Pace the mention of your product or service to the high points of a business lunch. • Paint pictures that tie your product to pleasurable experiences.

laugh. • Learning what makes it funny. • A practice session on identifying the style of humor. • The sales persuaders best type of humor: witicisms. • A 30-day program to improve your sense of humor.

Chapter 20:
The magic secret to remembering names. • Selective memory—how it works. • The trigger that makes you remember. • How to transpose from short-term to long-term memory. • Initial steps to burn a name into your memory. • Don't try to outdo the experts. • What's the lesson to learn here? • The key to remembering faces. • An exercise in memory discipline. • How important is it to remember names?

Chapter 21:
Use the other person's name at the beginning or the end of a sentence. • Make your request. • Tilt your head and smile as you say it. • Why the magic formula works. • How to use the formula.

Chapter 22:
Are you the target? • A magic expression. • Restating the objection. • That hasn't been my experience." • Handling the showperson. • Don't exacerbate the situation. • First find out what they want. • Charm them to death.

Chapter 23:
Figure out why won't they talk: obsession, inhibition, apathy, sulking, evaluation, penuriousness, time pressure, or fear.

Chapter 24:
The sales manager's doctrine. • How to develop the mission. • The four key elements of the mission. • The importance of informing the troops. • Using persuasion skills to sell the mission. • Building leadership credibility. • Building credibility when you're new on the job. • Leadership and the art of consistency. • Caring more about the success

of your people. • The mission is the most important thing. • Painting the picture of the mission. • The essence of persuasive leadership.

Preface

What You'll Get From This Book

F YOU'VE READ MY BOOK *SECRETS OF POWER NEGOTIATING FOR Salespeople*, you may be thinking "Okay Roger, so you know about negotiating—but what's the difference between *negotiating* and *persuasion*? Where does one end and the other begin?"

The two are very close, and the skills in each area will apply to the other, but for the purpose of this book, let's make this distinction.

Negotiating involves reaching an agreement on price or on the specific terms of an agreement. We negotiate the price of an automobile, or we negotiate an increase in pay. Clearly, there's a monetary amount involved. However, we also negotiate when there is no money involved. For example, we negotiate the terms of a nuclear arms reduction agreement, or we negotiate to get a kidnapper to release a hostage. In these instances, there's no money involved but there is a give and take involved in the specifics of the agreement.

Persuasion, on the other hand, is the art of getting people to go along with your point of view—to see it your way. Of course, you need negotiating skills to be a good persuader, and you need persuasion skills to be a good negotiator, but this definition will give us a blueprint for what we're going to talk about here.

That's what I'll teach you in this book: the skills to get people to see things your way.

We do this all the time, don't we? Any time we interact with another human being, there's an element of persuasion. As a salesperson, you may only think of persuasion skills when you're dealing with the buyer, trying to make a sale or solve a problem. I think that it's just as important to develop persuasion skills within your own organization. Salespeople often tell me that the entire sale hangs on their ability to persuade their own people to be flexible in the way they treat the customer. If the only way you can make a sale is to get expedited shipping, do you know how to sweet-talk the head of your shipping department? If a new customer's credit is shaky, do you know how to charm your accounts receivable manager? If you can't make the sales without a price break, do you know how to get your sales manager to see it your way?

Manipulation Won't Work Anymore!

First, let's accept that manipulation is no longer an effective sales tool. If you long for the "good old days" when you could count on a buyer "falling for" the alternate-choice close or the silent close, I feel bad for you. It was fun while it lasted, but buyers today are far too sophisticated for those kinds of tactics.

Let's face it, the world has changed. Selling is tougher than it has ever been. The world where we could take a product into the marketplace and name our price, because there wasn't any credible competition, will never be seen again. The world where sales are made and accounts maintained solely because of the bonding that takes place between buyer and salesperson only exists in Norman Rockwell paintings. Sorry Mr. Loman, but it's no longer so important to be liked.

We can't make sales anymore with manipulation; it just won't work. In the 21st century, we must learn to make sales by sitting down with buyers and persuading them to take our point of view.

The Dynamite Stuff
You'll Learn in This Book

The ability to persuade comes from a combination of skills, and I'll cover all of them in this book.

The first skill is the ability to use psychological pressure points that cause a buyer to be influenced. There are always underlying factors that affect the way the buyer is going to react to you. When we know about these hidden persuaders and have learned to use them, we not only become better persuaders, but we know how to protect ourselves when people use these factors against us.

You'll also learn about the importance of enthusiasm. This is not the phony excitement that pervades sales rallies, but is a genuine enthusiasm for your product and service. I'll teach you how to project enthusiasm to your buyers...and also how to develop enthusiasm if you don't have it.

Then, I'll teach you about credibility. No buyer will be persuaded unless he or she finds you credible and there is more to building credibility than you might believe. Some people are as sincere as they can be, and yet have trouble getting people to trust them. Others are outrageous con artists who should never be believed, and yet always seem able to persuade. I'll show you why and how you can build your credibility.

Next, I'll teach you the subliminal factors that cause one person to be persuaded by another person. You'll be fascinated when you read them and probably realize that all your life you've been persuaded by them, without perceiving what was going on.

I'll teach you specific verbal techniques that you can use to persuade. You'll learn a series of techniques that you can use word for word, which will get the buyer to see the sale your way. You'll develop the ability to say what you want to say in such a manner that it has irresistible appeal to other people.

You'll learn and use personal characteristics that cause a buyer to *want* to be influenced by you. I'm sure you've had the experience of meeting a truly charismatic salesperson. This person has an uncanny ability to draw people. I used to envy people like that because I assumed they were born with this magical gift. It was something they had and I didn't. Then I figured out that there really wasn't any magic involved—they were just using learned people skills. I will teach you some specific ways to improve your charisma and to develop the two key skills that charismatic people find so essential: the ability to remember names and faces and a sense of humor.

I'll talk about what to do when things go wrong and how to per-suade a difficult person. I'll teach you how to deal with the person who's so angry with you, he or she can't see straight. You'll learn how to deal with that perennial persuasion challenge—the clam, the buyer who won't open up and talk to you.

The power of persuasion! How much it means to success and hap-piness in our lives. And I can teach it to you. Really! If you'll stay with me, I promise you that by the time you lay this book down, you'll have acquired a new power that's so important to you, you'll wonder how you ever got along without it!

•••

The book is divided into four parts:

- In Part One, you'll learn how to play the persuasion game: what to say and what to do.
- In Part Two, you'll learn how to analyze the buyer: how to reach inside the buyer's mind and know exactly what will turn him or her on.
- In Part Three, you'll learn to develop the characteristics of a Power Persuader: an irresistible charisma, a dynamite sense of humor, and an uncanny ability to remember names. These things will make the buyer putty in your hands!
- In Part Four, you'll learn some magical persuasion techniques—how to move persuasion through four distinct stages, how to deal with impossible people, and how to use your new persua-sion skills to become a dynamic leader of people.

I promise you that by the time you finish this book, you'll have *everything* you'll ever need to get *anything* you'll ever want!

—Roger Dawson
La Habra Heights, California
RogDawson@aol.com

Part One

How to Play the Persuasion Game

A NYTIME WE DO ANYTHING, IT'S BECAUSE SOMEONE PLAYED THE persuasion game with us. That sounds like an overstatement, doesn't it? But it's true. Anytime we're doing anything, it's because somebody persuaded us to do it.

We get up in the morning because our parents persuaded us, at an early age, that it was the thing to do. We live where we live because somebody persuaded us to buy or rent a home there. As we move through our day, we abide by the laws of the land because we were persuaded to do so. We don't lie, cheat, or steal, because somebody persuaded us to adopt a set of moral and ethical standards.

We are surrounded by the things that people persuaded us to buy. The ability to persuade is the complex web upon which our whole world is suspended. Because our entire world is composed of the results of our ability to persuade others or their ability to persuade us, doesn't it make sense that we take the time to learn how to play the game well?

In the first part of this book, I'll teach you how to play the persuasion game.

1

6 Magic Keys That Control Buyers

SELLING IS REALLY A PERSUASION CONTEST, ISN'T IT? YOU'RE TRYING to persuade the buyer to buy. The buyer is trying to persuade you to buy his or her point of view that he or she:

1. Can't afford it.
2. Does not need it.
3. Can get it for less somewhere else.

One of you will succeed in your persuasion attempt. Will you end up as the persuader or the persuadee? What are the magic keys to persuading the buyer?

Do you know someone who has an incredible ability to influence people? Perhaps you're a salesperson in a competitive, price-conscious industry. You sweat buckets getting a new account to open up for you. However, the person who works the territory in the next state over never seems to have that kind of trouble. At every sales meeting, he's up there getting an award for the most new accounts. To rub salt into the wound, you bet that he doesn't work half as hard as you do.

Perhaps you're a salesperson who has become very good at prospecting for business and building rapport with the customer, but closing is your problem. You just can't get the buyer eager to "sign on the dotted line." Your sales manager can do it. Sometimes you've reluctantly called on your sales manager to help you close an account. She spends 20 minutes talking with the buyer. She doesn't appear to be selling hard, and she's certainly not closing hard. And she definitely doesn't tell the buyer anything that you haven't already told him. But the buyer suddenly says, "Okay then, how are we going to put this together? How is this going to work?"

What do these people know that you don't?

Probably, deep down in their subconscious mind, they have absorbed the following six magic control keys that influence buyers. If you asked them how they do it, they probably couldn't tell you. If you showed them this chapter, they would probably say, "Oh yes, I've been doing that for years, but I didn't understand the theory behind it."

So, let's start by examining the six magic keys that enable you to influence buyers.

Magic Control Key 1: Buyers can be sold, if you can reward them.

The first control key is obvious. Buyers can be persuaded to buy if they feel that they or their company will be rewarded. You can get a child to eat lima beans if you promise her ice cream afterward! Your young son strikes a deal with his mother that he'll go to bed if she lets him watch an additional half hour of television. As a salesperson, you probably work extra hard to win that Caribbean cruise.

Your first sales manager probably hammered into you, "Don't just explain the features. Translate those features into benefits for the buyer. Don't tell them that the car has power windows—that's only a feature. They pay money for *benefits*. With power windows you can cool the car must faster on a hot day. That's the benefit. That's what they'll pay for."

Superstar salespeople never take the approach that customers reward *them* by giving them an order. Superstars always think "win-win." "If I can give my buyers a win by solving their problem or serving them better, then they will be happy to give me the win of an improved income." Top salespeople in every industry project that they're so good at what they do that the buyer is rewarded by doing business with them.

Top attorneys can position themselves as being so valuable that they can pick and choose their clients. With good publicity, potential clients see them as so good at what they do, that the attorney is rewarding the client by being willing to represent them.

Top surgeons can pick and choose their patients because they have built a reputation for performing a specific operation better than anyone else.

Do you have that kind of reputation in your industry? Do buyers flock to do business with you because you're known as an expert in your field? Confidently projecting that you can reward your buyers is a powerful key to drawing buyers to you.

Neophyte salespeople believe that the buyer is rewarding them by giving them an order. If you think that way, you're probably communicating neediness to your prospects. Superstar salespeople project that the buyer is fortunate to have them there to solve their problems and serve them better. However, be careful how you get this across, because it could quickly turn to arrogance. You must still appreciate the business the buyer gives you.

How do you get away from projecting that the buyer is rewarding you by giving you an order? Here are five ways:

1. Understand that selling is a numbers game. If you're prospecting for new business as hard as you should be, there will always be a high percentage of people who will turn you down. There's no reason to feel rejection personally because they don't all buy.

2. Move away from what your product will do for the customer, and emphasize what *you* will *do* for the customer. Joe Girard, listed in the *Guinness Book of World Records* as the world's top car salesperson, says, "They don't buy Chevrolets. They buy me." The more you can convince customers how hard you're going to work for them, the less they can make the case that they're rewarding you by giving you the order.

3. Convince the buyer that what he is buying is scarce and he is lucky to get it. (There is more about this in Chapter 5: How Scarcity Motivates Buyers.)

4. Convince the buyer that you don't do business with everyone who asks to buy from you. Tell buyers that to become a

customer of yours, they must meet *your* requirements. That may sound like a stretch, but it can be done. Do you think that you could call up Boeing Aircraft and order a jet from them? I doubt it, even if you were paying cash. They would want to know why you want the plane, who's going to fly it, and what it's going to be used for (especially after September 11th).

5. Convince your customers that they have to qualify to reach certain levels with you and your company. Explain that your company has silver, gold, and platinum customers. The higher their level, the more privileges they get from you. Then, they have to work to reach the higher level or convince you to make an exception and treat them as though they were at the higher level.

EXERCISE: In the space provided, write three ways in which your buyers would be rewarded by doing business with you, instead of with your competitor:

1._____

2._____

3._____

I wonder if you included this: "They will be rewarded because they get me!"

That should be the *number one reason* that buyers want to buy from you. You must be a value-added salesperson! Your buyers need to believe in your ability to reward them *so* much that they insist on having *you* sell to them.

Magic Control Key 2: Buyers can be sold if you can exercise punishment power.

Punishment power is very powerful, because it triggers the most primal of instincts: fear. You're persuaded to give that big account the discount they want, because you fear losing the account. That's an obvious emotional reaction. However, what's really going on? Are you really so afraid of losing that account? Not really. What's really going on is that your mind is racing ahead. Your mind races faster than the speed of light, through a sequence of compounding tragedies. "If I lose the account I might get fired. I might not find another job. If I can't find another job, I'll lose my house. I won't have money for food, so I might starve to death." The fear of dying is a primal fear. As human beings, we must survive. It's our most basic urge, we'll do almost anything to survive.

However, you don't have to be threatened with death to be motivated by fear. Many of our fears are far more subtle.

The fear of failure causes a salesperson to give away things that may not be necessary in order to get the sale. All across the country every day, this is costing corporations millions of dollars of bottom-line profits.

Because of the negative aspects, fear is not a very good motivator, but there's no denying what a powerful persuasion force it is.

Salespeople usually get very good at projecting "reward power." They learn how to explain the features and then to project those features as benefits. Salespeople are usually very uncomfortable telling the buyer about the penalties of *not* buying from them.

In the space that follows, write three ways in which your buyers would be punished by doing business with your competitor, instead of with you:

1._____

2._____

3._____

I wonder if you included this: "They would be punished because they don't get me!"

That should be the number one reason that buyers won't buy from your competitors. Because if they do, they don't get you. You must be a value-added salesperson! Your buyers need to believe in you so much that they are afraid to buy from your competitor because they wouldn't get you.

Magic Control Key 3:
Combine reward and punishment.

Let's look at how Power Sales Persuaders make reward and punishment work *together* as a persuasion force. You should stress benefits to your customers to persuade them to buy and also try gently to imply the dangers of not investing. "Making this investment will do wonders for your bottom line. Do it now before the competition gets the jump on you."

In any persuasion situation, the elements of reward and punishment are always present. Let's say that you sell equipment, and part of the package is an extended service warranty. You project reward power by telling the buyer how the equipment will last longer if that buyer's equipment operators can call you for free service anytime they have a problem. Your service repair people will spot problems and take care of them before problems occur. The other side of this is to tell them the awful things that could happen to them if they don't invest in preventive maintenance. That's not so easy. You just convinced the buyer to invest a million dollars in your equipment because it's the best in the world, and now you're warning him that it may break down?

Power Persuaders know that the subtle application of both punishment and reward power is much more effective. They imply that things will get unpleasant if they don't get what they want. But then, when the other side looks as though they're going to give in, they quickly switch to reward power by showing their gratitude. "That's great, I really appreciate it. You're very nice."

Let's look at how reward and punishment power affect salespeople's attitude. New salespeople suffer because reward and punishment influence them too much. They think that every customer can reward them by giving them an order or punish them by turning them down—or worse yet, ridiculing them for what they've proposed.

Years ago, when I ran a large real-estate company, we had a terrible time getting people to farm. (Farming means to select an area of 500 homes and knock on doors in your farm regularly, until people get to know you as the real-estate expert for the area.) When I looked into the problem, I realized the salespeople weren't farming because they were afraid of people ridiculing them when they knocked on the door. Furthermore, their office managers weren't teaching them how to farm, because they were also afraid. And the regional managers weren't training the office managers to farm, because they were afraid of ridicule. So I went out with every one of our 28 office managers and three regional managers, one at a time, and knocked on doors with them. Once they found out that there was nothing to be afraid of, the whole company started farming, and the number of listings we were taking soared.

Magic Control Key 4:
Buyers can be sold, if you bond with them.

Bonding is a term that psychologists use to describe the change that takes place when a mother first touches her newborn baby. A bond develops between the two that never goes away. If you can learn how to bond with your buyers you will be a far more successful salesperson.

You bond with a buyer by moving your relationship from a business relationship to a personal one. Here are some suggestions:

1. Try to move the conversation from business to what's going on in his personal life. Switch the conversation to her hobbies, her vacation, or her family. One of the people who sells speaking engagements for me, tells me, "If I can get meeting planners to talk about their families or their hobbies, I know that I can close the sale." You must be subtle about the way you do this, and you *must* be skilled at reading the buyer's reaction. If you do it before the buyer is comfortable talking about her personal life the buyer will see you as manipulative or as a time waster. So try it, and back off if you meet resistance. You might say, "Is that a golf trophy over there?" If the buyer says, "Yes, but it was a long time ago" without even turning to look at it, you need to back off. If the buyer

passes the trophy over and tell you how he won it, you can continue bonding.

2. It's much easier to sell a friend than it is to sell a stranger, isn't it? One superstar salesperson told me, "I only sell to friends. I never sell to strangers." I asked him if that limits his list of prospects. And he told me, "Not really. If I meet a stranger I make friends with him. Then I sell him." How common sense can you get?

3. Try to move the meeting away from the office. As I taught in my book, *Secrets of Power Negotiating for Salespeople*, information flows much more freely away from the office. If you can get the buyer to go to lunch or dinner with you or play a round of golf, you will bond easily. Even if you can just get her down to her company coffee shop or across the street to McDonald's, information flows more freely and bonding can take place.

4. Let the buyer know that you "feel his pain." One of the things that made Bill Clinton so appealing when you met him was his ability to make you feel that he cared about you. You can project this by reacting to the buyer's emotions rather than what he is saying (more about this in Chapter 18, rule 11). If the buyer says, "The last time we did that we got sued," for example, you respond to the emotion, not the statement. "That must have made you really angry!" If the buyer says, "Our other supplier let us down," you respond with, "That must really have disappointed you."

5. Let the buyer know that you like her. I have the toughest time with this, perhaps because of my English upbringing. I didn't really learn it until I joined the Hacienda Golf Club, which is right next to my home in La Habra Heights, California. At first, I thought that the members weren't very friendly. Then I realized that I wasn't being friendly to them either. So, I made a point of letting people know that I liked them. I started going up to the members on the putting green or in the pro-shop and saying, "I really enjoyed playing with you the other day. You're great fun to be with!" Within a

couple of weeks, I realized that I was a member at one of the friendliest golf clubs in America. Try letting your buyers know that you like them by saying, "You're the most organized buyer I have," or "I always look forward to coming here. You are so much fun," or "You know why I like you so much? It's because you obviously have fun doing what you're doing."

H. Ross Perot, the Texas billionaire who founded EDS, is a leader at bonding with his employees. He had such deep concern and love for his employees at EDS that they were fiercely devoted to him. Remember what happened when some of his employees were trapped inside Iran as the Ayatollah Khomeini's revolution swept through the country? He risked his life by personally going into the country to get them out. (Ken Follett brilliantly described the escapade in his best selling book, *Wings of Eagles*.) Later, when General Motors bought EDS and Perot was forced out, the company lost its momentum.

We bond with other people simply because very few of us want to be hermits. We derive great joy and satisfaction from our relationships with other human beings, and it motivates us to sustain those relationships.

Magic Control Key 5:
Buyers can be sold, if they think you have more expertise than they do.

The next influencing factor is expertise. If you can convince the buyer that you know more about something than they do, you can use that as a very effective influencing factor.

Remember when you first got into your industry? You learned all the technicalities of it, but you still weren't yet comfortable with what you knew. Then you ran into a buyer who appeared to know more about it than you did. Remember how intimidating that was?

Doctors and attorneys project expertise power by developing a specialized language that you can't understand. Why else would doctor's write prescriptions in Latin? Why else would they write "post cibum" when they mean "after meals"? Because if we think the other person has a specialized knowledge that we don't, we tend to be influenced by them. Attorneys develop a whole new language that we can't understand in order to project expertise power.

Expertise power is not easy to acquire. It takes a lot of hard work to learn the technical side of your industry, but it's well worth the effort. For example, if you sell industrial air conditioning, you can develop a lot of power when you can calmly tell the buyer, "The problem with cutting corners like that is that it won't work well at high temperatures. You would either have to air condition your plant or you'd have to plan on closing every time the temperature passed 89.7 degrees."

Magic Control Key 6:
Buyers can be sold if you act consistently.

So what's the most powerful influencing factor of all? Is it monetary reward? Is it recognition? Is it fear? No. It's none of those. The most powerful influencing factor of all is one of which you may never have thought of before.

The most powerful influencing factor of all is *consistency*. Being able to successfully project that you have a consistent set of standards, and that you'll never deviate from them, has an awesome effect on people. I'll explain why later (in Chapter 9) but let me just point out for now why it's more powerful than the obvious influencing factors of reward and punishment. Although those two may have an immediate and dramatic effect on people, they cannot be sustained because they eventually will backfire on you.

The parents who are always persuading their children by offering them rewards quickly find out children learn to expect those rewards and will rebel if they don't get them.

You can pay a salesperson $200,000 a year, and in the early stages it will be a tremendous motivating factor for him. He will do anything to assure the continuation of that reward. But year by year the value of that reward starts to diminish.

You can motivate someone with punishment power—by threatening to fire that salesperson, for example. However, it always backfires if you keep it up too long. When you keep on threatening, she'll either find a way to get out from under the pressure, or she'll learn to live with it.

Yet, consistency power just grows and grows. The longer you project that you have a consistent set of standards from which you'll never deviate, people learn to trust you. From that trust grows a tremendous ability to persuade. (This is such an important part of Power Persuasion, that I devote an entire chapter to it.)

 # Key Points From This Chapter

1. Buyers can be sold if they think you can reward them. Instead of believing that your customers are rewarding you by giving you business, do this: Get so good at what you do that you are rewarding *them* when you accept them as a customer.
2. Buyers can be sold if they think you can punish them.
3. Power Persuaders know how to apply the dual pressures of reward and punishment.
4. Buyers can be sold if you bond with them. The closer you become to the buyer, the more you can influence him.
5. Work on projecting your expertise power. In today's high-tech world this is becoming more and more important.
6. The most important power of all is the power of consistency, which you'll learn about in Chapter 9.

2

Get Enthusiastic About Your Product

FRANKLY, I NEVER INTENDED TO INCLUDE A CHAPTER ON ENTHUSIASM in this book. The advice to be enthusiastic about your product or service seemed so trite, so "early-20th century." Surely you would expect something more sophisticated than that?

But this chapter is here for a very good reason. Every single one of the dozens of top salespeople that I asked listed it as the most important factor in sales persuasion. You cannot be a top salesperson unless you genuinely believe in the value of your product or service and can enthusiastically convey that to your buyers.

Let's be clear about what I mean by enthusiasm. I don't mean the mass excitement generated at rock concerts and sales rallies. That kind of frantic jump-up-and-down excitement is short-lived. What good does it do to get you all pumped up at one of those rallies if the thought of making a cold call gives you a migraine?

I'm talking about the genuine enthusiasm that comes from a sincere belief in what you're selling. All you have to do to develop enthusiasm is to start truly believing in your industry, your company, your product, and your ability to serve your customers. If you truly believe in your product, you won't need superficial excitement to motivate you. You'll be sitting in front of that phone thinking, "I can't wait to pick up the phone and start telling people how good this is."

But what if you don't feel that enthusiastic about what you sell? What can you do then? Here are some suggestions:

1. Get feedback from your customers. A lot of salespeople don't want to hear from people they have sold. No news is good news for that kind of salesperson. He thinks, "If a previous customer is calling, it must be a complaint that is going to tie up a lot of my time." Of course, that's the heart of his problem with lack of enthusiasm isn't it? If that salesperson truly believed in the product or service, she would be astonished to hear that there was an unhappy customer out there. Get feedback. The more you hear from your customers that they were delighted with their purchase, the better you will feel about what you do. That alone will nourish your enthusiasm.

2. Improve the quality of your customers' feedback with this mantra: "I'm going to promise my customers less but deliver more." If you are closing sales by exaggerating the worth or value of your product, you are always going to have unhappy customers. Of course they are going to be disappointed when your product or service doesn't come up to what you promised.

3. Stimulate your sales presentation with enthusiastic third-party stories. If you sell vacations and you can't get excited about going to Hawaii, you can still enthusiastically say, "Jay and Judy Coffee were so excited about their vacation in Hawaii. They called me to tell me that it was the best time they'd had in their lives." Perhaps you sell cars and wouldn't be seen dead in an SUV. You can still enthusiastically say, "Dave Brown brought one of these from me last month. He thinks it's the greatest vehicle he's ever owned. He keeps e-mailing me pictures of all the great off-road places he's taken it."

4. Learn a trick from the theater: It's the art of suspending reality. Gordon Davidson, the genius who runs the Los Angeles Center Theater Group, is a friend of mine. He told me about the ability of the theatrical director to suspend the belief of the audience. "The audience knows that they are sitting with 500 other people in a theater in Los Angeles about to watch *My Fair Lady*," he told me. "The director makes the audience willing to suspend that belief for a while and imagine that they are

really in a flower market in London." A good salesperson knows how to suspend a buyer's belief system. A vacation condo salesperson may be with buyers in a closing room in Amarillo, but he can have those buyers believe that they are walking on the perfect beach in Hawaii. Learn how to walk people into the dream. Let them feel the sand between their toes and feel the soft warm breezes through their hair. In the life insurance industry it's called "backing them up to the hearse and letting them smell the roses."

5. Stimulate your enthusiasm with simulations. A friend of mine who is a consultant to the military tells me that the reason the United States military is so effective in battle is that they work hard at simulating the battle-move with computer practice sessions. Before they go into battle, they have performed the maneuver thousands of times on computers and have learned to react to every possible counter-move of the opposing army. You can learn from that. Practice cranking up the enthusiasm level of your presentation in simulated selling sessions with your spouse, your significant other, your children, and anybody else who will listen. Encourage them to challenge you. "That's nonsense," they tell you. "No, it isn't!" you insist. "There isn't another company on the planet that makes a better product and backs it up better than we do."

6. Learn about your competitors and their shortcomings. Some salespeople are reluctant to do this because they have no intention of knocking the competition. That's fine, but hopefully the more you know about your competitor's problems and shortcomings, the more enthusiastic you will become about your own product.

7. Make a game out of projecting enthusiasm. After every presentation give yourself a grade for how well you projected enthusiasm. Reward yourself with a small gift if you can genuinely give yourself an A+.

8. Encourage the members of your mastermind group to hold role-playing sessions. Everyone gets to give his or her presentation in front of the group and gets graded by the other members on

enthusiasm level. If you don't have a mastermind group, read about it in Napoleon Hill's classic book *Think and Grow Rich* and develop one. Hill was convinced that the key to success is to develop a group of people who have shared values and similar success goals. The synergy of the members creates a powerful force that motivates the entire group.

•••

I've never met a more enthusiastic salesperson than my good friend Peter Shield. I first met Peter in Brisbane, Australia, when he introduced me to the audience at one of my Power Negotiating seminars. About 15 years later, Peter emigrated from Australia to Las Vegas, where he got involved in the timeshare industry. He has taken to the timeshare industry like a duck to water. He loves it. He eats it, sleeps it, and hungrily breathes the air of the timeshare industry. He has now managed timeshare projects around the world (even in communist China, if you can believe that. In fact he is the originator of the line, "And if you believe that, I've got a timeshare in communist China to sell you!").

For years now, I've tried to break Peter's enthusiasm for timesharing. I've never been able to do it. Every project he has worked on has been the most incredible bargain in the world. "Come on Peter," I'll tease him, "When I want to go on vacation I can pick from thousands of travel bargains on the Web. Why should I need to buy a timeshare?"

"Roger," he replies, "We've been friends for more than 15 years now and I'll tell you the truth from the bottom of my heart. You will never, ever find a better buy than the project that I'm working on now! And apart from which, you get my service. My service comes with every sale I make. And you can't buy me online." What does that teach me about Peter's approach? It teaches me that he will never ever let up on his belief in his product. Not even with his best friend Roger, who will probably never buy from him. Not with his children or his wife. Not with a complete stranger who will never buy from him and he will never see again. Never, ever, ever, ever, give up on your belief in your product and service. Not even to yourself in the wee small hours of the morning when the whole wide world is fast asleep and you lie awake and think about the sale and never, ever think of counting sheep. With that kind of enthusiasm for his product and his industry it's no wonder that Peter Shield is the best at what he does.

•••

People are persuaded by how well you can project your enthusiasm for your product or service. I'm not a big fan of evangelical preacher Jimmy Swaggart, but my goodness that man knows a thing or two about persuasion. Watch the sweat pour off his forehead as he forces his passion for religion out of his soul and into the hearts and minds of his congregation. When you can do that, brothers and sisters, no mere buyer is going to stand in your way!

 ## Key Points From This Chapter

1. Enthusiasm is not excitement. Enthusiasm comes from a genuine belief in your product or and service.
2. Get positive feedback from your customers. It nourishes your enthusiasm.
3. Improve the quality of the feedback by promising less and delivering more.
4. Stimulate your enthusiasm with simulations. Practice, practice, practice!
5. Never let anyone budge you from your belief in your product.
6. Buyers are not persuaded by logic. They are persuaded by how well you can communicate your belief in your product.

3

12 Magic Keys to Build Credibility

THE ABSOLUTE CORNERSTONE OF YOUR ABILITY TO PERSUADE—WHAT it all rests upon—is the level of credibility you have with buyers. When you speak, do they believe you? Unless they do, there is no possibility that you can get them to do what you want them to do.

People will listen to you, but they won't act—until they believe you. Let me stress that one more time. *People won't act unless they believe you.*

So if you're a salesperson trying to get an order, you should always be thinking, "Do they believe me?" Because if you haven't built enough credibility, they won't place the order.

It's important to understand the difference between credibility and trust. Credibility is intellectual. Trust is visceral. (I'll teach you how to build trust in Chapter 9 by acting consistently.) In this chapter I'll just deal with what makes the buyer believe you on an intellectual level.

A buyer can believe you and still not trust you. Imagine that you're mountaineering with a respected and accomplished mountaineer. You're roped together on a mountaintop in Peru, high above the snowline. You lose your footing and careen into a crevasse. You're partner pushes his ice ax deep into the snow and quickly wraps the rope around the handle. It stops your fall and you're now dangling in mid-air. Your partner yells down to you, "Don't worry. I sell this brand of rope. It will not break." You may well believe that person when he says the rope won't break. That's credibility. But what if the ice ax starts to pull out of the snow? If you fall again your partner will be dragged off the cliff with you. Now, do you trust him not to cut the rope?

Credibility is intellectual. Trust is visceral. You will need to know how to build both with your buyers, but for now let's concentrate on credibility.

In 330 B.C., the Greek philosopher Aristotle made the distinction by describing persuasion as requiring three parts. What Aristotle declared so long ago has become the basis for most Western thinking. Wouldn't it be fun to ask him what he has to say about 21st century selling? Here's what I think he would say:

> *"I believe that for a salesperson to be persuasive, she must be good at three things. She must have credibility with the buyer, something that I called "ethos" back in ancient Greece. Second, she must know how to project her feelings about the product or service, which I called "pathos" and you now call emotional appeal. Third, she must know how to explain the benefits of her product or service. I called this process "logos" and you now call it logic. Although logos is the least important of the three, it is significant, because if you don't present the benefits of your product or service logically, you leave the buyer thinking, 'I don't get this!"*

> *"This is their order of importance: ethos, pathos, and logos—credibility, emotional appeal, and logical appeal. I put credibility first because without that, nothing happens. It's the foundation of persuasion. How do you build credibility? I'm sure that in your modern world there are many more ways than I ever thought of, but here's what I came up with, more than 2,300 years ago. You must be knowledgeable about your product, in order to be believed. You must appear to be of good character. You need to be someone who tells the truth. And you must make an effort to understand all of this from the buyer's point of view, not yours."*

As a review, here are the three facets of successful credibility-building:

1. *Ethos:* Does the speaker have credibility with the listener? Aristotle further broke down ethos into three components:

    A.   The salesperson is knowledgeable and believable.

    B.   The salesperson appears to be of good character and someone who tells the truth.

    C.   The salesperson makes an effort to understand the buyer's situation and do what is right for the buyer.

2. *Pathos:* the emotional appeal that builds trust.

3. *Logos:* the logical appeal of the benefits that the speaker presents to get the listener's support.

•••

Fortunately, you can build credibility with a few simple techniques. In this chapter, let me teach you 12 tips to raise your level of credibility with other people.

Credibility Tip 1:
Never assume that the buyer believes you.

Let's face it, we get downright offended if someone questions our credibility. We hate it when a bartender cards us or when a bank teller asks us for identification. So, when we're persuading people, we don't like to admit that the buyer is sitting there thinking, "Prove it to me."

If you're a salesperson, you can present a glorious list of benefits that will descend upon the buyer when they have the common sense to make an investment in your product or service. It isn't even illegal to exaggerate your claims. (Lawmakers call it "puffing.") You can say you've got the greatest copy machine the world has ever known, even when you know it isn't, and you won't get into trouble. Just avoid any specifics and you're okay in the eyes of the laws. Still, it doesn't mean a thing until you've built the credibility needed to make the buyer believe it.

Don't be offended by people's natural unwillingness to believe you. Remember that we live in a world where a thousand advertising messages are screaming at us every day. We can't possibly believe everything we hear. To take everything at face value in today's world would be a shortcut to disaster. This is not a new phenomenon. When the *Declaration of Independence* was first published in an American newspaper, it shared the page with 10 advertisements. And that newspaper was competing with 29 other newspapers being published in the American colonies.

Power Persuaders learn instinctively to build credibility into their presentations. Never assume they believe you.

Credibility Tip 2: Only tell buyers as much as they will believe.

I was visiting my son John when he was a student at Menlo College in Atherton, California. He'd just completed a final and another student asked him how he did on it. "I think I may have aced it," John told him. "Alright!" the other boy said, and gave him a high five. A few moments later, another boy came by and asked John how he did on the test. "It was tough," John said, "but I hope to get a B."

"What's going on here?" I asked John. "You told the first boy that you got an A, and the second that you got a B."

"The first guy was the best student on campus, he'd believe I got an A. The second guy would never believe it. Haven't you learned that you should never tell anyone more than you think they'll believe?" Now that's smart!

I don't think a thousand psychologists with an unlimited research budget could come up with a greater truth than that. Even if you're telling the buyers begin to doubt it, your chances of persuading them fall like a rock.

Many years ago I was the merchandise manager for a large department store. We were heavily promotional, which means that our business went up dramatically when we advertised a sale, and business died when we didn't. So we'd run a big Sunday, Monday, and Tuesday sale, and then come back with a Thursday, Friday, and Saturday sale. The problem was this: How could we run the biggest sale of the year, twice a week, yearround? Soon, we'd lost all credibility with our customers. The salespeople would try to close a sale by saying, "Get it now, while it's on sale," only to have the customer respond, "Yes, but you'll have another sale next week."

You'll recall that Sears ran into the same problem. Eventually, they made the switch to yearround low pricing. The stores that dominate retailing today are Wal-Mart, Home Depot, and Target, all of which promote yearround low pricing.

The principle of "never tell them more than you think they'll believe" also applies to using fear as a motivator. I'm a professional speaker and I've always been surprised by the statistic that most people rate giving a speech as a bigger fear than dying. That's always sounded totally illogical to me. Surely dying is something to be feared more than giving a speech?! It turns out that the reason for this statistic is that most people think that they will have to give a speech one day.

It's a clear and present danger. Few people think that they're going to die before their time. That's why fear is not a great persuasion tool. A more serious threat is not a bigger persuader than a mild threat. Studies indicate that people are just as persuaded by mild threats as they are by strong threats. Finally the researchers realized that fear is a powerful persuader, only up to the point where people feel genuinely threatened by it. The moment they begin to doubt that the threat is as great as it is being made out to be, the power of fear as a persuader diminishes. So if you want to scare somebody, don't tell them more than they will believe!

So a fundamental rule for building credibility is this: Never tell them more than you think they'll believe. You may genuinely have a product or service that will far exceed their expectations. However, if you can't make them believe it, you're better off to temper your claims.

Credibility Tip 3:
Tell the truth, even if it hurts.

Some brilliant advertising people have taken advantage of telling the truth. Remember the old Volkswagen sedan, the one with a round-top that didn't change for 20 years or so? It was one of the ugliest cars ever made. It didn't have any extra features an advertising person could brag about. Only in later years did it even have a gas gauge. You could get so many miles per gallon of gas that you simply drove until it ran out of gas. Then, you switched to a small reserve tank, which was more than enough to get you to the next gas station.

When the Doyle, Dane, Bernbach Advertising Agency won this account, they must have groaned! What could you say about the car? It only had two features: It was cheap to run and it was reliable—but everybody knew that. What more could they say about it? Then they hit upon a brilliant flash of inspiration.

They decided to tell the truth!

I can imagine every advertising person in America coming off his or her chairs and saying, "You're going to what?!"

They ran a whole series of advertisements that said: "This car is ugly, it looks like a bug—**a beetle**." "This car is slow—you'll be lucky if you ever get a ticket."

The results were phenomenal. People loved the campaign, and sales shot up. The truth—the simple, pristine truth—is an astounding force.

Doyle, Dane went on to use the same principle with Avis rental cars. In a world where everyone was scrambling for some excuse to say they were the biggest and the best, the new Avis campaign proudly shouted "We're number two!" And followed it up with the sub line "so we try harder." It had an interesting effect on the employees of Avis and the number-one company, Hertz. A survey showed that the Avis employees really were trying harder, but the Hertz people were taking it easy on Avis. Even they were sympathetic to Avis's underdog positioning!

These two campaigns revolutionized American advertising. They were startling in their impact. Everybody was running around Madison Avenue saying, "Why don't we try a Doyle, Dane ad?" meaning, "Why don't we try telling the truth?" Nobody had ever pointed out the disadvantages of the product before. Nobody had ever paid millions to let the public know that the competition was more successful.

Telling the truth, even when it hurts, is an astounding force.

Credibility Tip 4:
Point out the disadvantages.

Many years ago, Benson and Hedges came out with a campaign for their new long cigarettes that bluntly stated, "Oh the disadvantages!" Mary Wells, at the ad agency, didn't go as far as saying, "These things are going to kill you!" But she did show scenes of people smoking in elevators and getting their cigarette caught in the door and other tongue-in-cheek situations where a long cigarette would be a disadvantage.

These advertising people had touched on a very important key to persuasion: If you point out the disadvantages, it makes everything else you say much more believable.

Research has shown that there are four sound reasons for also presenting the other side of the argument:

1.   It makes the buyer believe that you have objectivity.
2.   It flatters buyers that you believe they are intelligent enough to be aware of the disadvantages and still be persuaded in favor of your proposal.
3.   It forces you to anticipate objections and rehearse counterarguments.
4.   It gives credibility to everything else you say.

Credibility Tip 5: Use precise numbers.

People believe precise numbers more than they believe rounded numbers. The Ivory Soap people figured this out decades ago when they started claiming that "Ivory Soap is 99 44/100ths pure." Obviously we wouldn't challenge them if they told us that Ivory Soap was 100-percent pure; but the precise figure is subliminally more believable. We assume that somebody had gone to a lot of work to figure out that the soap wasn't 99 43/100ths pure or 99 45/100ths pure.

Why bother to say that Taster's Choice Decaffeinated Coffee is "99.7 percent" caffeine-free? They could probably get away with simply saying "caffeine-free." They do it because we believe specific numbers far more than we believe rounded numbers.

We can use the believability of the odd figure syndrome as a persuasion technique. Let's say you're buying a piece of property. They're asking $200,000. If you offer $200,000, it doesn't sound as firm a figure as if you say this: "We've done a thorough research on the property, and after running all the numbers, we feel that a fair price would be $198,700."

Studies have shown that when you take that approach, the seller will respond with a counter offer that is, on average, $4,720 less than if you start at $200,000. No! I have no idea what the real number is, but it sure sounds believable, doesn't it?

I once bought a hundred acres of land in the state of Washington. They were asking $185,000 for the land, and I asked Marge Winebrenner, the real estate agent, to make an offer at $115,050. She said, "Roger, what's this 50 dollars? Where did that come from?"

"Marge," I told her, "I've just been buying land for so long now that I have a formula that I use. I punched in the numbers and that's what came out." In fact I knew that I was less likely to get a counteroffer from a specific number like that. Marge did a terrific job of presenting the offer, and the seller accepted it.

So to build credibility, use precise numbers. Strangely enough, you're better off to claim that your new word-processing software will increase the productivity of their administrative assistant by 87 percent than to claim it will double his or her productivity.

Credibility Tip 6:
Let them know if you're not on commission.

Until it closed after over 70 years at the same location, my favorite furniture store was Angelus Furniture in East Los Angeles. It's right in the heart of the Mexican barrio where gang warfare is a way of life, and drive-by shootings are commonplace.

The store is in a terrible location. It's been there since the 1920s and used to be a furniture factory. The inside is like an ugly old barn. So why did I like it so much?

A big reason was because the salespeople weren't on commission. I felt I could trust the advice of the salespeople better if they don't have anything to gain.

Isn't that a strange phenomenon? A more logical approach would be to think: Commissioned salespeople make more money. Higher-paid people must be better at what they do. Therefore they would know more. Therefore their advice would be more sound.

However, as Power Persuaders, we have to accept that the buyer is probably sitting there thinking, "Oh sure, of course you'd tell me that—you're on commission" or that in other some way you benefit from persuading them.

So here's the rule: If you're not on commission, let the buyer know. Don't make a big deal out of it, but find a place to slide this into the conversation.

The first selling job I ever had was set-up that way. I was selling televisions and kitchen appliances in southern England when I was 18 years old. Instead of each individual salesperson getting paid a commission, they paid a bonus at the end of the month, based on our combined sales. I liked that. We were happy to help the other salesperson's customer if he or she came back, because it didn't matter which one of us wrote up the sale. We were just as aggressive in getting the business, but we were working *with* each other instead of *against* each other. Because we worked on a bonus system, not commission, we could say to people, "We don't work on commission, so our only interest is in finding exactly the right appliance for your needs."

Today many high-tech sales organizations are beginning to see the advantage of a team bonus, rather than individual incentives. As I travel around the country giving speeches to corporations in many different industries, I find that computer companies are the most advanced in their selling skills. Both hardware manufacturers and software vendors seem to be on the cutting edge of sales, for several reasons, I suppose. They are comparatively new industries, so they don't have a lot of old-time salespeople who cling to the old way of selling. Secondly, computers are so sophisticated that they call for above-average intelligence salespeople. Thirdly, computers call for a long-term relationship between vendor and client, so the selling is more needs-based. In plain language, that means you sell the customer what he needs, rather than what you want to sell him.

I run into many computer companies that reward their salespeople for team accomplishment, rather than individual sales performance. Yet I always wonder if the salespeople are being sure to let their customers know that they're not on commission. They should, because it's a big credibility builder.

So if you're not on commission let customers know that. Also, don't assume it's obvious that you don't work on commission. It may be obvious to you, but they may still have a question about it, and they don't feel comfortable asking you.

Credibility Tip 7:
Downplay any benefits to you.

If you are on commission, how can you overcome the problem of the buyer feeling that you'd say anything to make the sale? The key is to downplay any benefit to you.

The office equipment salesperson says, "John, I'm asking you to make an additional $500 investment to get the top-of-the-line equipment because it's best for you, not us. We've been in business for 28 years. We do more than $300 million a year. We're not going to jeopardize our reputation for one sale. We have to be absolutely convinced that every time we see you in the future, you'll thank us for getting you to invest in the best."

At the Power Negotiating Institute (which you can find at *www.rdawson.com*), which books me for speaking engagements, I've taught our people to deemphasize the importance of a potential booking by saying, "Please understand that Mr. Dawson turns down many more invitations to speak than he could possibly fulfill. Fortunately he's still available for that date. Of course, if he's not speaking for you on that day, he'll be speaking for somebody else. He just happens to be excited about working for you because he really feels he can make a big difference to your bottom-line profits."

This way, we let the meeting planner know that there's no particular financial gain to us in getting this booking, while still letting them know that we're excited about it. It also gives us an opportunity to reemphasize the benefits to them. We've also cut short any thoughts they may have about asking for a reduced fee.

That's why the sell-down close is so effective. The salesperson advises you to save money by buying the less expensive model. It is implied that he's putting your interests above his own, because he'll be making less commission. Never mind that this may not be true. The lower price model may have a "spiff" on it—a special bonus payment to the salesperson—that makes selling the cheaper model better for them also.

There is endless research to prove that the ability to persuade goes down dramatically if the other person thinks you have something to gain. Would you believe that a criminal could be more persuasive than a district attorney could? It's true. A study published by researchers Walster, Aronson and Abrahams had a criminal and a district attorney talk to the same audience. Both the district attorney and the criminal argued in favor of *more* power for district attorneys. The criminal was found to be far more persuasive because he appeared to be talking against his own best interests: He had nothing to gain.

They did the experiment again, with both of the speakers arguing *for less* power for district attorneys. Here, the district attorney was found to be far more persuasive, because he appeared to have nothing to gain.

It's a key point: If you want them to believe you, let them know you have nothing to gain.

Credibility Tip 8:
Dress the part of a successful person.

There's another subliminal way in which you downplay importance. Dress the part of someone who's above doing things for personal gain. Have you ever been in a restaurant and got the feeling the waiter is pushing expensive dishes to increase his or her tip? What if the owner of the restaurant came over and said, "So nice to see you again! You really must try the quail and lobster appetizer this evening. I know you'll love it."

We're less inclined to think the owner is hustling food than if the waiter were to say the same thing. Yet, that's strange, isn't it? The owner has more to gain than the waiter does. The waiter will make the 15-percent tip on the sale, whereas the owner will make 70 percent or more on the sale, depending on how well food costs were controlled.

We tend to trust the owner and be more easily persuaded by him or her, because our perception is that such people are above hustling food. So, by our manner and the way we dress, we project the image of Mr. or Ms. Success—a person who's far above recommending something merely for monetary reward.

Two questions salespeople ask me a lot is, "How should I dress, and what image should I project?" The answer is that you should dress well enough that you don't appear to need the sale to survive, but not so well that the buyer can't relate to you. That's where top-quality clothing comes in. It has a quiet elegance about it. It doesn't shout how much it cost. Take a $500 sports coat for example. People who wear $50 sports coats probably would have no idea how much it cost, but they know it looks good. People who wear $200 sports coats would know that you were wearing a top-of-the-line coat, although it wouldn't be so ostentatious that they'd think you were a drug dealer. People who wear $500 sports coats would simply admire your good taste. Of course people who wear $1,000 sports coats will think it's a potato sack! (However, you won't run into too many of those.)

There's no question that we are more easily persuaded by people who dress better than we do. Researchers Freed, Chandler, Mouton and Blake conducted a now-famous experiment on how easy it would be to encourage people to ignore a "Don't Walk" sign at a city intersection. When a well-dressed individual ignored the sign, 14 percent of the people who had been waiting for the light to change followed him across. When the same person repeated the experiment the next day, now dressed in sloppy clothes, only 4 percent of the people followed him across. Clearly, we are more easily persuaded by people who dress better than we do.

Credibility Tip 9: If you have something to gain, let the buyer know

The other way to handle the problem of diminished credibility due to personal gain factor is my favorite: Confront the problem head on.

Let's say you're a commercial real-estate broker. Your customer is undecided about making an investment in a new office building. You say "Mr. Jones, I want to be up-front with you: I work on commission. If you don't invest in this building, I lose money. However, the problem is, you lose too because the potential profits in this building are enormous. We both lose. But do you know what really bothers me, Mr. Jones? It's that I know to the *penny* what I'm going to lose, if you don't invest. What really bothers me, is that I don't know how much you're going to lose. It could be hundreds of thousands of dollars. Mr. Jones, if you went ahead, would you take title in your name, or in your corporate name?"

Credibility Tip 10: Confront problems head-on.

If something is bothering you, or bothering the buyer, you're much better off to get it out in the open and deal with it. It'll make you a better persuader. We often let problems fester simply because we're afraid to talk about them.

For example, you're meeting with a buyer, trying to get your sale approved, but it's obvious he's not listening to you. The body language isn't right. His head is vertical and his eyes never move from your eyes. If he were listening, his head would be slightly inclined, and his eyes would be active, reacting to what you're saying. Instead of plowing ahead with what will be a lost cause, have the courage to confront the problem. "I can see you're preoccupied. Do you have a problem I can help you with?" His eyes jump back into focus. "Oh, I'm sorry," he says, "I just got some bad news and it was distracting me, but this is important too. Let's go ahead and make a decision."

Perhaps you're a salesperson on your cell phone, trying to get an appointment with a business executive. He's being rude to you, saying, "I'm just too busy to waste my time with another salesperson."

Have the courage to confront the problem. "I can tell by the tone of your voice," you say, "that you've had a bad experience with a salesperson in the past. However, I promise you that this is important to you, and if it takes more than 15 minutes, it's because you asked me to stay. Fair enough? Would 10 or 11 o'clock be better for you?"

If something is bothering you or the buyer, it's better to get it out in the open. It'll make you a better Power Persuader.

Credibility Tip 11:
Use the power of the printed word.

One of the surest ways to build credibility is to use printed materials. Human beings do not give equal weight to their five senses (sight, hearing, touch, smell, and taste). We're all oriented to respond most to our primary sense. The two key ones are sight and hearing. More people are visual than are auditory. Most people believe more what they see in writing than they do when they just hear it.

To figure out your primary orientation, close your eyes and think of some friends you visited who lived in another town. Are you remembering what you saw? That means you're visually oriented. Or are you remembering what you heard when you were there? This would mean that you're aurally oriented.

When answering the previous question, you probably said that you remembered what you saw. Most of us are visually oriented. Most of us remember what we saw much more easily than we can remember what was said.

However, this doesn't include everybody. I have a friend who's a psychotherapist, and he can remember every word of a conversation, but has trouble remembering his patients when he meets them outside of the office. That's because he's an auditory person.

Visually oriented people remember better what they see, and most people are visual. That's why most people believe more what they see than what they hear.

People believe what they see in writing, when they won't if they just hear it.

Many types of businesses use presentation binders in presenting their goods or services. They're a great help to the new salesperson because then she doesn't have to memorize all the details. She can follow along and read with the customer. You remember your presentation binder, don't you? It was the book that your sales manager made you put together when you first joined the company. You used it for a week or two and then decided that your presentation was so good that you didn't need the crutch of a presentation binder anymore. Dig it out and start using it again! People believe what they see in writing! Don't wait until you get into a sales slump and your sales manager has to lecture you about getting back to the basics.

People tend to believe what they see in writing even when they know that you just came from the print shop with it. They might not believe the same thing when they just hear it. The power of the printed word is a key element in building credibility.

Credibility Tip 12:
Let the buyer know "who else says so."

Here's a key idea that Power Persuaders use to build credibility. When you're sitting across from someone else, imagine that he has a sign on his forehead that says, "And who else says so?" He knows you think your product or service is good, but you're paid to say that! Who else says so?

Without a doubt the key element in building credibility is to let the buyer know that somebody else, besides you, thinks that you've got the greatest product or service in the world.

If you're marketing a product or service, you should maintain a display binder of letters from happy customers. Be sure the letters are current, with the writers' telephone number so they can be called for verification.

How do you accumulate these letters? Some of them will come to you because your customers are so thrilled about what you did for them that they write you about it. But very often you have to ask for the testimonials.

Whenever somebody compliments you on what you've done, simply ask, "Would you mind putting that in writing?"

If you promise not to tell anybody, I'll share a little trade secret about this with you. Sometimes they'll say to you, "Well, I wouldn't know exactly what to say." What a great opportunity for you!

You should say, "I can imagine how busy you are. Would you like me to draft a letter for you that you can approve and have your secretary type up?"

Because this is going to save them the work of having to think about it, they usually say, "That'd be fine." Now you can let your creative juices flow, as you prepare a dynamite reference letter. Print it out on blank paper, with a cover note. As long as you don't go too far into fantasyland, your customer will chuckle when it gets there and send it on to the secretary to be typed on letterhead.

While I am sharing trade secrets, here's a dynamite way to get a key endorsement. If you're in a business where you prepare a brochure about your services, which would include almost any self-employed person or independent contractor, this technique will do wonders for you. How would you like to have a famous person give you a great endorsement? It might be a celebrity or a top business leader in your industry. Write that person a polite letter and ask for his or her endorsement of what you do.

To save the person time, offer three different options: three different sentences endorsing you. Ask to initial approval on one of them and mail it back to you in the enclosed stamped, addressed envelope. Here's how you get the person to give you the endorsement that you really want: The first endorsement should be outrageous, something to which nobody would ever lend his or her name, such as: "Joe Smith is the greatest financial advisor in the world." The second endorsement is a strong one, and the one that you hope to get. It might say, "Listen to Joe Smith. I did, and I'll never regret it." The third endorsement is far less than he'll be willing to go along with. It might say, "Joe Smith appears to be a very qualified financial advisor."

When he gets the letter, he'll quickly glance at the three suggestions. He'll quickly eliminate choice one as too strong. Choice two is more than he'd like to say, but choice three is far too weak. So he comes back up to choice two, initials it, and mails it back to you. And you get exactly the testimonial you want.

In selecting the person that you want to endorse you, don't pick a person who can market his or her endorsements. Even if Tiger Woods wanted to help you out, he has a business manager who would expect to get a piece of the action and would veto it. (Unless of course, you're asking him to endorse a charity or a political candidate, which isn't an endorsement for which he could get paid.)

And look for people who have given endorsements before. Some people are very willing to help; others don't like to do it.

Key Points From This Chapter

A key part of Power Persuasion is making buyers believe what you're telling them. You can do that if you'll remember these key points:

1. Never assume the buyer believes you.
2. Only tell the buyer as much as he or she will believe.
3. Tell the truth, even if it hurts.
4. Point out the disadvantages.
5. Use precise numbers.
6. Let the buyer know you're not on commission.
7. Downplay any benefits.
8. Dress the part of a successful person.
9. If you do have something to gain, let the buyer know.
10. Confront problems head on.
11. Use the power of the printed word.
12. Let the buyer know who else says so.

4

Creating Buyer Desire
by Creating an Obligation

I N THIS CHAPTER I'LL TEACH YOU SIX WAYS TO CREATE "BUYER DESIRE." This consists of six ways of making the buyer want to buy from you. You need to learn the art of creating an obligation in the buyer's mind. This is such a powerful persuasion tool that it's like creating a vacuum that causes what you want to flow to you.

Creating an obligation works because, in this country, we have an enormous sense of fair play. We Americans have a set of scales for mental fairness, much like the scales of justice. If we don't think the fairness scales are fairly balanced, we tend to want to do something about it. That's why, in this country asking, "What do you think would be fair?" is a powerful persuasion technique!

Most corporations are so aware of the power of this technique that they have created rules to *stop* you from creating an obligation in their buyer's minds. For example, you are not permitted to buy the buyer a gift. If you take the buyer to lunch, many companies will insist that the buyer split the check with you. Doesn't that tell you how powerful this tool is?

So, I'm not talking about bribing the buyer. I'm talking about far more subtle ways of creating an obligation.

Method 1:
Ask for more than you expect to get.

A great way to create an obligation in the buyer's mind is to ask for more than you expect to get. Then, when you back off on your demand, you have tilted the scales of fairness in your favor. Your concession in reducing your demand creates an obligation on the part of the buyer to make a reciprocal concession.

Unfortunately, most inexperienced salespeople are too intimidated to do this. They're so unsure of their ability to be persuasive that they actually reduce their demands before they start.

Power Persuaders know that it's not enough to have the courage to expect and confidently request what we want. We must be willing to have the courage to ask for more than we expect to get. Then, when we scale back our request later, it will create an obligation in the mind of the buyer.

Here are some of the things an experienced salesperson will ask for that a new salesperson might not have the courage to ask for:

1. Full list price.
2. Payment in advance, or a deposit with the order.
3. Extended warranty fees.
4. An extended service contract.
5. Penalties if annual volume doesn't reach a targeted level.
6. Design or engineering fees.
7. Charges for samples.
8. Charges for custom packaging.
9. Bar coding charges.

Asking for more than you expect to get is a *very* important persuasion technique. However, it's so simple that I'm concerned that you'll overlook it. Or, I'm afraid that you'll think, "Oh sure, I understand that. Let's move on." It may be a very simple principle, but there are many reasons for doing it.

1. You might just get it. You may be misinformed about how much the buyer wants your product or how few options he or she has.

2. It gives you some negotiating room. You can always come down, but you can never go up.
3. It creates a climate where the buyer can have a win with you.
4. It raises the perceived value of your product or service. If you say, "List price is $1,000, but for you we'll do it for $950," you've immediately discounted the perceived value.
5. It prevents deadlocks with an egotistical buyer who is determined to beat you down on price.

To see how truly effective this method can be, let's consider a group of people in the world who almost *always* get what they want. These people are legendary for their incredible persuasion skills. Wise men have written volumes about their mystical ability to get what they want, under the most challenging conditions. Their talents are so unique that thousands of psychologists have devoted their careers to studying them. Of course, I'm talking about your children!

How naturally they slip into the technique of asking for more than they expect to get, instinctively knowing that it creates an obligation.

For the last 21 years I've lived in La Habra Heights, a little town about 10 miles north of Disneyland in California. During that time, I've raised three children, which means umpteen trips to the Magic Kingdom. If you're going to let your children go to Disneyland, expect to pay about 50 dollars per person for admission and lunch. When they ask for a trip to Disneyland and then back off and settle for a movie and popcorn, you think you've died and gone to heaven.

Many years ago, when my daughter Julia was working for a stockbroker in Beverly Hills, she called to ask if I'd like to go to lunch. My youngest son John, who was home from college, had a summer job at her office and she thought it would be great if we could all go to lunch together.

That's fine, except that Beverly Hills is an hour and a half drive for me, and it was already 1 p.m. This would mean taking an entire afternoon away from a book I was writing, to say nothing of the fact that lunch to Julia means the Polo Lounge and a $150 check.

I told her, "I'd really love to, Julia, but I just can't spare the time."

She replied, "Then would you mind if I took John to lunch?"

Relieved, I replied, "Oh, sure, that's fine, and I'll reimburse you." When I'd hung up, I thought, "She's done it to me again. I fall for that *every* time. She had no intention of me joining them for lunch. She was just asking for more that she expected to get."

More recently, my older son Dwight asked me if he could borrow my Corvette for the evening. I said, "Dwight, that's a pretty fast car. I don't know if I'd feel comfortable with you driving around all night in the Corvette."

He looked really disappointed, and said, "Could I borrow the minivan, then?"

I said, "Okay, I guess I don't have a problem with you borrowing the minivan." I didn't think any more about it until half an hour later when I looked out into the driveway. Dwight plays bass guitar with this group and he was loading these huge loudspeakers into the back of the minivan. There is no way could he have put all that equipment in the Corvette!

He'd been very smart. If he'd have asked to borrow the minivan in the first place, I might have said no. Because he had to have it to move his equipment, an argument might have followed. Once people have made a decision on something, they hate to back down...and I'm no exception. We all tend to dig in to our positions. By asking for the Corvette instead, he knew that he could always back down to the minivan, and I would feel that I'd had things my way. I'd feel that I'd won. How smart!

A classic example of asking for more was the divorce of Johnny Carson from his third wife, Joanna. At issue was the amount of money that Joanna should get to maintain her lifestyle until the divorce could be settled. Johnny's lawyers offered $15,000 a month. Joanna's attorneys produced papers to showthat it would take $220,000 a month to maintain her lifestyle! Did he expect her to settle for $15,000? No way! Did she expect to get $220,000 a month? Of course not!

You ask for more than you expect to get because it creates an environment where the buyer feels that he's the recipient of a concession—and that you are due a reciprocal concession.

How Unions and Management Get Each Other's Goat

Here's how asking for more than you expect works in a more serious setting. Many years ago I helped negotiate a renewal of a union contract at a retail store. During the prior contract period, the union pay raises hadn't even kept up with the increases in the Federal Minimum Wage.

Management genuinely felt the union was doing a disservice to its members, who are also employees.

The union's initial demand was absolutely outrageous. Their proposal was to put store clerks' pay on a par with the Teamsters in Alameda County, California. We had trouble even figuring out why they'd picked Alameda County, which was more than a hundred miles away. But it wasn't that complicated when we analyzed it. The Teamsters in that county simply had the best contract in the state.

I thought that proposal was outrageous enough, but it was timid compared to the company's first proposal—that union membership become voluntary. With the union's dismal track record of obtaining benefits for the employees, it was a proposal that would destroy the union at that location.

We were so far apart that outsiders thought we'd never be able to get together, but both sides were experienced negotiators. We worked our way in toward the middle and reached an agreeable solution.

Why had the union asked for so much, knowing it would never get it? Why had the company asked for an open shop, knowing that it would never get it? Because both sides wanted the other side to feel they'd won. Really, the perception of thinking they'd won may have been far more important than the reality of the settlement. Both sides had to report on the results of the agreement: the union to the members, and the corporate attorneys to the company management. Each side did the other a favor by asking for so much, and then conceding most of it. The union negotiators could say to the members, "We didn't get you a huge increase, but they were insisting on an open shop, which would have left you without any protection at all. We forced them to give up on that idea."

The corporate attorneys could say, "Sure we had to concede an increase in pay that was larger than we hoped for. But you should have heard their initial demand."

Sometimes They Give You What You Want Anyway

When I first began to understand the idea of always asking for more, I decided to experiment with the owner of the company at which I worked. Abandoning any sense of reason, I worked on a list of demands and then kept expanding them.

When I met with him about them, I thought that I'd be lucky if he agreed to any of my demands. But to my amazement, an hour later I walked out with a substantial promotion, a 60-percent increase in base pay, a bonus program, a new suite of offices, and permission to hire an assistant for my secretary.

Unethical Ways of Using This Concept

A national chain of department stores devised a completely unethical scheme for marketing major appliances that worked this way:

For each type of product—such as televisions, ranges, and washing machines—they developed a good, a better, and a best, consisting of a low-end product, a middle-of-the-line product, and a top-of-the-line product. They'd advertise the low-end product at a very attractive price and then, through salesmanship and creative display work, sell customers on the more expensive model when they came into the store.

Bait and switch is a serious enough ethical offense. But besides that, they'd developed an interesting new wrinkle: They structured the line so the maximum profit wasn't on the most expensive model, but rather on the middle-of-the-line model. They trained the salesperson to sell up to the top of the line, but then in a confidential whisper, tell the customer he didn't think the extra money was worth it. The salesperson would "confess" that, if given the opportunity, he or she would purchase the less-expensive middle model. Unknown to the customer, this was the model on which the store made the most profit and the model on which the salesperson made the biggest bonus. Of course this is completely unethical and they deserved to be brought to task. And eventually they were, by the Federal Trade Commission.

Of course, you shouldn't do things such as this. However, as a Power Persuader you must understand these techniques so you won't be vulnerable to other people's efforts to exploit you.

Yet in this example, we see why asking for more than you expect to get is a powerful technique. When you back away a little bit from the initial demand, you actually create an obligation in the mind of the buyer. You've made a concession to the other side and therefore he or she should make a reciprocal concession to you.

When the salesperson mentioned previously went ahead to suggest to customers that they use some of their "savings" to invest in a service contract on the appliance, the acceptance rate was remarkably high. This store probably would've got away with it for a long time if it hadn't been so outrageously successful. The incredibly high percentage of business they were doing on the middle-of-the-line products drew the attention of consumer activists, along with a subsequent federal action that ended the practice.

The Oliver Twist Syndrome

There's a big danger to be aware of when asking for more than you expect to get. Oliver Twist, the Charles Dickens character in the poor house who had the nerve to ask for more food, might put it this way: Asking for more is one thing; demanding more is another.

Remember that this is a persuasion technique. If you raise your demands to beyond what's reasonable and then convince yourself you're going to get all of it, you may be heading for trouble.

When you ask the buyer for more, be sure it doesn't come across as a demand. Imply some flexibility. You've got plenty of room to give a little. Let the other side know that you think the request is reasonable, but that you have their interests at heart too. If need be, you're willing to listen to a counterproposal.

Method 2: Volunteer concessions— but only those that won't hurt you.

If you can help the other side without it taking away from your position, why not? Power Persuaders look for concessions they can make, as long as it doesn't hurt their position.

One of the most powerful thoughts when trying to persuade people is not, "How can I get them to give me what I want?" Rather, it's more along the lines of "What can I give them that wouldn't take away from my position?" Giving something that's of value to them creates an obligation in their minds. If you give people what they want, they'll give you what you want.

When we get into trouble, it's because we've assumed that the other person wants the same thing that we want. I used this principle to help James Woodberry get his brother out of Kuwait when Saddam Hussein was holding his brother captive.

When Saddam Hussein invaded Kuwait, James called me right away. He told me that he had been listening to my negotiating tapes for years and that he wanted to hire me to help him negotiate his brother's freedom. His brother was an oil worker in Kuwait and was now being held as a human shield. James explained to me that he was willing to pay me for my expertise and also pay whatever ransom was needed. I told him that I'd be happy to help him, but of course I wouldn't take any money from him. I also told him that I didn't think that we would have to pay a ransom to get his brother back. "We've got to look at this from Saddam Hussein's point of view," I told him. "He will only release your brother when it is in his interest to do so. Saddam doesn't need money; he needs good publicity. If you can give him that, I think that he will give you back your brother."

I gave James my suggestions, and he followed through beautifully. He called the four major networks and told them that he was going to Iraq to negotiate his brother's release. He implied that the other networks were excited about the chance to cover the story, which had a great human-interest angle. CNN, NBC, and ABC were interested but didn't bite. CBS thought it was a great story, particularly because we were ignoring the advice of the State Department, which was telling us to stay out of it. In fact, Dan Rather liked the idea so much that he wanted to go with James to cover the story in person. Unfortunately, the executives at CBS didn't think that it was smart to send their multi-million dollar anchorman into the middle of a war, and they nixed the idea.

Disappointed but not defeated, James decided to fly to Amman, Jordan, where the reporters had set up their base of operations. He found the hotel where most of them were staying and started buying them drinks in the bar. He spread the story of his wanting to go to Baghdad and negotiate freedom for his brother. Several of the reporters showed interest and offered to go with him to Baghdad and introduce him to government officials. He started the rounds of government offices and let everyone know that he was there to appeal to Saddam Hussein for his brother's release. After many anxious days he finally got the call that he had been waiting for—Saddam Hussein wanted to meet with him at his palace.

When James got there he found that television cameras had been set up and the interview was to be filmed and released to the world media. Hussein launched into a long speech. About 15 minutes into the tirade, it became clear to James that Hussein was going to release his brother. "From then on," he told me, "All I wanted to do was get out of there." The speech droned on for an hour and a half, but finally James was reunited with his brother and allowed to leave the country.

Why was James successful in negotiations when our state department negotiators had failed? He was working with a critical principle of Power Persuasion, which is to understand that the other side will only do what you want them to do when it is in their best interest to do so. Learn to look at things from the buyer's point of view, not yours. Because when you give people what they want, they'll give you what you want.

Method 3: Give a Small Gift

Another way to create an obligation is to give a small gift to the other person. The fact that giving a small gift creates an obligation is why Fuller Brush salespeople and Avon ladies were so successful with their free sample at the door technique. Even if it's something we don't particular want, we feel obligated enough to let them into our homes, and present their wares.

Why do we feel this way? Because it was drummed into us at an early age. When you were six and your cute little classmate sent you a valentine, didn't you feel that you should return the favor? When you get a Christmas card from someone, don't you rush to send one back? Don't you feel awful when someone gives you a Christmas or Easter gift when you hadn't thought to get one for that person? I know that when I attend a wedding I feel obligated to take a gift that at least equals the cost of the dinner.

Yes, I know that it's stupid. That's the point. It doesn't make any sense. It has just become part of our personal culture.

The Hare Krishna Society took ruthless advantage of this with their collecting techniques at airports. The Hare Krishna is a Hindu sect founded in a small town about halfway between New Delhi and Agra in India. In the 1960s, the devotees of this sect could be seen in Hollywood and other exotic parts of this country with shaven heads and long robes. Usually they'd be pounding on small drums and dancing up and down like Native Americans doing a rain dance.

During the turbulent years of the Vietnam War, they attracted some fairly affluent followers. But during the 1980s they started having a terrible time raising money. The world had changed from rebellion to respectable conformity. The hippies of the '60s became the yuppies of the '80s, and the Hare Krishnas had turned into a weird blight on society.

They hit upon a brilliant scheme to collect money. Using members dressed in more conventional clothing, they set up shop in the major airports. Their method was to approach someone, stick a small flower into his or her lapel, and then ask for a contribution. The results were phenomenal and enabled the sect to fund more than a hundred temples and centers around the world.

It turned out that very few people could resist the obligation they created with even so small a gift as an unwanted flower. To further underscore the power of creating an obligation for persuasion, remember that if the public would have been able to resist it, the problem of airport solicitation would quickly have gone away. Airports wouldn't have been a profitable place to solicit funds.

Method 4:
Use the magic in a gift of flowers.

Power Persuaders know there's magic in the gift of flowers. I remember when my business manager was working on a sale of my services that would eventually lead to more than $200,000 worth of business for us. She'd had an encouraging meeting with the man who would take our proposal to his executive committee for consideration.

I told her to send a dozen roses to the man, to be delivered on the morning of the meeting. She didn't think it was such a great idea. She felt foolish and was concerned that it might be seen as manipulative. However, she went ahead...and we got the contract. Later she told the executive that she hoped he hadn't seen the roses as a bribe. He laughed and said of course he did, but he was appreciative anyway.

If you deal with customers from China you must understand that giving flowers is an art form in the Orient. Outside of every new business you see mountains of flowers that have been sent to the business owner to wish them good luck in their new venture. For example, I recently did five days of seminars in Taiwan. At each stop I was presented with a huge bouquet of flowers. Remember that it's the personal touch that makes this effective.

Remember that it's the personal touch that makes this effective. Flowers make a great gift for two reasons. First, flowers have the personal touch because the perception is that somebody selected them. They also come with a handwritten message (even though the recipient knows the sender dictated the message to the florist over the phone).

Florists know it would be a big mistake to type out that message. It would lose its personal touch. How would you feel if you'd attended a wedding and received a printed card thanking you for your gift…without a signature? It's probably worse than getting no thank you at all.

Second, flowers get around the perception of bribery problem. I doubt that any buyer would have to refuse flowers because of a conflict-of-interest problem. A bottle of booze, which would cost much less, might cost them their job.

A non-personalized gift, such as a paperweight or a letter opener, doesn't create the personal obligation, because people perceive it as coming from the company, not the individual. Flowers don't have that problem.

I had learned how effective this can be when I bought a four-unit apartment building several years ago. An investor had purchased a whole street-full of these rental units and subdivided them so they could be sold individually.

He ran a small ad in the Sunday paper and I drove by to look at them. When I got there, the place was in an uproar. It was a very hot real-estate market in California at the time, and hundreds of investors were there to check these units out. Frantic buyers crowded the sales room.

Over the heads of the crowd, I yelled to the salesperson, "Do you have any left?"

"Only one," he yelled back "It's $129,000 with 20 percent down."

"I'll take it!" I screamed back.

And he started tacking up a "sold out" sign. Sure, I was taking a risk buying a building I hadn't even seen. Yet if they'd sold that many in the first couple of hours after putting them on the market, it couldn't be too bad a buy.

The next morning I was having an acute attack of buyer's remorse at this rash purchase, when a florist delivered a bouquet of flowers. There was a handwritten note from my salesperson that said "congratulations on your wise investment." Suddenly, I forgot all thoughts of backing out. As does everybody, I like to think of myself as a person who keeps his commitments. This salesperson was working on commission and was depending on me. He could have sold it to somebody else if I hadn't jumped in. What a brilliant move by the developer! For 20 dollars or so, he'd locked in a $129,000 sale. And I was much better off for being persuaded. Three years later I sold the building for $190,000.

Method 5: Give the gift of thoughtfulness.

The gift of thoughtfulness creates a powerful obligation for a buyer. I heard of a salesperson who developed a strong bond with a key client, simply by finding out that the man's grandson collected foreign stamps. Whenever he came by, he'd be sure to have a few new stamps with him. This powerful executive, known to chew up salespeople and spit them out, was so impressed with the man's thoughtfulness. He'd get his calls held and enthusiastically go over the new arrivals every time the salesperson came in.

Another more subtle gift is the cheerful willingness to stick around if the person you're waiting to see is delayed, even rescheduling the appointment if necessary. This inconvenience can be one of the best things to happen to you, as long as you handle it well. With it, you create an obligation.

And don't think that you can act irritated and annoyed in front of the person's secretary, and charming and compliant in front of the boss, and get away with it. Most bosses trust their secretaries and value their opinions. Many a big sale has gone completely down the tubes because the secretary whispered to the boss, "That salesperson is a real pain. You can't believe what a nuisance he's been."

And many a relationship blossomed because the secretary reported, "He's so nice, he's been sitting there for hours and hasn't complained once."

Method 6: Make it win-win.

You may be thinking that all this is very manipulative and rather unethical. I disagree with you. If your heart is in the right place, if you're absolutely sure that you're acting in the best interests of the buyer, I say that you have an obligation to understand and apply the principles of Power Persuasion.

W. Edwards Deming, the famous business guru who many credit with reviving Japanese industry after World War II, was a big believer in that. He would tell you that it's not enough for you to identify your customers' needs and fulfill them. It's not enough for you to identify your customers' problems and solve them. You have to identify your customers' future needs and problems. If you're at the top of your game it's very possible that your customer has no idea that she needs your goods or services. You're thinking well ahead of her present needs and problems. In that case, selling her something that she doesn't think she needs is not manipulation; it's an obligation that you have to your customers and your industry.

The art of creating an obligation is a key Power Persuasion factor for all salespeople to understand. That obligation creates a vacuum that causes what you want to flow to you.

 ## Key Points From This Chapter.

Knowing how to subtly create an obligation in the mind of the buyer is a powerful persuasion tool. The best ways to do this are:

1. Ask for more than you expect to get. You might just get it. It gives you room to negotiate, and it makes the buyer feel obligated when you back down. Don't fall into the trap of turning the request into a demand; you must imply flexibility.

2. Volunteer concessions that don't take away from your position. When you give people what they want, they'll give you what you want.

3. Give a small gift. In our society, even the smallest gift demands a reciprocal concession.

4. Use the magic in a gift of flowers. Because they have such a personal touch, a small gift of flowers can put together— or confirm—a huge transaction.

5. Give the gift of thoughtfulness. Don't get irritated when people make you wait or in other ways break a commitment. Recognize that by responding with thoughtfulness, you can create an obligation.

6. Make it win-win. If you genuinely have the buyer's interests at heart, you needn't feel guilty about "manipulating" him. You're acting in his best interests.

5

How Scarcity Motivates Buyers

IN THIS CHAPTER, I'LL TEACH YOU HOW TO USE A PRESSURE POINT THAT persuades buyers to act: the perception of scarcity. Putting a limit on what you're offering gives you the power to persuade them. It creates a sense of urgency, which makes them move quickly to seize the opportunity. It motivates buyers to *buy*!

Whenever I think about this principle, I'm reminded of a visit to the Soviet Union during the early days of Gorbachev's reforms. Standing on a second-floor balcony, I was watching an incredible scene take place below: a new phenomenon in Soviet life. The new policy of *perestroika*, or restructuring, was permitting a very small amount of entrepreneurial activity. Before perestroika, all sources of supply were government-controlled; now a few people could buy and sell goods and keep the profits. Below me a man had just opened up a cardboard box and was selling the contents. They appeared to be very poor quality wristwatches. In seconds, the word spread of something new for sale, and a panic started. Buyers mobbed the man, fighting their way through the crowd to thrust rubles at him. Then the buyers would fight their way back out through the crowd to unwrap the packages and find out what they had just bought.

It made me think of a trip I'd made into the upper reaches of the Amazon. One day, we stopped in a little backwater to catch and fry some piranha fish for lunch. I've never been an Ernest Hemingway when it comes to fishing, but even I can catch piranha. All you need is a hook on the end of a piece of string. The minute you toss it in, the water boils with frenzied activity as the piranhas attack the bare hook. That's the kind of frenzy I was watching in Moscow that day.

The scene is Moscow was a graphic demonstration of the power of scarcity. The man may have had access to many more watches, but he was smart enough to bring in only one box. The implication that there is a limited supply is a powerful persuasion force. The buyer feels that she must act quickly before it's too late.

Even Smart Buyers Can Fall
for the Scarcity Pressure Point

Don't think for a moment that only unsophisticated buyers are panicked into buying in times of scarcity. I once taught negotiating skills to a company that manufactures bearings for aircraft engines. Their normal lead-time for production of a bearing is about 10 weeks. However, there had been rumors that there would be a shortage of a raw material needed to manufacture the bearings, and the aircraft manufacturers weren't about to stop production on a $30-million jet because they couldn't get a relatively inexpensive bearing.

Despite the company's assurances of supplies, the aircraft manufacturers started increasing their orders in order to build up an inventory. As word got out about what one manufacturer was doing, the others jumped on the bandwagon. Soon the orders far exceeded the bearing company's ability to produce them. So it started telling its customers that deliveries would be delayed, which only increased the panic. Soon they had to quote delivery dates almost two years out!

Imagine the havoc that this created with this small bearing company, especially because it knew the pendulum would have to swing the other way soon. When the aircraft manufacturers began to realize the panic wasn't justified, they had 10 times their normal inventory on hand. Then would come many months when the bearing company wouldn't get any orders at all.

Scarcity Drives Value and Prices Sky-High

Scarcity increases the value and makes you want to act quickly. Let's say you're in an appliance store. You can't bring yourself to spend all that money on a new refrigerator, and the salesperson is getting impatient. He may finally say, "Look, before we go any further, I'd better be sure that we've got one of those left in the warehouse. They've been going like hot cakes."

He calls out to his manager, "Charlie, do we have any more 7256s left?"

The manager calls back, "I just checked on that one because I've got a customer who's interested. There's only one left. You better grab it now if you want it. I really goofed pricing those things so low."

And you yell, "I'll take it, I'll take it!"

Now, you might think you're too sophisticated to fall for this, but appliance salespeople are a breed apart when it comes to persuading customers. I used to be a merchandise manager in a large department store, so I know what I'm talking about.

I'll always remember a sizzling hot summer's day in Bakersfield, California, when we were having a sidewalk sale. It was 100 degrees at 9 o'clock in the morning, and the mercury was heading for 110. Bob White, my appliance manager, was manhandling slightly damaged appliances out to the sidewalk and taping sale price tags to them. Sweat was pouring off him.

"How much is that refrigerator?" asked an early-bird customer.

"The store's not open yet."

The customer ignored this and persisted, "Yes, but how much is it?"

"It's exactly what it says on the sign. One of a kind—$399."

The customer responded hopefully, "Could you knock a little more off?" The heat and the frustration finally got to Bob. He reached into his toolbox, pulled out a hammer and whacked the side of the refrigerator, chipping off a piece of the porcelain finish.

"There," he said "I knocked some off. Do you want me to knock some more off?"

"No, no!" screamed the customer, "I'll take it, I'll take it!"

Buyers and Salespeople Fight on the Battlefield of Scarcity

Buyers go to seminars too, you know. Just as you go to seminars and read books to develop your selling skills, they work on improving their buying skills. Guess what they get taught at their seminars? That with proper skills, they can convince any salesperson that what they are selling is a commodity. I'm not just talking about things such as steel, corn, or pork bellies. They brag that if you were selling space shuttles or a cure for cancer they could make you believe that they can get it from someone else at a lower price.

So the buyer's job is convince you that there is no such thing as scarcity. You job is to convince the buyer that your product or service is unique and in very short supply. This is much easier to do if you believe in value-added selling. You yourself add value to your product. Never just sell the product alone. Sell the package: your product and the value that *you* add to the product. You are unique. When the only way that they get you is to buy your product, and they only want to do business with you, you have taken ultimate advantage of the scarcity principle.

Scarcity is a powerful sales persuasion tool. Never give the buyer the open-ended opportunity to take advantage of your proposal. Let your buyer know that an opportunity such as the one you're proposing only comes along once in a blue moon, and that it should be now. Whenever you're trying to persuade someone, always project that if he doesn't accept your proposal, there's a scarcity of options available to him. It will give you control!

Key Points From This Chapter

1. Scarcity is a key pressure point in persuasion. If you can convince the buyer that the opportunity you're offering him is limited, you can persuade him to act quickly.

2. Scarcity increases value. Buyers will pay more for something they perceive to be in short supply. It is an obvious principle that can be validated by a visit to any antique store.

3. You may hear from your buyers that you're selling a commodity; they can get what you have to offer in many other places. That's their job: to downplay the importance of scarcity and convince you that you're selling a commodity. Your job is to convince them that the combination of your product and your value-added service is unique.

4. By implying scarcity, you can raise the value of your product or service in your buyer's mind.

6

Making the Sale With Time Pressure

IN THIS CHAPTER, I'LL TEACH YOU ABOUT THE POWER OF "TIME PRESSURE." The faster you can persuade the buyer to decide, the more likely you are to get what you want. The longer you give the buyer to think about it, the less chance you have of getting what you want.

It amazes me that it has become the custom in the real-estate industry to give the seller two or three days to "think about" the buyer's offer. The longer you give someone to think about a proposal, the less chance you have of it being what you want.

The faster you can persuade the buyer to decide, the more likely you are to get what you want. The longer you give him or her to think about it, the less chance you have of getting what you want.

If we lived in a world of trained negotiators, with both sides genuinely interested in seeking creative solutions that also benefit the other side, there would be an advantage to giving the buyer time to think about it. If he truly has your interest at heart, he may think of a benefit he could give you, one that doesn't detract from his position.

Unfortunately, we don't live in a world like that. The reality of the situation is that if you give the buyer time to think of a change to your proposal, it will probably be a change that benefits him and detracts from your position.

The faster you can get the buyer to decide the more chance you have of getting what you want. The longer you give the buyer to think about it, the less chance you have of getting what you want.

How Children Use Time Pressure

Don't your children use time pressure on you all the time? Don't they always ask you for something? Just as you're leaving, or just as they're rushing out of the house. Once, when my youngest son was living at home, he drove me across town to Los Angeles airport for a speaking tour. We didn't talk about anything of consequence on the way over. We were curbside, and the skycap had my luggage on his cart. John said to me, "Dad, I'm sorry, I forgot. I need $50 to fix the muffler on my car."

I said, "John, don't do this to me—I teach this stuff! How come this didn't come up before? Why are you waiting until now?"

"I'm sorry, Dad, but I got a fix-it ticket, and it has to be done before you get back from your trip. Let me have the money, and I'll explain it when you get back. Okay?"

They're not really that manipulative. It's just that, over the years, they've instinctively learned that they stand a better chance of getting what they want under time pressure.

Moving People With
the Power of Time Pressure

So the question becomes, does the person you're trying to persuade feel he must act quickly and seize the opportunity while he still can?

If you're applying for a job, have you let the company know that, although it's your first choice, you have three other offers to choose from? That's time pressure, isn't it? You won't be in the job market very long.

If you're a sales manager trying to get a salesperson to accept a transfer, have you put it this way? "Bob, I hate to put any pressure on you...." I call that a preparer: You've just prepared Bob for pressure and likewise have given yourself permission to put pressure on him. "Bob, I hate to put any pressure on you, but the president is insisting I fill this spot right away. Of course, you're my first choice, but if I can't convince you that this move to Guam is great for you, I'm just going to have to go with my second choice. I don't want to do that, Bob. So where are we, on a scale of one to 10?"

That's time pressure, isn't it? You're letting Bob know that this opportunity won't be around for long.

Secrets From Inside a Timeshare Closing Room

If you really want to experience what a powerful persuader time pressure can be, take a tour of a timeshare real-estate development.

On the face of it, timesharing is a win-win idea. It takes the condominium concept one step further. The condo concept says that sometimes you're better off not owning the *entire* building. If you only own the portion of the building you occupy, the cost of the portions that have mutual benefit for all the owners can be shared, such as the exercise room and the swimming pool. Timesharing says that for a second home, you don't have to own all the building, all the time. If you just owned it for the weeks when you'd be using it, you'd be better off.

Unfortunately, in the early days of timeshare, the idea got into the hands of some unscrupulous promoters, and what could have been an outstanding concept got a bad reputation. (If you had a bad experience with timeshare in those early days, don't let it color your feelings of the industry today.) Today's timeshare industry is controlled by some of the biggest and most ethical names in the travel industry, such as Fairfield, Hilton, Marriott, and Disney. One thing hasn't changed: The timeshare sale must be made when the prospect first tours the property. There are no "be-backs" in timeshare.

I was once privy to the inside workings of a Florida timeshare operation. Let's face it: Nobody knows how to close using time pressure the way that timeshare people do. They know how to take unsuspecting people off the street and have them make a $20,000 investment before their free breakfast hits their stomachs.

Here's how they do it. The hook is an offer of free tickets to Disney World. You can't buy gas, or go to a store or restaurant in Orange County, Florida, without being approached with this offer. To a vacationer on a budget that's almost irresistible: At eight in the morning, you can get a free breakfast, take a quick tour of the timeshare project, say no, and pick up $50 worth of tickets. By 9 o'clock you'll be walking down Main Street, U.S.A., feeling good that you've beaten the system.

Not exactly. The free breakfast puts you under an obligation to listen, just as I taught you in Chapter 4. The salesperson who escorts you isn't the kind of person you expected at all. You had braced yourself to resist a high-pressure sales pitch, but this isn't high-pressure at all. She's the sweetest person in the world, and she reminds you of your favorite aunt.

She explains the timeshare concept over breakfast and deliberately understates the appearance of the unit you're to see. Remember what we talked about in Chapter 3, about credibility? Never tell a person more than you think he'll believe. Here, she's done even better than that. The image the sales agent has created in your mind is that the unit's a good value but nothing to get excited about.

Then you're taken over to see the model. And, wow! Is this thing ever fantastic! It looks like the ultimate in luxury. It has a sunken whirlpool bath, mirrors all over the place, and all the latest appliances. By now you're excited. Maybe this is something you *should* think about.

You go back to the closing room to get your free tickets. There are 20 other families crowded into a small room, seated at tiny cocktail tables. You tell them you'd like to think about it. They drop the price for a today-only special. They're applying the potent effect of time pressure. If you could buy it today, for $5,000 off the regular price, would you wait to think about it and then be willing to pay the full price three days from now? Of course not.

Their whole presentation is dependent on the credibility of this one issue. That there are no "be-backs" in the timeshare industry. Unless they can persuade you that the offer to sell at $20,000 is no good tomorrow, they're sunk.

Let's say you're still resisting. If this is the case, you'll now be dealing with a turnover (T.O.) person (as they're known in the trade). If the first salesperson can't close you, you're turned over to a hard closer. Nobody gets their free tickets until they've dealt with the T.O. person, and this person is a master at closing with time pressure.

Now a different persuasion factor is taking over in the closing room. Other couples have made the decision to invest. They're being introduced to the group as the "proud new vacation owners." Everyone's applauding. There's something more powerful than ether in the room that's intoxicating people. That intoxicant is peer-group pressure. It's devastatingly powerful.

Swept up in all the excitement, the feelings of obligation, and the time pressure, it isn't long before you're the proud owner of a time-share week—a $20,000 investment that you hadn't even been considering three hours before.

But wait a minute. Hasn't Florida, along with many other states, passed rescission laws to protect the public against time-pressure selling? Oh sure, in Florida you can call back 15 days later and tell them that you've changed your mind, and they must refund your deposit. But a very small percentage of people do that.

Why is this? The timeshare people have perfected another persuasion technique called "bringing them back off the mountain." Just as a mountain guide knows that getting her clients to the top of the mountain is only half the battle, the timeshare salesperson must bring you back from the heights of giddy excitement. She must get you to confirm your decision in a more rational mood. She does this with all the care of an anesthesiologist bringing you off ether.

She'll pre-state every one of your possible reasons for wanting to rescind. "You'll probably think that you made a rash decision in the heat of the moment. You'll probably wake up in the middle of the night wondering if you've overspent your budget. You may even start wondering if I talked you into making this investment just so that I could earn a commission. Probably your brother-in-law will tell you you've made a mistake. However, none of these are true. The truth of the matter is, you've worked hard all your lives, and you deserve a little luxury on your vacations. Isn't that right?"

I'm not suggesting that you need to adopt the sales techniques of the timeshare industry, which depends on the salesperson closing the sale on the first contact with the prospect. However, you should be aware that under time pressure, people become more flexible. Your chances of persuading them are much greater if they feel even the subtlest effect of time pressure.

The faster you can get people to decide, the more of a chance you have of getting what you want. The longer you give them to think about it, the less chance you have of getting what you want.

 ## Key Points From This Chapter

1. The faster you can persuade the buyer to decide, the more likely you are to get what you want.
2. The longer you give the buyer to think about it, the less chance you have of getting what you want.
3. If you give the buyer time to think of a change to your proposal, it will probably be a change that benefits him, not you.
4. Learn from your children. They ask you for things at the very last moment, because they instinctively know that, under time pressure, you become more flexible.
5. Let the buyer know that the opportunity you're offering won't be around for very long.
6. Put teeth into it. If you say that a special price is available today only, you must mean it. The moment they suspect that they could still get the same price tomorrow, you have neutralized the effect of time pressure. You may lose some sales as you put this policy into effect, but in the long run you'll win.

7. If you've made an emotional sale, learn how to "bring the buyer back from the mountain." The buyer may regret the decision later and want to rescind the transaction. When you do get a decision made under time pressure, you must have the buyer affirm the decision in a less-emotional atmosphere.

7

The Zen-like Art of Sharing Secrets

THE NEXT POWER PERSUASION TECHNIQUE IS THE ART OF SHARING secrets, and it's something that will really fascinate you. Interrogators use it to break people's resistance to sharing information, and you can also use it as a remarkable persuasion tool. It is almost zen-like in its ability to influence buyers.

It's a three-step process, and the results are nothing short of magical:

1. Tell a secret.
2. Make a confession.
3. Ask a favor.

This process was developed from a technique taught to our spies in World War II that would help them if captured. A spy who completely denies any wrongdoing antagonizes the interrogator and causes him to try even harder to get a confession. Instead, the prisoner tells a secret by making a confession. For example, he confesses that he's been visiting a married girlfriend or transporting merchandise stolen from his friends. Then he asks the interrogator the favor of keeping it secret. It draws the other person into a conspiracy, and this makes it harder for the questioner to abuse the prisoner.

Here's how it works in business. Harry sells luxury yachts. He says, "Mr. Buyer, I think we know each other well enough that I can share a little secret with you. This model has been outfitted with an upgraded radio by mistake, and the owner of the boatyard didn't notice it yet. If you promise not to tell a soul, I'll let you have it for the base price."

Charlie is a sales manager who has just had one of his key people hand in his resignation. He uses the tell a secret, make a confession, and ask a favor technique.

He says, "Fred, I can understand exactly how you feel right now. If you promise to keep it a secret, I'll tell you why I know exactly how you feel. Fair enough? Do I have your word that you won't repeat what I'm about to tell you?"

Fred leans forward like a conspirator. "Sure, Charlie," he says, "just because I'm leaving, it doesn't mean you can't trust me."

"I quit this company once. I've never told anybody about this before, but just like you I was the top salesperson in the region. A competitor offered me a higher commission split and a new Cadillac if I'd go with them. I thought I was so well liked by my customers that they'd follow me whichever company I went with. Boy, did I make a mistake! Sure, they liked me, but I found out they liked what I'd been selling them even better. There was no way would they change suppliers. That was back in the days when this company was willing to bend the rules about rehiring people. When I came crawling back, they were good enough to give me a second chance. That wouldn't happen today. Do me a favor, Fred, and don't make the same mistake that I did, please?"

What's the key to this technique? It's the fact that secret information always seems more valid. If you want to convince people of something you doubt they'll believe, start by saying, "I shouldn't be telling you this, but..." or "I'm telling you this in strictest confidence...."

People who have mastered the art of large corporation politics have used this to engineer their own promotions. They corner the company's biggest gossip in the lunchroom, and they lean toward him and whisper confidentially, "Bob, can I trust you to keep a secret?"

Bob, blissfully unaware that David singled him out solely because he could be trusted *not* to keep a secret, whispers back, "Of course you can, David. You know me."

Then David continues, "I really shouldn't be telling you this. It was told to me in strictest confidence. No, I'm sorry, I really shouldn't."

By now Bob is drooling at the thought of some new juicy piece of gossip. "Go ahead," he encourages. "You know I won't tell a soul."

"You're right," David says. "I can trust you, can't I? Actually I was going to ask you a favor. Somebody told me in strictest confidence that I was up for promotion to vice-president of sales. Have you heard anything about it?"

Bob's eyes widen in amazement, "No, I haven't, David, but I'll ask around and see what I can find out."

"No, no, Bob, you mustn't do that. Don't mention a word of this to anyone. You have to promise."

In fact, there never was a rumor about a promotion. However there will be, and, by the end of the day, it'll be a big one. Everyone will be talking about David's impending promotion. Eventually, somebody in top management is going to say, "I've been hearing a lot lately about David Smith getting a vice-presidency. What have you heard about this?"

The other person will say, "I haven't heard anything official, but everyone's talking about it, so there must be something to it. He's doing a good job for us. I guess he's due." Soon, David's name has come to the top of the list for people getting promoted to vice-president.

•••

I think our founding fathers were blessed with extreme insight when they wrote such strong guarantees of freedom of speech into the Constitution. Censoring anyone from doing anything clearly makes them want to do it more.

Judges face a peculiar problem when it comes to what juries see as secret information. Very often, during a trial, attorneys introduce information that shouldn't be considered by the jury. The judge can do two things: declare a mistrial, which would be extreme, or instruct the jury to disregard the evidence. The problem with an instruction to disregard is that it has the opposite effect on the jury. Information given in secret tends to be especially believable.

An extensive study at the University of Chicago Law School proved this. The professor impaneled juries to decide the amount of damages in an injury lawsuit. When he introduced evidence that the defendant was insured against the loss, the average award went up 13 percent. Yet, when the judge told the jury they must disregard this piece of information, the average award shot up 40 percent.

Clearly, there's persuasive value in letting buyers in on confidential information. Try drawing buyers into your confidence by sharing a secret with them. If you want the buyer to *really* pay attention to what you're saying, tell her how much trouble you'd be in if you got caught telling her.

 # Key Points From This Chapter

1. The magical three-step formula for getting cooperation from the buyer is to tell a secret, make a confession, and ask a favor.
2. Sharing a secret draws the buyer into a conspiracy and makes it harder for him to oppose you.
3. Censored information always seems more valuable. If you want people to really take notice of what you're saying, explain that you shouldn't be telling them and that you'd be in trouble if you got caught.

8

The Power of Association: Tie Your Persuasion Effort to Something Good

WHAT IF, AS WE TRIED TO PERSUADE THE BUYER, WE WERE ABLE TO conjure up in his or her mind thoughts that were very pleasant and warm? Wouldn't it make the buyer very receptive to what we were saying? Of course it would! Power Persuaders do it all the time, taking advantage of this flaw in human thinking: Once we associate one thing with another, it's very hard for our mind to break that association. I call this the power of association, and it's a critical persuasion technique.

Singer Robert Goulet points out that early in his career, Ed Sullivan got it in his head that Goulet was from Canada, despite strong denials from the performer. "Ed Sullivan introduced me on national television so often as being from Canada, I began to wonder if it wasn't true," Goulet would quip.

Business genius Harold Geneen has a similar obsession, but his iswith numbers. A president of one of his companies told me that when Geneen first bought their company, they were intimidated by his reputation and didn't know how to handle him. "He shot a question at me, and I didn't know the answer. Rather than having the courage to tell him I didn't know the number, I made an educated guess. When I researched it, I found that I was way off. On his next visit I told him what had happened and gave him the correct figure. That was fine with him, except that I could never budge him from the original figure he'd set in his mind." Once

Geneen heard that number associated with that statistic, he wasn't able to break the association.

How can we use the power of association to influence other people? We don't have to search far for examples. Look at the celebrity ads on television. It is no coincidence that your teenager wears the same basketball shoes as Michael Jordan and drinks the same soft drink. If you're seeing too much of your teenager daughter's belly button these days, blame Britney Spears.

I once spoke to the Undergarment Association of New York. They told me that Madonna had single-handedly saved their industry by promoting bustiers. Nike signed Tiger Woods to a $100-million contract before he won his first professional golf tournament.

Manufacturers don't pay fortunes to celebrity spokespeople because they're credible experts on the qualities of the product. They pay because we have trouble disassociating their product from the celebrity. The product itself becomes warm, friendly, sexy, desirable, super-masculine, or whatever other traits we see that celebrity as having.

Another example is the way that sports fans associate with their teams when they're winning. "We're number one! We're number one!" is the chant. I'm sure the players must be thinking, "What's this 'we' stuff, buddy? Where were you last year when we went in the toilet?"

When a football or baseball team fights its way to the Super Bowl or the World Series, and then loses, we're treated to the spectacle of fans screaming at the television cameras, "*We* had a chance to win the championship, and *they* blew it!"

Listen to your local radio station. The station name is announced right after the most popular hits. The program director wants to hit you with their identification signal when you're feeling good in order to create a positive association.

Sale persuaders can use these kinds of association techniques. For example, people react more favorably to a proposal when they're doing something that they enjoy, such as golfing, skiing, or sailing.

I remember a salesperson who tried to apply this principle with me but didn't think it through. He invited me out to play golf at the beautiful Coto de Caza Golf Club in Orange County, California. A golf course is a good place to build association power with a potential customer. With luck, I would always associate him and his company with the fine feeling I would get from that round of golf. The problem was that this course was a killer! Rated one of the toughest courses in the country, it was far beyond my playing capability. I lost two balls and took a 10 on the first hole, and it only went downhill from there!

As hard as I tell myself it was all my fault, not his, I'm well aware that when I think of that salesperson and his company, I associate them with that miserable day on the golf course. Why on earth would *any* salesperson do that? Unless you're sure you've got a par golfer on your hands, go to a course where everyone can have a good time (and perhaps shoot the lowest score of their lives).

When I wanted to close a big sale I used to think that it would be a good idea to take the buyer out on my sailboat. It seemed like a perfect sales location. Picture it: The sun is shining. You're gliding past the mansions of Malibu. The cockpit table is laid out with a fine picnic and a chilled bottle of wine. And there's no possibility of the buyer walking out on me!

Everything would be perfect, except for one thing. If he gets seasick on me, it turns into the most miserable experience of his life.

Very often salespeople offer to buy their clients lunch, but they do it for the wrong reason. It's true that buying something for the client creates an obligation—I talked about that in Chapter 3—but that's not the reason you buy someone lunch. Chances are, the client is perfectly capable of buying his own lunch. You do it because you want to associate you and your product with the pleasurable experience of a fine lunch. That's why astute businesspeople spend a fortune on business lunches: It creates an obligation, and the pleasurable act of eating will be linked with the proposal.

It's amazing to me that psychological researchers misunderstood this principle for decades. Any salesperson will tell you that it's easier to sell a customer over lunch. "A well-fed customer is one who will buy" is a salesperson's standard belief. Nobody bothered very much to find out *why* this works so well.

Curious researchers conducted studies and came to the conclusion that when people are distracted by something, they are more likely to be persuaded than if you have their total concentration. Studies far back as one done in 1964 by Leon Festinger and Nathan Maccoby seemed to prove it. However, subsequent studies finessed this by researching exactly *what* distraction worked best. They found that food and sex are the two best distracters. Stick a plate of good food in front of someone while you're trying to persuade him, and you'll do better than if you have his undivided attention. Show up with a beautiful assistant, and you can sway his opinion more easily than if there is no distraction. Conversely, if the distraction is an unpleasant one, your persuasive ability goes down. So researchers became convinced that distracting the buyer makes it easier to close the sale.

It seems clear to me that what is really going on is that buyers associate your presentation with the distraction. If it's a pleasant distraction, such as a fine lunch, they associate your presentation with that pleasure and are more likely to buy.

Power Persuaders know how to finesse the business lunch experience even further. Let's imagine you're taking a key client to lunch. However carefully you plan, there will be high points and low points to the meal. There may be an unexpected wait for the table (a low point). Once seated, the waiter comes promptly and quickly serves generous drinks (a high point). A chosen item on the menu is sold out (a low point). And so on.

Power Persuaders are careful to pace the mention of their company's name, or talk about their product, to the high points. Don't magnify the problem by shutting up during the low points. However, be careful to avoid mention of you, your company, or your product. You'll be amazed at how subliminally associating your message with other pleasurable moments will build a positive base for your persuasive abilities.

Watch how auto manufacturers use this technique in their TV commercials. Have you ever seen a car commercial that shows how well the car does in gridlock traffic during the evening rush hour? No! It's always zooming around on a beautiful mountain road, free as a bird, with a beautiful person at the driver's side.

Smart salespeople know how to paint mental pictures of the pleasurable feeling that comes from using the product. People don't buy $1,000 worth of new ski equipment because of the latest technical advances. They buy them for the sheer joy of zooming down a mountainside on a crystal clear morning.

People don't buy RV's because of the money they'll save. They buy them for the sheer joy of waking up alone in a meadow next to a pristine alpine lake.

Power Persuaders know how to associate their message with pleasurable images in the buyer's mind.

 # Key Points From This Chapter

1. Once we associate one thing with another, it's very hard to break that association.

2. Manufacturers don't pay fortunes to celebrity spokespeople because they're credible experts on the qualities of the product. They pay because we have trouble disassociating their product from the celebrity.

3. Buyers react more favorably to a proposal when they're doing something that they enjoy, such as eating, golfing, skiing, or sailing.

4. Pace the mention of your company and product to the high points of a business lunch.

5. Learn how to paint pictures of your product or service that visually tie it in to pleasurable experiences.

9

The Power of Consistency

BUYERS ARE DRAWN TO YOU IF YOU ACT CONSISTENTLY AND ARE repelled if you act inconsistently. It's a concept that takes only seconds to learn, but it may take a lifetime to fully appreciate its power.

Why do we admire this characteristic so much? Our need for consistency comes from the tremendous need we have to develop a predictable world in which to exist. Your most basic and intense need is the desire to survive. This is a key reason humans, above all other species, have survived and prospered on earth. When our backs are against the wall, we will adapt, change, or do almost anything to assure our survival.

Our next strongest instinct is the need for security in our lives. Security is the assurance that we can continue to survive.

Think of the being shipwrecked on a desert island. Your first concern would be to figure out if you could survive on the island. Is there enough food and fresh water? Having established that, you can survive on a short-term basis. Your next concern would be to assure the continuance of your survival. You might develop a system to store rainwater, so you wouldn't run out of drinking water. You might build a compound in which you could store supplies of food, protecting it from the elements and any rodents or animals that might be in the area.

The same basic need for survival and security, which would be obvious to us on a desert island, still drives us in modern civilization.

We surround ourselves with an environment that is consistent and predictable. Instead of foraging for food on a day-to-day basis to assure our survival, we store it in huge freezers. Additionally, instead of daily looking for ways to make money, we prefer an association with an organization that consistently offers us predictable rewards.

So in our minds, we equate consistency with our two most basic needs: survival and security. If there is consistency in our world, we feel secure. When faced with inconsistent people and circumstances, we feel insecure. So, in our relationships, we admire people who act in consistent patterns of behavior. We are much more likely to be persuaded by someone whom we see as consistent.

Abraham Maslow, a psychologist, came to see this need for consistency in our lives as the very highest of human needs. Maslow is famous for his Hierarchy of Needs, which follows:

1. Survival.
2. Security—the need to assure our continued survival.
3. Social—the need to interact with other humans.
4. Self-Esteem—the need to be respected by others.

After he'd developed this pyramid, he came up with three needs higher than those:

5. Cognitive needs: the need to know.
6. Aesthetic needs: the need for beauty and consistency.
7. Self-Actualization: the need to feel fulfilled.

Our cognitive needs are clear. Human beings have a tremendous need to know what's going on: We can't stand a mystery. We plan to spend billions of dollars to fly to Mars, because we've just *got* to know if there is microscopic life on that planet. On the other hand, you can put a cow in a field, and it will stay in that field all its life and never wonder what's on the other side of the hill.

Our aesthetic needs factor into consistency as we are attracted to beauty and order. We can't stand a painting that isn't hanging straight; we have an inborn need to straighten it.

The need for consistency in our lives is a powerful force because it bonds the sophisticated need for an aesthetic environment—for beauty in our lives—with the most basic of needs: the need for survival.

This need for consistency is an awesome force, and Power Sales Persuaders can ride that force to get what they want from buyers.

Consistency Can Be an Awesome Force

Remember the movie *The Bridge on the River Kwai*? What a brilliant portrayal of the power of consistency! It was David Lean's superb adaptation of Pierre Boulle's book about prisoners of war in the Asian jungles during World War II. You'll recall that Alec Guinness played the role of a British officer, persuaded by the Japanese to build a bridge over the River Kwai. He determines that it will be the finest bridge that he and his men can possibly build.

Boulle based his book on a true incident, when the Japanese crossed the border into neutral Thailand to construct a supply line built with prisoner of war labor.

The fascinating thing to me is that David Lean made the movie in 1957, some 15 years after the incident. Today, several decades since the movie was released, the actual location of the bridge is still a major tourist attraction. Even the place where Lean filmed the movie, a thousand miles away in Sri Lanka, is a must-see location for tourists visiting that country.

Why this extraordinary fascination? It was a fabulous movie, but I think that part of the fascination was because the movie vividly portrayed one of the most vital traits you can develop: consistency.

The British colonel suffered incredible torture because of his initial refusal to let his men work on the Japanese bridge, which was vital to the Japanese war effort. He finally agreed with the justification that it would be good therapy for the men. The men under him assumed that this was some kind of trick and that he wanted them to sabotage the bridge with poor workmanship. They obviously didn't understand the mindset of the British Army officer. Having spent a lifetime standing for pride in his country, in his regiment, and in his service to his king, he simply found it inconsistent to do less than his best in building the bridge. Although it would aid the enemy, he urged his men to show the Japanese just how fine a British bridge could be.

So here we have the irony of British prisoners of war laboring to build a bridge that would help the combat efforts of their mortal enemies. When escaped prisoner William Holden returned to blow up the bridge, did Guinness cheer him on? Not at all! He did everything he could to stop Holden from blowing up "his" bridge.

Here's the fascinating question for persuaders: Who was the hero of the movie? The American who was risking his life to destroy the bridge? Or the Englishman who was aiding and abetting the enemy? The British officer, played by Alec Guinness, was clearly the hero.

Why? Because we revere people who behave consistently. We fear and dislike people who are erratic. You should understand that exhibiting consistency in behavior is an incredibly potent force, because it conditions the buyer to trust you.

Consistency Makes You Appear Strong

In our minds a high degree of consistency is synonymous with intellectual and personal strength. We'll overlook almost anything if a person is consistent in his or her behavior. Winston Churchill was a bellicose, belligerent person. His desire to impose total control on the British Empire beyond the end of World War II was hopelessly archaic and could have led to anarchy. However, we love and respect him for his strength of convictions.

Similarly we've come to love Harry Truman, and we forgive him for his salty language and outbursts of temper.

John F. Kennedy spoke in grand terms of a new frontier, of the mantle of power passing to a new generation, born in this century. He projected a consistent set of standards. He did it very well. Bobby Kennedy, in his last years as a presidential candidate, learned to do it well. Remember his slogan? "Some men look at things the way they are and say, 'Why?' I look at things that never were and say, 'Why not?'"

One of the most beloved presidents of the 20th century, Ronald Reagan, was brilliant at projecting the power of consistency. He could get away with some outrageous acts because of it. Executive order 12333 prohibits us from assassinating foreign leaders. Reagan ordered our Air Force to drop a load of 2000-pound bombs on Muammar al-Qaddafi's tent, and we loved him for it. Why? Because he was acting consistently. He told us he *was* that kind of person, and he lived up to his image. Conversely, the low point of Reagan's popularity was when he appeared to have been negotiating with the Iranians for the release of the hostages held in Lebanon, when he'd told us he'd never do that.

The Senate spent $50 million on the "Irangate" hearings, and couldn't prove any presidential wrongdoing. Yet, public opinion reacted in completely the opposite manner. We loved him for the apparent show of strength in trying to send Qaddafi into the next world as a martyr, and we maligned him for his apparent inconsistency in trying to trade arms for hostages.

Using Consistency to Move Merchandise

Here's how all this applies to the power of sales persuasion.

We like and admire consistent behavior in other people. They like and admire it in us. If we're willing to take a stand for our principles, especially if it appears we're risking financial loss, it builds trust in the buyer and they love us for it.

For example, you might sell computers, and you've got the courage to say to your customers, "Of course you'd like to save money. And I'd favor it too, if it were the right thing for you to do—but it isn't. I know that you won't be completely happy unless you get the model with the larger hard drive. I'm sorry, but I won't sell you anything less."

They will love you for that! Of course it'll raise a few eyebrows, but if you've done your homework and you're right, you'll have power with that customer. If you back down, how are they going to respect you?

Suppose your doctor told you that you needed triple bypass heart surgery, and you said, "I think I can get by with a double bypass."

If he said, "Okay, let's try a double and see how it works out," how would you feel about him then? You'd probably want a second opinion, wouldn't you?

Why Carter's Downfall was Reagan's Windfall

Inconsistency was President Carter's downfall. He was one of the nicest, most moral and ethical presidents we've ever had. He was also one of the hardest-working men who ever occupied the White House and probably among the most intelligent—he majored in nuclear physics, after all! However, he lost his ability to persuade because he appeared to vacillate on different issues. We never knew if he felt strongly enough to follow through, if the going got tough.

Take, for example, his handling of the visa for the Shah of Iran. After he was exiled, the Shah lived in his beautiful villa on Acapulco Bay. He became seriously ill and requested a visa to come to this country for medical treatment. At first Carter said no, fearing repercussions in Iran. Then, he changed his mind and approved the visa so that he could get cancer treatment in New York. This created a surge of anti-American protests in Iran. Carter changed his mind again and made him move to Panama in order to take the pressure off the situation.

I don't think Ronald Reagan would've done that. Reagan would've made a decision, one way or the other, and stuck with it. Take, for example, Reagan's decision to deny Yasir Arafat a visa so that he could accept an invitation to address the General Assembly of the United Nations in New York. How would you react if you got voted down 150 to 2 in the United Nations—and one of the two was *your* vote? The United Nations eventually decided to move its entire assembly to Geneva to go around your decision! Wouldn't you think that you'd want to take another look at it? Wouldn't you tend to think, "Maybe I goofed on that one?" No! You make a decision and you stick with it, because projecting that you're consistent in your behavior is the most powerful persuasion factor you have going for you.

During George H.W. Bush's first few years as president, he was all over the board on his level of consistency, and you could see his popularity ratings move in direct relationship to it. At first, he was very consistent in his opposition to new taxes. "They're going to come down from Capitol Hill," he told us, "and tell me we've got to have new taxes. And I'm going to tell them, 'Read my lips: No new taxes.' So they'll go back and talk about it, and they'll come back and say, 'Mr. President, we've got to have new taxes' And I'll say, 'Read my lips. No new taxes.'"

We loved him for it...until he backed down on that issue and allowed new taxes. We castigated him for it; his popularity dropped from 80 percent to 45 percent almost overnight.

Then along came the Persian Gulf War. How would you rate him for consistency on his handling of the war? A perfect score, right? Nobody could have been more consistent in the way they handled Saddam Hussein. And we loved him for it! His popularity soared from the 40s up to the 90s.

Then he was faced with the problem of the Kurdish refugees. One day he was saying, "I will not send American troops into the middle of a civil war that's been going on for centuries." That's great, take a stand, but stick with the stand you've taken. The very next day, he changed his mind and sent troops into northern Iraq. His approval rating dropped immediately from the 90s down to the 50s.

What clearer proof could we have? People want to follow, they want to be led, by someone they see as consistent in his or her behavior.

If you're a sales manager or employer, I can tell you one thing with absolute certainty about your sales force: They'd rather you got them together and said, "Hey gang, this is what we stand for around here. These are our moral and ethical standards, and you can count on it that we'll never deviate from them." They'd rather you say that than have you vacillate on every little issue that came along.

We don't want to be influenced by people with inconsistent standards. Power Persuaders understand that consistency is an awesome force. If you act consistently, your buyers will be persuaded to follow you. If you understand how strongly your buyers need consistency in their lives, you can use that to mold their behavior.

Key Points From This Chapter

1. Buyers are drawn to you if you act consistently and are repelled if you act inconsistently.

2. Our need for consistency comes from our tremendous need to develop a predictable world in which to exist.

3. In our minds, we equate consistency with our two most basic needs: survival and security.

4. This need for consistency is an awesome force, and as a Power Persuader you can ride that force to get what you want from other people.

5. Exhibiting consistency in behavior is an incredibly potent force, because it conditions the buyer to trust you.

6. We only trust strangers when they've established a consistent pattern of behavior.

7. Make a decision and stick with it, because projecting that you're consistent in your behavior is the most powerful persuasion factor you have going for you.

8. People want to follow, they want to be led by someone they see as consistent in their behavior.

10

Bonding: The Magic Key to Persuasion

BONDING IS A TERM THAT PSYCHOLOGISTS USE TO DESCRIBE THE change that takes place when a mother touches her new baby for the first time. A bond forms between the two of them that lasts for the rest of their lives.

Power Persuaders use the term to describe the movement of getting a person to commit to a position. If we can get people to commit to a position—any position—we can then build on their need to remain consistent to that commitment. We've bonded them to that behavioral pattern.

We bond people with expressions such as, "I've always thought of you as a fair person, and you see yourself that way too, don't you?" Get your buyer to commit to that, and you've almost pre-scribed his future behavior toward you. It's very hard for him to do anything unfair.

"Harry, you do believe in 'win-win,' don't you? If I show you how you can win, you don't mind me having a win too, do you?" Get commitment and you've bonded Harry to that behavior.

Verbal reinforcement of a person's behavior is a powerful tool. Can you change the way people behave by complimenting them when they behave the way you want them to and withholding compliments when they don't? You bet! At Hollins College, 24 students in a psychology course decided to see if they could use compliments to change the way the women on campus dressed. For a while, they complimented all the female students who wore blue. It caused the wearing of blue outfits to rise from 25 percent to 38 percent. Then they switched to complimenting any woman who wore red. They caused the appearance of red on campus to double, from 11 percent to 22 percent. You're doing the same thing when you comment favorably on a person's behavior.

By bonding with people slowly, layer by layer, we can persuade them to do almost anything. Of course we'd never use persuasion bonding to get somebody to do something illegal or immoral, but it's fascinating to see how powerful it is in action.

In the movie *Wall Street*, Michael Douglas used it to subvert Charlie Sheen to the illegal use of insider information. As you may recall Sheen played a Wall Street account executive anxious to get some of Michael Douglas's business. He tells Douglas of an airline company that's about to be exonerated by the FAA in a crash investigation. He helps him make a killing investing in the company's stock. He doesn't tell Douglas that he got this inside information from his father, who works for the airline. However, Douglas finds out and reminds Sheen that he's committed a criminal act—which bonds Sheen to that new self-image. His next step is to get Sheen to follow another investor to find out which company he's about to take over. This is objectionable to Sheen, but Douglas has skillfully pushed him into thinking of himself as someone who's capable of breaking the law in that manner.

Had Douglas come right out at the start and tried to persuade Sheen to become an overt inside trader, he wouldn't have been successful. But by bonding him one step at a time to this new behavior, he could subvert him.

How to Sell up a Storm Using the Principle of Bonding

The principle of bonding tells you that you shouldn't be too concerned if you can't get full compliance in the early stages of the persuasion process. If you can get the buyer to agree to even a watered-down request, you'll have more success later. While you get the person to agree to the reduced request, you bond the buyer to a new self-image.

Perhaps you sell office equipment. A big profit item for you would be the service contract that extends the warranty. You may initially have trouble getting the customer to agree to this. The customer says, "We know you make profit on those service warranties. We're a big enough company to take the risk ourselves." If you'll go back to this after you've reached initial agreement, you may find that his attitude has changed completely.

Before you leave, have the courage to say, "Mr. Buyer, could we take another look at this extended warranty? I really believe it's the way for you to go. The issue isn't cashflow, it's preventive maintenance. If your equipment is covered, your employees will call us much sooner, because the call doesn't cost you anything. We'll spot problems before they get worse, and your equipment will last longer."

The customer had just made a big commitment to you, and what you stand for, by agreeing to purchase your equipment. You've got a good chance of him responding with, "Well okay, if you think it's really that important, let's go ahead."

Any time people bond to a behavior pattern, they have a mental momentum to reinforce that decision. Although they may have rejected the idea out of hand before, it may be a completely different story now. All over America, salespeople are walking away with half a piece of pie when they could have it all. Always make a second effort, once the buyer has bonded by agreeing to part of your proposal.

How People Bond to Their Mental Investments

Let me give you an example of how the process of bonding causes the mind to reinforce decisions it has made earlier. As do many other states, California has lottery fever. One week, the prize in the weekly "pick 6" drawing was $39 million. The day of the drawing, lottery tickets were selling around the state at the rate of 5,000 per second! The odds of winning were 14 million to one, but nobody seemed to care.

My golfing buddy, Michael Crowe, bought $50 worth of tickets. Just to see his reaction, I tried to buy his lottery tickets from him. He turned down $150 for his tickets, although he had plenty of time to rebuy them...and pocket a $100 profit!

There's far more going on here than gambler's superstition. Before he bought the tickets, I'm sure that Michael was reluctant to invest $50 on a 14-million-to-one shot. However, having made the decision to go ahead, he now had mentally bonded to that decision. Because he turned down $150, you could conclude he was now three times more sure of his investment than he was when he bought the tickets.

Think of that the next time you're using your powers of persuasion. Whether you're a salesperson marketing a product or a sales manager persuading a salesperson, after you reach initial agreement, say this to yourself: "This person is now three times more sure of the decision than he or she was when we met. Now I can nibble for the extra items that really put the icing on the cake."

If you work for a large corporation, look at its annual statement and compare net earnings to gross revenues. Probably, your company is lucky to be bringing 5 percent down to the bottom line. With profit margins so slim, it's probably true that you lose money on the first item you sell a customer. You have to amortize all your development costs, fixed production overhead, and marketing costs against that first item. It's only on the add-on items, and the repeat purchases, that your company really makes any profit.

In the shoe business, they say that when you buy a dozen pairs of shoes from the manufacturer, you lose money when you sell the first 11 pairs. It's only when you sell the 12th pair without marking them down that you make any money. In the supermarket business, if you buy $50 worth of groceries and tip the bagger a dollar for carrying them out to your car, the bagger made more profit from the transaction than the store.

In light of this, let's take another look at the salesperson selling office equipment. The add-ons, such as the service contract or supplies, may be the only thing on which he's making any money! Having the courage to go back for more after you reach that initial agreement is one of the most profitable things that you can do.

Remember That the Buyer Has Bonded With His Previous Decisions

As you try to get the buyer to bond with the decision to do business with you, remember that he has already bonded with his decision to buy from his existing supplier. Be careful that you don't directly attack that decision. Saying, "My product is far superior to XYZ's product," may be a direct attack on that buyer's ability to make a good decision. Phrase your attack more courteously by saying, "Ten years ago when you first started doing business with XYZ, I think you made a smart decision. With today's technology there are far better choices available to you."

How Interrogators Use the Power of Commitment

Here's how interrogators at prisoner-of-war camps use bonding to persuade their captives to betray their country.

Chinese interrogators during the Korean War had remarkable success in getting the prisoners to cooperate with their demands. Faced with determined troops drilled to give nothing more than name, rank, and serial number, they developed a deceptively simple program: Start small and build—the law of bonding. If you can get someone to take even the smallest stand on something, you can build on his desire to remain consistent with the previous position.

A prisoner might be asked in a friendly manner to agree that not everything in the Western world was perfect. The interrogator would concur that unemployment was lower in communist countries. These apparently harmless and accurate comments subtly commit the prisoner to a pro-communist point of view.

Later, he might be asked to elaborate on his comment that things were not perfect in the West. Would he mind listing a few of the things that caused him to say that? And why did he state that unemployment wasn't a problem in communist countries? Where had he heard this?

Building on these seemingly inconsequential bondings, the Chinese got many prisoners to sign petitions condemning the war and have them record statements for broadcast that seemed blatantly pro-communist.

Dr. Edgar Schein, who spent years investigating the Chinese interrogation methods, stated that nearly all prisoners of war in the Korean conflict collaborated in one form or another with the enemy—a remarkable change from World War II, when very few did so.

The Essay Contest Phenomenon

Have you ever wondered about those manufacturers' contests where your entry requires an essay of 25 words describing why you like a particular brand of ketchup or potato chips? Who cares? Surely they don't expect you to come up with some brilliant piece of prose that their advertising agency overlooked? Not at all. They're using the power of bonding. If hundreds of thousands of consumers go on record as liking the product, they're bonding to a position. In all likelihood they'll reinforce that position by continuing to like—and buy—the product.

Getting the Buyer to Bond to Your Product

How can you get the buyer to bond to you and your product or service? Certainly getting her to buy from you is one way. But there's another step that is even more powerful: getting her to recommend you. I'm sure that whenever you make a sale, you ask the buyer to suggest other prospects to you. This is a wonderful way to develop prospects.

Having gotten the buyer to give your some names, try to get the buyer to call that person and suggest that you get together. Yes, it makes the chances of your selling the prospect much better, but it also does a very important thing: It makes the buyer public commit his support you. That makes far more difficult to have him change his mind about you.

An experiment conducted by Hobart and Hovland and published in *American Psychologist* clearly shows this. They took 100 high-school students and exposed them to a speech in favor of reducing the voting age. They then asked them to write an essay expressing their point of view. They told half the students that their essays might be published in the school newspaper. The other half were told that their essays would be confidential. Then they had all the students listen to a very convincing speech that the voting age should *not* be lowered. It changed very few of the minds of students who had written for publication. But most of the students who thought their articles were confidential changed their minds. It was one of many experiments that have shown conclusively that if you can get people to publicly commit to a position, they will rarely change from that position.

Key Points From This Chapter

1. If we can get people to commit to a position, any position, we can then build on their need to remain consistent to that commitment. We've bonded them to that behavioral pattern.

2. By bonding people slowly, layer by layer, we can persuade them to do almost anything.

3. Any time a person bonds to a behavior pattern, he has a mental momentum to reinforce that decision. That's why you should always make a second effort, once the buyer has bonded by agreeing to part of your proposal.

4. Having the courage to go back for more after you reach that initial agreement is one of the most profitable things you can do.

5. Bonding is so powerful that Chinese interrogators could use it to get American troops to write statements condemning their country's own actions.

6. Get the buyer to go public with his support of you by having him call the potential customers and recommend you.

11

Selling to a Committee

ONE OF THE MOST DAUNTING CHALLENGES A SALESPERSON CAN FACE is being asked to make a presentation to a buying committee. Being a professional speaker for more than 20 years, I've learned a thing or two about persuading audiences.

In this chapter I'll teach you all I've learned, from personal experience and research—on how to persuade a group of people. It will teach you what you need to know to make persuasive presentations to buying committees.

Know What Caused
Your Committee to Be There

The first point to consider in persuading the member of the committee is this: How did they get there? Are they there because they were told to be there, or did they choose to be there? For example, at the corporation, management may have told the committee members that they must attend, whether they want to or not. They may even be hostile toward you because they don't want to be there. On the other hand, if attendance was voluntary, they have chosen to come and hear you.

What's the significance of this? Obviously, you stand a better chance of having a friendly audience if they chose to be there. Yet, there's something even more important to you as a persuader. If your audience chose to be there, you can almost count that they're already sold on what you have to say.

Who do you think attends speeches when the speaker is a Democrat running for office? They're usually all Democrats, who are already sold on what the speaker has to say anyway. Republicans, who are the ones the speaker really wants to talk to, rarely come.

Who do you think attends PTA meetings? It isn't the parents of bad students, who are the ones who could really benefit from the meeting. It's the parents of good students, the ones who aren't having trouble anyway.

Researchers call this the selective exposure syndrome. Guess who are the largest readers of ads for any particular model of car. It's people who already own that car, not the people that the advertiser is paying money to reach. It's a reason why television is such a powerful advertising medium: You reach everybody, not just the people who have an interest in your product.

This happens because people like to stay in their comfort zone. Given a choice of listening to a speaker who will say things that they already believe or someone who will challenge their existing views, they nearly always pick the one with whom they'll be comfortable.

So the first thought of the persuasive speaker should be: Did the members of this committee choose to be here? If they did, you can almost assume they already support what you have to say. You don't have to be so concerned with presenting opposing points of view and you don't have to worry about converting them. All your persuasive power can be concentrated on your call to action. Be clear and strong in telling them what you want them to do.

Should You Put Your Strongest Argument at the Beginning or the End?

Researchers call this the primacy-recency issue. Are you better off making your strong argument up front and then following up with supporting evidence, or should you save your big guns for last?

You are smart to be concerned about this. There's no question that people remember what they hear first or last best. Your strongest argument should be either at the beginning or the end. Just as the first and last paragraphs of a sales letter should be the strongest. And the first and last chapters of a book should be memorable. However, if you have 20 minutes to persuade a committee, are you better off hitting them between the eyes with your best argument first? Or, are you better off finishing with a rousing call to action by putting your strongest points last?

It depends on the audience. This is why you need to know whether your audience chose to be there or whether they were required to be there.

If the audience is friendly, and already believes in what you have to say, save the strongest argument for last. They'll be supportive enough to listen to what you have to say. You can then save the big guns for the call to action at the end.

If the committee isn't already sold on the issue you're presenting or if they're either passive or hostile, put your big argument up front. You need a strong attention-getter, so they'll listen to what you have to say. You need to shock them into realizing the size of the problem or opportunity. You might start out, "You might not like what I have to say today, but somebody has to have the courage to say it. If we don't take action today, you will be exposing this organization to more danger that it has faced in the 34 years since your founder started this company."

If Several Salespeople Will Present, Should You Go First or Last?

The right way may surprise you. Let's say that you sell hardware. Home Depot is having its biannual line review. You're sitting in the lobby with five other salespeople, all of whom are your direct competitors. Home Depot's review committee is going to listen to all six presentations and decide which of the six lines it will carry. Would you prefer to present first or last?

I always thought that I'd be better off to be last. It is good to be the person who presents her argument last, just before the committee votes. However, research in this area proved me wrong: You're better off going first. (Because of primacy-recency, if you can't go first, go last.)

Researchers have done extensive studies on this topic. They very carefully created an environment where arguments of equal persuasive strength were presented in different sequences to perfectly balanced audiences. These studies proved conclusively that you're better off to go first. You'll be more successful if you present your argument first and then let the other salespeople shoot you down if they can. Sure, you have the disadvantage of not knowing what the other salespeople will say. Another salesperson could effectively dispute your argument, but you're better off to have first shot at the hearts and minds of the committee.

A Simple and Effective Way to Get the Committee on Your Side

It's really easy: Start by supporting an issue about which you know the audience is enthusiastic. Let's say that you're making a presentation to an oil company, and you know that their corporate culture is strongly against any government intervention in industry. You sell computer technology and custom software. You start your presentation by talking about the Fortune 500 companies with whom you have done business and how well you work with a wide variety of industries. Then you say, "In fact, the only segment of commerce that we haven't done well with is government. We've always had a problem seeing eye to eye with government agencies." What does this do for you? It doesn't get members of the committee who are neutral to support your project. But it does silence some of your potential critics.

Researcher W. Weiss, reporting in the *Journal of Abnormal and Social Psychology*, showed why this works. He took a group of 120 college students and split them into two groups. His persuasion topic was the government fluoridation of water, which he knew by conducting a previous questionnaire the students favored, but not by a strong majority. Before the talk on fluoridation, the speaker told one group of students how strongly he supported student freedom, which was clearly an issue they enthusiastically supported. The speaker didn't tell the other group of students this. The speaker asked both groups of students to support a ban on fluoridation. Remember that the students actually supported fluoridation, so the speaker was asking them to change their minds. He could persuade the first group, who had heard him speak out for student freedom. He couldn't persuade the second group.

It's important to understand what was going on here. Further research told him that speaking in favor of a popular issue didn't get the audience to support the other issue. But it did diffuse many potential critics, and therefore gave him the majority.

The lesson to be learned is that if you want to minimize opposition to your argument, start by supporting an issue that you know the committee is enthusiastically behind.

Know Whether to Use Emotion or Logic to Persuade

Most salespeople will tell you that people buy with emotion. If this is true it follows that a speaker would be more persuasive when he presents an emotional appeal, rather than one that is logical.

The problem is that there is no credible research showing that people are more easily swayed by emotion than logic.

The truth is that it depends on the committee members to whom you're speaking. Some of them will be very emotional and swayed by emotional appeals. Other members will think so logically that emotional appeals seem phony to them and turn them off.

Research has shown that the intelligence level of the audience makes a big difference. Logic sways highly intelligent people, who are turned off by emotion. Logic baffles people of low intelligence, who are vulnerable to emotional appeals.

Research was also done on what's called Integrative Complexity, which compares how hard it is to persuade people who think concretely, versus those who think abstractly. Concrete thinkers are more rigid in their attitudes and have trouble using information in new and meaningful ways. Abstract thinkers, the creative people in our society, are much more open to new ideas.

From this you'd conclude that it's easier to persuade creative people, such as artists and writers, than it is to persuade non-creative people, such as accountants and engineers. In reality, the opposite is true. Although the creative person is more likely to seek out new opinions and listen to your arguments, she is harder to persuade. The accountant or engineer may be very reluctant to hear your message, because his mind is made up. However, he'll very quickly change his minds, if you can prove him wrong, because he has no emotional attachment to preconceived ideas.

A Power Persuader knows how to read the committee. Take the time to do extensive research. Who will be there? What are their positions in the organization? Take the time to shake hands with all of them and get a feel for who they are.

Should You Have a Question-and-Answer Session?

A positive question-and-answer session, dramatically improves your ability to persuade. A negative question-and-answer session could be a disaster.

What you hope to accomplish is to have a majority of the members take a position supporting your point of view. Even if it's only game playing, people will support an issue of which they've spoken in favor.

Always be supportive of people who have the courage to ask questions. You don't have to agree with them, but tell them it was a good question and treat them warmly.

If you're uncomfortable throwing the meeting open to questions, you probably don't know your product or service well enough. Or you don't believe in your product or service well enough. If you totally believe that they need to buy from you, you will welcome objections because they give you a chance to correct the misunderstanding the audience may have. Don't be afraid that you'll get a hostile questioner who will make you look like a fool. Unless you've been hostile toward the committee, they're not going to pick on you like that.

Research shows that not only are people much more easily persuaded when you've actively involved them, but they also remain convinced for much longer. People quickly forget what they hear, but they remember what they've done for a long time.

Power Sales Persuaders understand the importance of getting actively involved in a question-and-answer session.

Constructive Distractions Can Improve Your Ability to Persuade

Don't be too concerned about distractions. People are more easily persuaded when they're moderately distracted.

Sounds strange, doesn't it? But it's true. People are more easily persuaded when they're being distracted than when they're being forced to concentrate on the matter at hand. However, to work, the distraction must be moderate, and it must be pleasant. A business lunch is a perfect example of pleasant but moderate distraction—it's an ideal setting in which to persuade someone. In Chapter 8, I told you the prime reason business lunches are effective, but the fact that it's a pleasant distraction also helps.

When you think about it, the reason a pleasant distraction helps you persuade is obvious. When people are forced to concentrate on making a decision, it seems like hard work. Pleasant, but moderate, distractions create a warm, friendly environment where the buyer is much more receptive to your message.

Humor is a good way to distract an audience, so a few pleasant witticisms help. Don't tell a joke, because if it bombs it could kill you. If a committee member wants to crack a joke, encourage her and laugh along with her.

Humor by itself is not a good persuader. Satire, for example, can cause people to think about the problems of society, but it seldom causes real change. However, humor can be very valuable as an adjunct to your persuasive message. It helps for several reasons:

1. It acts as a pleasant but moderate distraction, which, as I told you previously, is an aid to persuasion.
2. It stops the committee from becoming bored.
3. It stops their minds from wandering.
4. It puts the committee in a friendly and receptive state of mind.

Humor stops becoming an aid to persuasion when the message itself becomes the humor. I've seen novice salespeople fall into this trap a lot. As they enjoy having the committee laugh at their jokes, they use more and more humor in their presentation. Just because the committee is having a good time, and listening carefully to every word, doesn't mean that they're being persuaded.

Power Persuaders know how to use humor, but not to let humor become the message.

Interesting visual aids are another way to pleasantly distract. In my seminars, I use color cartoons in my PowerPoint presentation to illustrate the point I'm making. They stop the audience from being bored and provides a pleasant but moderate distraction.

Should You Present Both Sides of the Argument, or Only One?

I could bore you with scads of research on this topic, but let's just cut to the chase and give you the rules:

You Need Only Present One Side of the Argument if:

1. The committee is friendly.
2. Your argument is the only one to be presented.
3. You're looking for fast approval, rather than long-term support.

You Should Present Both Sides of the Argument if:

1. The committee is hostile.
2. They'll subsequently hear opposing salespeople.
3. You seek long-term support.

Overstating Your Case Is Detrimental

A little exaggeration for the sake of emphasis may be all right, but don't overdo it. In persuasion there's a clear case of diminishing returns when you do this.

Let's examine just two of the motivating factors (I talked about these, and others, in Chapter 1.) Your ability to persuade increases as you increase the perception of reward for agreeing with your proposition. On the other side of the coin, it also increases with your ability to project greater penalties for disagreeing. However, more important than the amount of the reward or punishment is the committee's belief that the pluses and minuses are real.

The moment you push it to the point where the committee no longer believes you, your ability to persuade with reward and punishment drops off dramatically.

Learn the Art of Getting the Most Effective Introduction

If you're going to make a sales presentation to a committee, it may not occur to you that the way you are introduced is critical, but it is. Your introduction can either be verbal, with the client introducing you to the group, or visual, through a handout that you give to the group.

To be persuaded, the committee must see you as an authority. The authority may come from your title, your credentials, or your expertise in the topic. If you're introduced as "the person who solved the luggage problem at Denver Airport," and they all nod their heads appreciatively, you're halfway home.

What can you do if you don't have strong credentials that can be brought out in your introduction? If that's the case, you're better off to have your credentials presented *after* you're through. Research has proven that if they listen to your introduction and see your credentials as weak, it almost eliminates your chance of persuading them. However, the opposite applies. If you speak without an introduction and they like what you have to say, finding out later that you have poor credentials has almost no negative effect.

Research has also shown people very quickly forget who said something, even if they can remember what was said. Doesn't that ring true? You frequently hear people saying, "I heard that so and so did this and that." They remember what they heard, but they can't remember who said it. What does this have to do with your introduction? It means that the credibility given you by a good introduction is very important in *short-term* persuasion, such as when you want them to buy or vote for something. However, as time passes, the credibility of the speaker becomes less and less important. Researchers call this the sleeper effect.

Let's say you're introducing a new program for automatic inventory replenishment to the marketplace. It's revolutionary—nobody has seen anything like it before. In the early stages of promoting the program, get as many people as possible talking up your product. The credibility of the speaker isn't that important. What you want is a large number of people who have heard about the program. You want everyone in the industry saying, "I heard that XYZ company has a great program for increasing inventory turnover with automatic replenishment." They won't remember who said it, or where they heard it, but they know they heard it somewhere. As you get into making specific sales presentation to companies, and you want them to take specific action by buying your product, the credibility of the people making the presentation becomes much more important. A good introduction is very important if you intend to ask for immediate action. It's less important if you are after long-term change in attitude.

Here's an insider tip: I always have my introducer use a prepared introduction that I've given him or her. Most professional speakers do it this way. The reason isn't to assure we get a flattering introduction, but to be sure the introducer doesn't get too carried away. Given free rein, an introducer usually will. They'll tell the audience you're the greatest speaker on the face of the earth and how lucky the audience is to have the privilege of listening to you. This damages your ability to persuade, because it builds a wall between you and the audience. When you eventually get your hands on the microphone, the audience is sitting there, thinking, "I can't believe he's that good. He's going to have to prove it to me." You have a wall between you and the audience that has to be torn down before you can start.

The Most Important Thing
You Can Do to Persuade a Committee

Presenting information alone doesn't change minds. You must draw conclusions, and ask the committee to do something, even if it's only to change their minds about something. Here's something that will surprise you: Researchers have spent a lot of time analyzing the effect of the news media on public opinion. Here's what they found out: When the news media presents news in an unbiased manner, it has almost no effect on public opinion.

Let's say that the news media reports that a policeman shot a teenager in a traffic stop. As it only presents information, and doesn't ask people to change their points of view, the story only serves to reinforce existing opinions. People who think that police brutality is rampant will continue to think that. People who think that teenagers don't respect the law will continue to think that way. Opinions are swayed *only* when the writer makes an effort to write a convincing piece.

If you want to persuade that sales committee (or a buyer one on one, for that matter), it isn?t good enough to present the information and hope it causes a change in them. You must draw conclusions, ask them to change, and tell them what you expect them to do. And when I say *tell them* what you expect them to do, I mean exactly that. Many times I've seen salespeople do a brilliant job of bringing the buyer to the brink of a decision. Then they lose it because they don't take the final step of telling the buyer how to do. They don't tell the buyer what they want the buyer to do next. They don't say, "I just need you to tell me to ship it." Or, "I just need you to give me a purchase order number and a deposit check for $5,000."

Once, I attended a church service in a strange town and I was prepared to contribute when the offering was taken. In the middle of the service, the minister started telling us that it was time to put a special message in an envelope and bless the work of the church. While I was still trying to figure out what this meant, huge plastic salad bowls appeared from nowhere and were passed along the pews at lightning speed. It flashed across my mind that this might be the collection, but I didn't see much money going into the bowls, mostly envelopes. Less than five seconds after the bowls first appeared, one came to me, and I simply passed it on. All this may have had some spiritual significance that escaped me, but from a persuasion point of view, it wasn't smart. The minister should have done a better job of telling us what was expected. "Now is the time that we get money out and put it into the plastic bowls," would have done nicely.

Power Persuaders know that it isn't enough to ask for the sale. You've also got to tell people what you want them to do.

 Key Points From This Chapter

1. Know what caused your committee to be there. If they chose to be there, they're probably already sold on what you have to say. All your persuasive power can then be concentrated on your call to action. Be clear and strong in telling them what you want them to do.

2. Your strongest argument should be either at the beginning or the end.

3. If the audience is friendly and already believes in what you have to say, save the strongest argument for last. If the audience isn't already sold on the issue you're presenting, if they're either passive or hostile, put your big argument up front. You'll be more successful if you present your argument first and then let the other salespeople attempt to shoot you down.

4. Start by supporting an issue about which you know the audience is enthusiastic.

5. There is no credible research that people are more easily swayed by emotion than logic. It depends on the audience.

6. Logic sways highly intelligent people, who are turned off by emotion. Logic baffles people of low intelligence, who are vulnerable to emotional appeals.

7. Although the creative person is more likely to seek out new opinions, and listen to your arguments he or she is harder to persuade.

8. The logical thinker may be reluctant to hear your message because his mind is made up. However, he'll quickly change his mind if you present a convincing and logical argument.

9. Get your audience involved. Having a question-and-answer session dramatically improves your ability to persuade.

10. People are more easily persuaded when they're distracted. However, for the distraction to work, it must be moderate and it must be pleasant.

11. Humor alone is not a good persuader. Humor, as an adjunct to your persuasive message, can be very valuable.

12. Learn whether to present both sides of the argument, or only one. Present only one side if the committee is friendly with no competition and if you're only looking for a fast approval. Present both sides if the committee is hostile or if you're competing against other salespeople.

13. If you have strong credentials, get them in front of the committee *before* you start. If you don't have strong credentials, you can minimize that disadvantage by selling them on the product or service first. If you don't have strong credentials for your introduction, you're better off to have the committee told who you are *after* your talk.

14. Most importantly, draw conclusions, ask for the sale, and tell them what you want them to do.

12

8 Verbal Persuasion Tools to Control the Buyer

L ET'S MOVE INTO SOME REALLY NITTY-GRITTY WAYS OF GETTING the buyer to see things your way. In this chapter, I'll teach you verbal persuasion tools. These are specific things you can say that will persuade the buyer to your point of view.

Some of them may sound very sneaky to you. You may also be upset when you read them because you recognize that they've been used on you. However you feel about them, it's essential that you're familiar with them and understand *why* they're effective persuasion tools.

Verbal Persuasion Tool 1: Diffusion

Let's start with the skill of diffusion, which is one of the simplest methods of bringing an angry person along to your way of thinking.

When someone has taken an opposing position to you, make the case that there isn't any conflict and that you're really out for the same thing.

Consider a situation that every sales manager has faced, at one time or another. Two of his salespeople have stormed into his office and said, "Okay, you're going to have to decide which one of us is right and which one of us is wrong. We've been arguing all morning, and we can't agree."

The Power Persuader diffuses the friction by first getting them to agree that their purpose is identical, even if they can't agree on the method. He listens to both sides and then says, "Wait a minute. First, I don't see you being so far apart on this thing. As I see it, you both want to do the same thing. You want to see the company increase its market share, and do it profitably, right? That's what we're all here for, right? Now Joe, you're one of the greatest sales promoters I've ever met. I want you to keep coming up with these great ideas for pumping the business. Susie, you're a terrific numbers person. I want you to work with Joe to be sure that it's going to be profitable and we don't bite off more than we can chew. That's what Joe wants too, Susie. Now let's get our heads together and see how we can put this thing together and still minimize the downside risk. Fair enough?"

Or, it could be the manager who has the challenging assignment of persuading one of his people to accept a transfer. "Bob," he says, "I really don't understand why you're upset about this. We're all after the same thing, aren't we? Don't forget the strength of this company is with its people. It is not the factories, the warehouses, and the office buildings that make this company great—it's the people. Believe me, we want what's best for you, just as much as you do. We're really in total agreement. Bob, I wish you could see this from my perspective. You'll look back on this move to El Paso as the greatest thing that ever happened to you."

Here's how a salesperson would use diffusion: Mary is trying to sell the top-of-the-line photocopier to a car rental company. They're strongly opposed to spending that much money. She'll say, "Mr. Jones, you're acting as if we're on different sides on this matter. Really, we're not. We're both out for the same thing. We both want what's best for your company. I can only grow and prosper if you grow and prosper. Mr. Jones, I'm absolutely convinced that this is the right thing for you to do. If I let you do anything less, I'd be letting you down."

•••

Nothing works the way sincerity does! The next time you're faced with a persuasion task that's beginning to turn into conflict, try diffusion. A lot can be accomplished when you ask, "We're really both out for the same thing, aren't we?"

Verbal Persuasion Tool 2:
"Yes, I take it personally."

This is powerful tool. Someone who's trying to persuade us to do something we don't want to do will very often start with the expression, "I don't want you to take this personally."

Whenever I hear that, I can't help thinking of the Woody Allen movie *Play It Again, Sam.* In one of the opening scenes, his wife is leaving him. She's calmly packing all her stuff into her old Volkswagen bug as he desperately tries to talk her out of it. As she gets into the car, she says, "Now, I don't want you to take this personally!" How else are you supposed to take it when your wife walks out on you?

Whenever someone tries to lay bad news on you that way, be sure to challenge him or her. Power Persuaders know that you don't give up your hold on the warm emotion that exists between you.

A key salesperson comes to you and says, "Don't take this personally, but I'm going to work for the competition."

You say, "Charlie, there's nobody in this company I care for more than you. And if it's the best thing for you, I'm happy for you." This is diffusion, isn't it? You're positioning both people on the same side of the disagreement. "But don't ask me not to take it personally. After all we've meant to each other, of course I take it personally that you wouldn't talk it over with me first. Charlie, you have an open mind, don't you? If I could show you why you should stay with us, you'd be open-minded enough to listen to me, wouldn't you, Charlie?"

Incidentally, I'm always amazed when I hear a sales manager tell me that he wouldn't take the time to talk an salesperson out of quitting, however good he was. "Just as a matter of principle, if they want to leave, I let 'em," they proudly tell me.

Let me tell you something: You can ride those principles into oblivion in today's business world. I can understand a principle that you won't increase their pay to keep them or make any other concessions under that kind of pressure. Still, a Power Persuader makes the effort to keep them and knows how to make employees want to stay without making any concessions to keep them on the payroll.

Verbal Persuasion Tool 3:
Being "Nixonesque."

Being Nixonesque in your statements means never making a statement that's so specific you can get nailed for it. I call it being Nixonesque because it really came to the fore during the Watergate hearings. All the defendants were very careful not to make specific statements. If you examine the testimony, you'll see that it was full of responses such as, "I can't recall ever saying that," or, "I don't think that it's possible that we could have discussed that," or, "To the best of my knowledge, I didn't approve that."

That's a whole lot different than saying, "I didn't say that," or, "We didn't discuss that," or, "I didn't approve that." (So, I don't lead you astray, it's still perjury to say, "I don't recall" when you really *do* recall.) When you make a statement that specific, the attorney may have been setting a trap for you. The attorney could have been up front and said, "In his deposition, Mr. Jones says that you approved the action. Did you?" Instead, the attorney says, "Did you approve the action?"

You now fall into the trap of assuming that he's asking a question to which he doesn't know the answer. And you respond, "Absolutely not."

The attorney can nail you! "But we have a sworn deposition from Mr. Jones that you did approve this, on April the 14th, at 3:12 in the afternoon. Are you saying that Mr. Jones was lying under oath?"

One of my first bosses drilled into me the value of being deliberately vague when I was only 20. I'd taken a summer job at a resort hotel in southern England. They asked me to box up and ship a piece of equipment. A week later, the boss called me into his office. "Roger," he said, "it doesn't look as if you did a very good job of boxing up that piece of equipment. It was damaged when it arrived."

I was new on the job, and I wasn't particularly eager to get fired over this. Because he didn't seem clear on his facts, I decided to try to bluff my way out of it, feeling I had a good chance of getting away with blaming the freight company.

"Well, sir," I said, looking him straight in the eye and holding his gaze, "I can assure you it wasn't my fault. Nobody could have done a better job of packing it. It must have been the freight company's fault."

"Really," he responded casually, "I'm surprised to hear you say that. Look at this."

From his desk drawer he pulled out an 8-by-10 glossy picture of the shipment as it had arrived at its destination, clearly showing that I'd done a sloppy job of packaging it. An 8-by-10! Was that overkill or what?

If I had been more Nixonesque, I would've said, "I can't recall exactly how I packed it for shipment, but if my memory serves me correctly, I did it well."

Salespeople and managers get caught up in this all the time. It's the salesperson who rashly says to the buyer, "But nobody in the industry will give you 60-day terms!"

The buyer calmly reaches into his desk drawer and says, "Oh really? Your major competitor will. Look at this proposal from them." The salesperson suddenly knows he's lost all his credibility.

The manager faced with the tricky problem of getting his people to take a cutback in expense per diem makes the rash statement that everybody is having to take the same cut. Specifics can nail you! The salespeople may know perfectly well that when the top salesperson in the company threatened to quit over this, you made an exception and swore him to secrecy.

Why leave yourself vulnerable by making absolute statements, when a little Nixonesquequisity can protect you?

Verbal Persuasion Tool 4:
"I'm not offended."

Here's an interesting little verbal tool. How do you let people know that you're upset with them without actually having to come out and say it? I call it the "I'm not offended" tool.

Let's say that one of your employees is upset with the company. He's blows off a little steam one day and says something along the lines of, "It seems like every time we turn around the company is sticking it to the employees!" Let's assume this is a good employee who's always been loyal and is a good worker; he just happens to be upset right now.

You don't want to ignore this, but you don't want to let it go either. How do you avoid confrontation (which might lead to him quitting) or getting so out of line that you'll have to threaten to fire him, while still letting him know you're not going to put up with that kind of thing?

To do this, you can use the "I'm not offended" tool. "Harry," you say, "many people would be really offended by that, but I want you to know that I'm not. I know that deep down you don't mean it. You've always been a loyal employee and I refuse to believe you're doing a complete about-face over a little matter like this."

Perhaps it's the salesperson faced with the unpleasant job of facing a customer who's been over-billed for a shipment. It was a mistake caused by an oversight on the salesperson's part. He forgot to let the billing office know of the special deal he'd cut. Even so, the buyer is making a mountain out of a molehill. He screams, "You're trying to %#(*ing cheat me! I never should have trusted you in the first place!" The salesperson doesn't want to raise the level of confrontation, but also he wants to tell the buyer he's not going to put up with that kind of treatment anymore.

"Mr. Buyer," he says, "I want you to know that I'm not offended by your anger, or by your use of profanity. You're got a right to be upset—I would be too. However, is it fair to accuse us of a lack of integrity, when in reality what happened here was a clerical error?"

The beauty of "I'm not offended," is that it enables you to say one thing, while making it clear to the other person that you mean exactly the opposite!

Verbal Persuasion Tool 5: "Easy to deny"

Here's a cute little verbal tool that would have saved many public figures a great deal of embarrassment if they had known about it. I hope you never have to use it but, just in case you do, here it is. I call it the "easy to deny" tool. This tool is for those times when you are caught doing something you shouldn't be doing. You don't want to lie by denying it, but, on the other hand, you don't want to admit it either. It's time for the "easy to deny" tool. "It would be easy for me to deny the accusations and simply put the matter to rest. That would obviously be the easy thing for me to do. Still, sometimes the easy way isn't the best way. There's a larger question at stake here. That question is this; Does my sales manager have the right to make me answer to every rumor that might come his way, regardless of who might start that rumor?"

Verbal Persuasion Tool 6:
"I'm not suggesting..."

"I'm not suggesting" is when you know perfectly well that you caught the other person with his hand in the cookie jar. However, you don't want to cause a confrontation by accusing him. However, you want to make him aware you know what he was up to. "Joe, I'm not suggesting for one minute that you put earning a commission ahead of the best interests of the company."

Or, "Harry, I'm not suggesting for one moment that there was anything immoral about you spending the weekend in the Bahamas with your secretary. I'm just asking you to see how it might look to people who don't know you as well as I do."

Harry knows exactly what you're really saying, which is, "Harry, I know what you're like better than anybody. I'm going to look the other way this time, because I don't want to fire you over this, but do it again and you're out on the street."

Verbal Persuasion Tool 7:
Give the buyer options.

To many foreigners, the most obvious American characteristic is the need for personal freedom. In Tanzania, I met a German who's a top executive with Mercedes Benz of North America. Although he's lived in America for 20 years, he still thinks of himself as German, and his company has sent him home to Germany every two years on vacation. We became good friends and ended up climbing Mount Kilimanjaro together, with his son and my daughter.

On the fourth day of the climb we were at 16,000 feet on the great saddle of the mountain that lies between the two peaks, watching the sun set on the vast African plain. At the equator, the sun sets very quickly because it goes down vertically. (Did you realize that in America, the sun doesn't set straight *down*? It sets at about a 45-degree angle.) It's a grand experience to watch that great ball of fire dive straight down for the horizon.

"Rolf," I asked him, "after 20 years of living in America, what do you think is the strangest characteristic of the American people?"

He proceeded to tell me how wonderful he thought the country was and how he loved living here. "Yes, I agree with you about all those things," I said. "What I'm curious about is this: Is there anything about Americans that you haven't figured out yet?"

Reluctantly he told me, "To my way of thinking, Americans have an incredible need for personal freedom. It's the best thing about them, and yet it's the worst thing. In my country we're willing to accept gun control because it reduces crime. We're willing to accept stricter building codes because it makes our cities more beautiful for everyone. Americans want personal freedom, however destructive it may be."

What would you do if you suddenly realized that you had burglars in your house? I hope you'd do what every law enforcement officer would tell you to do. Give them a way to escape. Never corner criminals so they have no way to get out. They're liable to turn violent.

The same principle applies in persuasion. You should always let the buyer have a way to get out. You should always let her have options.

Because we value personal freedom so much, you can very often sour a persuasion attempt, for no more reason than this. That the buyer feels trapped, and has no choice other than to comply with your demands. That may sound like checkmate to you, but when you force people to give in—rather than persuading them to do so—they very often do self-destructive things out of sheer frustration. This may include quitting your company, buying from your competitor, or, in the case of your children, doing something against your wishes out of a sense of rebellion.

It's an interesting point to remember in persuasion: We have a tremendous need to feel free. We don't want to feel that someone has outmaneuvered us and we have only one choice left. So Power Persuaders work with this and understand that you should always give the other side two options from which to choose.

The essence of the option tool is to be sure that the options you give them are both acceptable to you.

The salesperson closes by saying, "Well, I don't think there's any question that you need to go with the top-of-the-line machine. The question becomes, how do we work it out so you can live comfortably with the investment? Look at these two plans, and tell me which would be best for you. One is an extended purchase plan, and the other is a lease with an option to buy."

The sales manager says, "There's no question that as head of our West Texas division you should be a senior district manager. The question is: Should we make the announcement before you transfer to El Paso, or is it better to let you settle in there and make the announcement in 90 days? Which do you think, Bob?"

The "give them options," tool tells us two things. Never back somebody into a corner by saying things such as, "Take it or leave it. We're not going to reduce the price," or, "Anne, it's the only slot we've got open for a sales manager. Take the transfer or we're going to part company."

Remember that, in this country, we prize our freedom so much that we're likely to do dumb things when people try to deprive us of that freedom.

The second thing it tells us is that we should always offer the buyer two options, both of which we can live with. "We may be able to come off list price a little, provided you prepay the order. Would you rather do that?" Or, "Anne, the only way I can keep you in Chicago is as an assistant sales manager on straight commission. Would that be a better way for you to go?"

Verbal Persuasion Tool 8:
The Innocent Question

Let's say you're a sales manager and you've got a key salesperson who's threatening to leave. The salesperson is all worked up about it. You've refused to give him an increase in pay, and he says, "If you don't give me more money, I'm going to quit!"

You could do this: Lean back in your chair, thoughtfully think of your home telephone number, and mentally recite it backward, including the area code. This makes you appear to be deep in thought. Or, you might take off your glasses, if you wear them, and put the tip of one of the earpieces in your mouth. The body language signals a need for more information. A quizzical expression comes over your face. You finally say slowly, "But Bob, why would you want to do that?"

Bob might say, "Because I can't afford to go on working here for the money you pay me!"

You reply, "But Bob—wouldn't quitting without another job to go to just make your financial condition worse?"

"Well, I'll find somebody that will appreciate what I do for them!"

"But Bob, we appreciate what you do for us! It's just that we can't afford to give you any more money right now. Let's talk about ways that you could improve your productivity so we could afford to give you more money in the future. Fair enough?"

That little expression, "But why would you want to do that?" is magical. It's particularly magical if you know the buyer just blurted out a statement without giving it much thought.

For example, your best customer may suddenly lose patience and say, "Well, I'll just give the order to your competitor—that's what I'll do!"

You think of your home telephone number backward and calmly ask, "But why would you want to do that, Joe?"

"Because they care about our business. They can get the parts here next week."

"And if we weren't so fussy about quality control, we probably could get them here next week, too! Joe, we've been doing business together for 12 years, right? Have you ever had to shut down an assembly line because we didn't have the parts for you? Trust me, Joe, it's gonna be okay"

The beauty of the "innocent question" is that it forces the buyer to clarify and restate her objection. Often when she's forced to do that, the strong position she's taking won't make as much sense the second time around.

Key Points From This Chapter

1. Diffuse the opposition by making the case that there really isn't any conflict. You're both after the same thing.
2. Diffuse friction between people by getting them first to agree that both sides' purpose is identical, even if they can't agree on the method for solving the problem.
3. When someone asks you "not to take it personally," don't agree to.
4. Be "Nixonesque." Don't make a statement that's so specific that you can get nailed for it.
5. When people offend you, use the "I'm not offended" tool.
6. When you don't want to lie by denying the truth, it's time for the "easy to deny" tool.
7. Use the "I'm not suggesting" tool when you know perfectly well you caught the other person, hand firmly placed within the cookie jar.
8. Always let the buyer have a way to "escape." You should always let the buyer have options, because we all have a tremendous need to feel free.

9. When people are threatening to do something rash, think of
    your home telephone number backward and calmly ask, "But
    why would you want to do that?" Show yourself as the per-
    sonification of calm and poise.

13

Exposing and Destroying the HAGS

I N THIS CHAPTER, I'LL TEACH YOU HOW TO EXORCISE A BUYER'S NEGATIVE emotions. The word *exorcise* means to draw out: to expose and to banish. When people have bad feelings about you, or what you're doing, you're always better off to get those feelings out on the table. Have them acknowledge the bad feelings, and agree that they should be banished. An unexpressed emotion is akin to a festering wound: Unless exposed and treated, it always gets worse.

I call these four negative emotions the HAGS (Hurt, Anger, Greed, and Suspicion). They are the bane of a salesperson's life.

Negative Emotion 1: Hurt

Hurt is probably the emotion people least like to admit. It means a side of them trusted you, and now they feel let down. Hurt is a difficult emotion with which to deal because the hurt person always feels that he, too, was at fault for trusting you. Treat it gently, but you're always better off to exorcise it. Obviously this can happen a lot with personal relationships, but let's stick with a sales example.

Let's say that your best customer caught your company giving a lower price to his competitor. You never would've approved it if you'd known about it, but you're the one he's been dealing with, and he's hurt because he trusted you and, in his eyes, you let him down. Promising that you'll never do it again just doesn't get it. The problem is that the buyer doesn't trust you anymore. Why would he trust you that you're not lying to him now? You need to bring out the hurt, and treat it.

"Charlie, I can see you're hurt by this. I can see it in your eyes. And you've every right to be. You've trusted me for the eight years that we've been doing business together, and this is the first time we've ever let you down. Of course you're hurt, and you've every right to be. I don't want only to get your business back, Charlie. What's more important to me is getting your trust back. What would it take to do that, Charlie? You tell me."

Negative Emotion 2: Anger

Now let's take anger. The buyer hasn't come out and said she's angry with you, but it's obvious that she is. You say, "Jill, it's clear to see you're angry about this. And believe me, I agree with you. You've got every right to be angry. And maybe, I've got a right to be angry with your people too. However, staying angry with each other isn't going to solve the problem. Why don't we both put that behind us and look at ways we can rebuild our relationship. Fair enough?" (Incidentally, in Chapter 24, I'll share six more ways to persuade an angry person.)

Negative Emotion 3: Greed

The third emotion, greed, takes a little more finesse. Here we'll have to use a combination of exorcism along with a technique I call "Many people would feel...." Let's say that you're selling something because you desperately need to raise cash. You're vulnerable and you feel the other side is taking unfair advantage of it.

You say, "Sally, could I get something out on the table here? I appreciate your need to drive a hard bargain, and I don't have a problem with that. Many people would feel you're taking advantage of a difficult situation. However, I've known you for years and I know you're not a greedy person. Let's talk about a figure that would be fair for both of us."

What have we accomplished here? We've brought the problem out into the open. We've let them know that we're on to them, but we've done it without being confrontational.

Negative Emotion 4: Suspicion

How would you identify suspicion? A good clue is when people want to hide something from you. Perhaps you're dealing with two or more buyers and they ask for privacy to discuss something, or one passes a note to the other.

Another clue is when they don't feel comfortable answering your questions. Perhaps you've asked them a question and they haven't wanted to answer it yet. You ask, "How much business does your company do a year?"

They come back with this: "We wouldn't feel comfortable sharing that information with you." This is a polite way of saying, "It's none of your business, Charlie."

However, if you detect suspicion, confront it and **don't** overlook it, lest you'll make it worse. "Forgive me, but apparently, you don't trust me yet. Perhaps I haven't given you any reason to trust me. However, if we're to work together, it's important that we trust each other completely. So let's talk about it. What's bothering you?"

You may say, "Wait a minute, Roger. I might not want to know about this. If they start unloading on me, it could sour the relationship completely."

Trust me. You're always better off to know. Ignorance is never bliss. Ignorance may result in poverty and disease, but it is never bliss.

 # Key Points From This Chapter

1.   When people have bad feelings about you or what you're doing, you're always better off to get those feelings out on the table. Have them acknowledge the bad feelings and agree to deal with them.

2. Hurt means the other side trusted you...and now they feel let down. Hurt is a difficult emotion with which to deal because the hurt person always feels that he was at fault for trusting you.

3. When buyers haven't come out and said they're angry with you (but it's obvious they are), bring it out. Say something like "Sally, it's clear to see you're angry about this. Why don't we both put that behind us and look at ways we can rebuild our relationship. Fair enough?"

4. Handling greed takes a little more finesse. Let them know you're on to them, without being confrontational.

5. Suspicion on their part means they don't trust you yet. You can detect this if they avoid answering your questions or conceal things from you by passing notes or asking for privacy. If you detect suspicion, confront it. Don't overlook it, or you'll make it worse.

6. When you encounter the negative emotions of hurt, anger, greed, and suspicion, don't learn to live with them. Learn to exorcise them instead.

P~art~ T~wo~

Analyzing the Buyer

I THINK THIS SECTION ABOUT ANALYZING THE BUYER WILL FASCINATE YOU.

Power Persuasion would be a lot easier to learn if everybody reacted the same way, wouldn't it? We could simply learn what to say that would make our proposal irresistible, and go out there and lay our story on the buyer. Buyers would clap their hands, jump up and down with joy, and yell, "I can't wait!"

Unfortunately, they don't.

Everyone reacts in his or her unique way. That's what makes persuasion challenging, but it's also what makes it fascinating. We will look at the dimensions that affect the way you should persuade, and how you can read them in the buyer.

We'll look at these three questions in this section:

How do buyers react to what you tell them?

Is the buyer a "matcher" or a "mismatcher"?

What motivates the buyer?

Is she drawn to possibilities or does she react only to necessity? Does she sort your input by how it affects her or how it affects others? Does she seek pleasure or resist pain? Are they field-dependent or field-independent?

How does the buyer decides?

You know how if you understand his buyer personality. Is he assertive or non-assertive? Is he emotional on non-emotional? Is he

141

open-minded or close-minded? Is the buyer conscious or unconscious in they way information is received? And what is his neuro-linguistic orientation? Is he visual, auditory, or kinesthetic?

14

Matchers Versus Mismatchers

EVERYONE EITHER TENDS TO BE A "MATCHER" OR "MISMATCHER," and being able to recognize which your buyer is makes you a better persuader.

Matchers like their world to stay the same. They're likely to stay on the same job for a long time and stay married to the same person for life. They vacation in the same place every year and seldom change their mind about anything. They are the "know what I like and like what I know" brigade.

Mismatchers like the excitement of change, and they frequently change jobs and spouses. They have a high level of discontent, which can be healthy and make them very ambitious. Or it can be negative and lead to great frustration and failure.

Note that matchers and mismatchers don't always translate into positive and negative thinkers. At first you might think that the matcher is more the positive, because he is happy with his pattern of doing things and doesn't want to change. And that the mismatcher must be negative, because he doesn't like to repeat the same experiences. But you could also make the case that the mismatcher is the positive one. He's eager to try new things because he's confident that he can make things work and so is not afraid to try new things.

Let's start by figuring out whether you are a matcher or a mismatcher. Take a look at the next page.

In the lines that followthe bills, list five things that you observe about the relationship between the three pieces of paper. Be sure to do this before you read beyond that, or you'll miss the benefit of the exercise:

1._____

2._____

3._____

4._____

5._____

When looking at these images, a matcher will see the similarities:

1. They're all U.S. currency.
2. They're all the same size.
3. They're all written in English.
4. They all have their value in all four corners.
5. They're all made of paper.

A mismatcher, on the other hand, will see the differences:

1. They're all different values.
2. One is face down, two are face up.
3. There's a serial number on the front, but not the back.
4. Only the five is green in color.
5. The five has a building on it, the others have faces.

It's unlikely that you're either a *pure* matcher or mismatcher—there are varying degrees in-between. You probably listed some similarities and some dissimilarities. But which did you list first? If you listed the similarities first, that's significant. You're a matcher who *also* sees exceptions. If you listed the dissimilarities first, you're a mismatcher who sees exceptions.

Let's see how you can identify this trait in people. Let's say you want to discuss your industry with a friend of yours who is also a salesperson. You may say, "Tell me what you like about being a salesperson." Note that you've taken a position in the way that you asked the question. You came at it from a positive point of view. You asked "What do you like?" and not "What do you have the biggest problem with?"

It's up to your friend to match or mismatch that statement. He or she might say, "I love the big commission checks and the freedom of not having to go to an office." Or he or she might mismatch you by saying, "I like it so much, it's easier for me to tell you what I don't like. I could do without the airplanes and the taxis."

Let's say that you sell office equipment and you're upgrading a customer to the latest version of your equipment. This company has been a good customer for years, and they are happy with the equipment you sold them last time. However they're now ready to trade the old one in and invest in the latest model.

Ask a matcher why she's thinking of making the investment. This person will tell you, "This one has been such a great machine for us, we know we'll be even happier with the latest model."

Ask a mismatcher and this person will tell you, "This one's getting old, and we want to trade it in before it starts giving us trouble. And the new model can do so many things that this one can't."

Your sales approach should be different. With the matcher, you'd stress that the new machines are every bit as reliable as the old ones. Even though they do more, they are just as easy to use and maintain. And all the supplies or software that they've been using will work with the new equipment.

With the mismatcher, you'd want to stress the differences. Tell them how the machine has been completely redesigned. How it's way ahead of its predecessor, and once they have it, they'll wonder how on earth they ever got along without it.

How does this help you become a Power Persuader? If you know whether they match or mismatch, you'll know how to appeal to them. For example, reverse psychology only works on a mismatcher. If you've raised children, I'm sure you've had at least one who's a mismatcher. If you want your daughter to finish her homework before she goes to bed, you have to say to her, "Why don't you get up early and finish your homework in the morning when you're fresh?"

She'll say, "Daddy, I told you, I have to finish it tonight!"

If you want your son to ride his bike to school, you have to say, "Why don't I give you a ride to school, and you can catch the bus home?"

He'll say, "I don't want to ride the bus. I'll ride my bike instead." This only works with a mismatcher. Try it with a matcher and he or she will say, "Sure, if that's what you want me to do."

My literary hero Ernest Hemingway was a classic mismatcher, known for his cantankerous outbursts against anyone he didn't like. So when young journalist A.E. Hotchner was told by his editor at *Cosmopolitan* to find a way to get Hemingway to write an article on the future of journalism, he had a huge challenge on his hands. Hemingway only wrote what he wanted to write and had a reputation for verbally destroying any journalist with the nerve to approach him.

Hotchner flew down to Havana, where Hemingway was living in his country home just outside of town. He spent two days at the Hotel Nacional in what he described in his great book *Papa Hemingway* as a "semicomatose state induced by pure cowardice," trying to come up with a plan. Knowing that Hemingway, as a world-class mismatcher, was liable to oppose anything he said, he sent him a note explaining why he was there. He told Hemingway he didn't expect him to write the article, but he'd be obliged if Hemingway would let him have a note saying he'd tried, so that he wouldn't get fired from *Cosmopolitan*. The strategy worked. The next morning he got a call from the great author, who said he couldn't permit Hotchner to lose face with the Hearst organization (which owned *Cosmopolitan*) because it would be like "getting bounced from a leper colony." Their meeting turning into a lifelong friendship, with Hotchner adapting many of Hemingway's stories for television.

Similarly if you were a sales manager trying to persuade your top salesperson that a transfer from Boston to El Paso is the most wonderful thing that will ever have happened, you'd want to consider whether this person was a matcher or mismatcher. With the matcher, you'd want to tell how El Paso is a thriving metropolis that has everything Boston can offer! With a mismatcher you'd stress the excitement of a new culture along with new friends and new challenges.

 ## Key Points From This Chapter

1. Everyone either tends to be either matcher or mismatcher. Being able to recognize which one of these your buyer is helps you become a better persuader.

2. Matchers look for similarities; mismatchers look for differences. Most people are a combination of both. Some look for similarities and then see the exceptions. Others look for dissimilarities and then look for exceptions.

3. Matchers would like their world to stay the same and form lifelong attachments to things and people. Mismatchers are always discontent and frequently move on to what they hope will be greener pastures.

4. To persuade a matcher, stress the improvements over the pre-vious service or product, but not the differences. To persuade mismatchers, stress how different your product or service is from what they've had in the past.

5. Reverse psychology works well with the mismatcher. Antici-pate that he'll disagree with you and want to move away from your proposal.

15

What Motivates the Buyer?

I
N THIS CHAPTER, I'LL TEACH YOU ABOUT THE INTERNAL FRAMES OF
reference that motivate the buyer to do what you want him or her to
do. In this context, there are four paradigms that explain how people
view their world:

1. **Possibility versus necessity.** People are either motivated by
    the possibility of reward as the result of acting or by the feel-
    ing that they must take action out of necessity.
2. **Self-centered versus externally centered.** People either see
    the change in light of how it would affect them or how it would
    affect others.
3. **Pleasure versus pain.** People make decisions to either move
    toward pleasure or move away from pain.
4. **Field-dependent or field-independent.** This is psychology-
    talk for questioning whether people care about what others
    think. Some people are very much influenced by what others
    think. Other people could care less.

In this chapter, we shall take a look at these one at a time.

Possibility Versus Necessity

Put yourself in the shoes of movie producer Mike Todd in October of 1956. It was the night before his movie *Around the World in 80 Days* premiered. He was flat broke and millions of dollars in debt. He had high hopes for his new movie, but he also knew it could bomb.

The phone in his Park Avenue apartment rang. It was Otis Chandler, the publisher of the *Los Angeles Times*. He offered to buy 50 percent of the movie for 15 million dollars. Todd told Otis he wanted to take a vote among the people there: wife Elizabeth Taylor, son Mike, and friend Eddie Fisher. His son and friend both told him to jump at the money. His wife told him to gamble.

He took his hand off the mouthpiece and turned down the offer, in effect betting 15 million dollars that his movie was worth much more— at least 30 million. What kind of person would take a gamble like that? A possibility thinker, that's who.

We are all either possibility thinkers or we are necessity thinkers. (Just for the record, Robert Schuller coined the phrase *Possibility Thinker*.) The first are motivated by what might happen. The second only take action when they have to.

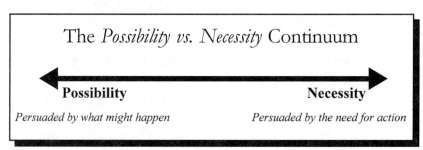

The *Possibility vs. Necessity* Continuum

Possibility ◄——————————————► Necessity

Persuaded by what might happen   *Persuaded by the need for action*

Possibility thinkers are not the plodders of the world. They are always taking great soaring leaps, and very often they come crashing down. Necessity thinkers would never quit a job because of practical reasons ("I can't quit now, I've only got 10 years to go until retirement"). The possibility thinker always has half a dozen pipe dreams going for him...which may take him to another job altogether.

Where do possibility thinkers come from? Probably from feelings of security or insecurity that build up in us very early in life. Until I was 18 years old, I lived in nine different homes and changed high schools four times. That gives you a completely different perspective on life, over kids who live in the same house until they leave for college. You become more comfortable with change and feel more secure taking risks.

That's why the unknown fascinates possibility thinkers. Their minds race ahead to all the exciting things that lay out there, beyond their present frame of reference. Necessity thinkers anchor to the world they know.

Let me give you a simple test to determine where you are on this scale. Answer this question: How old were you when you first started earning money outside your home? In asking this question to literally hundreds of job applicants over the years, I've found a very direct correlation. The younger you were when you first started earning your own money, the more initiative you'll have. And the more initiative you have, the more you will function on possibilities rather than necessities.

It's easy to see how Power Sales Persuaders use this. Your buyers who are possibility thinkers are always looking for what they could gain by buying from you. By realizing this, you know that the key is to paint an exciting picture of the great things that could happen if they buy.

Your necessity-based buyers are more concerned about what they might *lose* by making a move. You need to talk to those buyers about how this move will enable them to maintain what they already have.

Self-Centered Versus Externally Centered

The next dimension is how people reference their world in terms of self-interests or external interests. On the extreme ends of the scale, you have Mother Theresa, whose interests were totally external with almost no self-interests, and on the other end of the scale you have Donald Trump, who seems only capable of considering things in terms of self-interests.

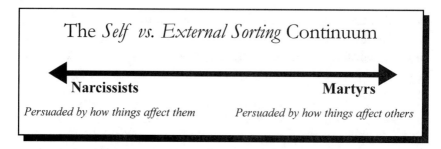

The *Self vs. External Sorting* Continuum

Narcissists   **Martyrs**

Persuaded by how things affect them   *Persuaded by how things affect others*

Few people are that extreme—most of us are somewhere in the middle of this self-importance scale. We are neither martyrs (I am nothing compared to my cause) to narcissists (I am the center of the universe). Because we admire externally oriented people, and condemn people for being self-centered, we tend to think of ourselves as less self-centered than most. When we do act in a self-centered way, we tend to justify. For example, we say, "The situation called for someone to make tough choices."

It's interesting how the differences between us and other people pop into our minds during conversations. Once I was talking to a friend about marriage proposals she had received. She told me that she'd been proposed to several times and almost accepted one of them.

"Why didn't you," I asked her.

"Because at the last moment, I started thinking to myself, *Why I am I doing this? I'm not lonely, I don't want to have children, and I don't need financial support.* So I thought 'what's in it for me,' and told him no."

This was so far from my thinking about marriage that, for a moment, I couldn't put it together with my frame of reference. To me, you don't marry someone because of what's in it for you. You marry someone because you love her so much that you just want to give everything to her. In this instance, she was sorting internally and I was sorting externally.

If you know whether your buyers sort internally or externally, you know how to persuade them. Let's say you sell temporary help services to corporations. If their human resources director sorts internally, you'd want to tell him how much work and hassle this will save him. If he sorts externally, you'd want to stress what a big help it will be to the company.

If you sell cars, you'd tell the internal sorter how good she is going to feel as she drives it. To an external, you'd stress how safe and comfortable her family with be.

Analyze the way your buyers talk, and decide whether they sort internally or externally. If they are internal, appeal to their self-interests. If they are external stress the benefits to the people around them.

Moving Toward Pleasure or Away From Pain

We all are somewhere on the pleasure/pain continuum. When faced with a decision, we will always decide based on where we are on that continuum. The extremes would be the hedonist (pleasure seeker) and the coward (pain avoider). But few people are that extreme.

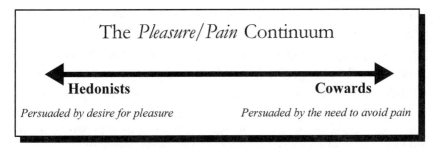

The *Pleasure/Pain* Continuum

Hedonists   **Cowards**

Persuaded by desire for pleasure   *Persuaded by the need to avoid pain*

The pleasure/pain continuum is often the key to motivating your buyer. If your buyer tends to seek pleasure rather than avoid pain, he'll buy if he thinks it will bring him pleasure. If your buyer tends to avoid pain, he'll buy when it saves him pain or discomfort.

I didn't understand how the pain/pleasure continuum motivates people until I was climbing the Matterhorn in Switzerland with my son John. My French climbing guide Guy, (pronounced *Gee*, with a hard *G*), gave me the finest motivational talk of my life. At one point, I couldn't see any way to make the next pitch. The rock was perfectly smooth. Guy was above me, belaying my rope. I could call out to him, but I couldn't see him. I yelled, "Guy, this isn't going to go. There's no way."

He called back, "Roger, you will find a way to make it go. If you don't we will 'ave to spend ze night on zis mountain." That's when I really understood motivation, as it relates to avoiding pain, for the first time. When the pain of doing nothing exceeds the pain of moving on, you will move on. I swung out onto the rock and somehow made it up.

Where are you on this continuum? It has a lot to do with how much discipline you have. I remember having dinner with some business acquaintances when they said, "Roger, we need a fourth for golf tomorrow. We're playing at Monarch Bay, which is a beautiful course right on the ocean. Want to join us? Please come as our guest." I'm sure you've been in a situation similar to that, haven't you? When you're torn between the pleasure of doing something that would be really fun, and the pain of all the work that will pile up while you're out goofing off? If you were in my situation, what would you have done? I'm self-employed, so I was free to take the day off. However, I was under a deadline to get a manuscript to my publisher. If I played golf, I knew I'd have to burn some midnight oil to get caught up. What would you have done?

Perhaps the answer is clear to you. You might be thinking, "Are you crazy? Go play golf! Don't pass up a great opportunity like that." Or you may be at the other end of the scale, saying, "Roger, you'll never achieve your full potential if you goof off like that. Keep working, and there'll be time for fun later." I guess I'm somewhere in the middle. I played golf with them, but I felt guilty about it!

This is an underlying key to all human behavior. Do you exercise because you enjoy it or because you want to prevent a heart attack? Do you do what your boss tells you because you want to be on the team or because you don't want him or her angry at you? Do you mow the lawn because of how great it's going to look or because if you don't do it this week, it'll be murder to do next week?

It's easy to see how Power Sales Persuaders can use this to get what they want. If you see that the buyer is a pleasure-seeker, you paint a picture of how good it's going to make him feel. If you know he's a pain avoider, paint a picture of the penalties of not making a move.

How do you find out which of these your buyers are? Ask them, "How do you feel about that?" It's open ended, so they can't answer with a yes or no, and it goes to their feelings—which is what you're trying to uncover.

Your buyer says, "We're thinking of expanding our line of sporting goods equipment to include tennis rackets."

You ask, "How do you feel about that?"

If the buyer's a pleasure-seeker, he'll say, "I think it'd be great. It'll expose us to a whole new class of customer." If he's a pain avoider, he'll say, "I'm concerned by diversifying we'll lose focus on our core business."

You might have a sales manager, who says, "I'm thinking of expanding into Florida."

Instead of jumping in with your opinion about it, you ask, "How do you feel about that?" If he's a pleasure-seeker, he'll say, "It's a dynamite idea, and I know someone who'd die for the opportunity to run the district down there." If he's a pain-avoider, he'll say, "I'm not convinced we should expand in this soft market. But if we don't, our competition will beat us to the punch."

Field-Dependant Versus Field-Independent

Next let's take a look at something by which we all are all influenced. Some people care very deeply what other people think, and others could care less what other people think. Psychologists call this being field-dependant versus field-independent.

The lives of field-dependant people are constantly being affected by what's going on around them. They quickly take on the mood of the people around them. If everybody's happy and excited, they tend to be that way too. They often avoid watching the news on television, because they're so deeply affected by bad news.

Field-independent people seem oblivious to what's going on around them. They can be in Times Square at midnight on New Year's Eve and still not get caught up in the excitement. The film *Roger and Me* portrayed then–General Motor's chairman Roger Smith as field-in-dependent and completely oblivious to the affect plant closures were having on the people of Flint, Michigan. That wasn't accurate, but it was filmmaker Michael Moore's perception.

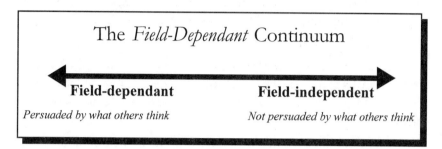

The *Field-Dependant* Continuum

Field-dependant   **Field-independent**

Persuaded by what others think   *Not persuaded by what others think*

Both ends of the continuum have pluses and minuses. Let's first consider the person who is very field-dependent, who cares very much what other people think. On the positive side, this is a person who is considerate and thoughtful of others. On the negative side, this is a person who never takes a stand on anything and is constantly being blown back and forth by the winds of change. This person is a joiner and never a leader.

Conversely, consider people who are field-independent, who doesn't care what others think. On the positive side they are the leaders of society, always in the forefront of change. Also they are what Abraham Maslow described as "self actualizing" people, unfettered by the need to be liked or looked up to by other people. On the negative side, they might be considered as bombastic and self-centered.

You first need to learn how to identify the buyer on this continuum. Here's an excellent way to do it. In some way find out how the buyer knows he or she is doing a good job. Let's say you sell furniture to hotels, and you're meeting with the vice president in charge of operations for a medium-sized regional chain of hotels. At some point in the conversation, you might find it appropriate to ask, "Something has always interested me about large companies such as this. How do you know when you've done a good job?"

A field-dependant person will tell you, "I get an annual review just like all the other employees, and the president of the company lets me know. Usually he doesn't pull any punches!" A field-independent person will be more likely to say, "Oh, I don't need anybody to tell me, that's for sure. If I don't meet the criteria I've set for myself, I know I've failed."

You probably won't have to be as direct as that to find out where he or she is on this continuum. If you're aware of it and are listening carefully to the other's person's responses, you'll quickly pick up on how much he cares about what other people think of him. Field-independent people say things such as, "It's my neck that is in the noose on this one," or "I'm going to go with my gut instinct," or, "They just don't know what's best for them."

Field-dependant people say things such as, "I want to survey our people on this before we go ahead," or "I have to take several options to the committee," or "I don't want everybody breathing down my neck on this."

Having identified the buyer as field-dependant or field-independent, you can then plan your persuasion strategy. To the field-independent hotel furniture buyer you'd say things such as, "You can't expect your guests to be the mattress expert that you are. All they care about is if they get a good night's sleep. You are the one who has to do what's in their best interests." To the field-dependent person, you're better off to say, "Nobody's going to write you to complain about a soft mattress, but believe me, they know whether they've had a good night's sleep or not. And they quit staying at your hotels. You don't want that, do you?"

 ## Key Points From This Chapter

1. Buyers are either motivated by the possibilities of your proposal or by the perceived necessity of making a move. When talking to a possibility thinker, stress the exciting benefits of making a move. When persuading a necessity thinker, stress the penalties of not changing.
2. People are either persuaded by self-interests (internal sorters) or by concern for others (external sorters). In some it's extreme—

Donald Trump, Mother Theresa—but in most of us it's much more subtle. Analyze the way your buyers talk, and decide whether they sort internally or externally. If they're internal, appeal to their self-interests. If they're external, stress the benefits to the people around them.

3.   The pleasure/pain continuum is often the key to motivation. If we seek pleasure rather than avoid pain, we will move if we think it will bring us pleasure. If we avoid pain, we will be motivated to move when it will cause us to avoid pain or discomfort. If you see the buyer as a pleasure-seeker, paint a picture of how good your proposal is going to make him feel. If you know that he is a pain-avoider, paint a picture of the penalties of not making a move.

4.   Some people care very deeply what other people think, and others could care less. Psychologists call this being field-dependant versus field-independent. To the field-dependant buyer, stress how much people will appreciate his going along with your proposal. To the field-independent buyer, emphasis how he must take a leadership role and make bold decisions.

16

How the Buyer Decides

I N THE PREVIOUS CHAPTER, I TAUGHT YOU ABOUT THE INTERNAL FRAMES OF reference that cause people to analyze your proposal in different ways. Now that you know this, let's say that you have skillfully determined their internal reference points and made your presentation in such a way that it has maximum appeal to their way of thinking. Great!

Now we're down to the actual point where the buyer makes a decision to go with your proposal or reject it. In this chapter I'll teach you some of the processes that buyers go through before they decide whether or not to be persuaded.

Assertive Versus Unassertive

Assertive people tend to make decisions quickly. They take a look at your proposal and either go for it or don't go for it. Less assertive people need time to make up their minds.

This facet is very important when you're trying to persuade someone to buy. If you don't ask the assertive person to buy, he or she will think something is wrong. This person may ask why you don't feel strong enough to push for an approval. Conversely, if you push an unassertive buyer for a decision before he or she is ready to make it, you're creating a problem. This person will either resist what is seen as a high-pressure tactic, or think you're trying to push the sale before half the needed information is given to make the right move.

So, it's very important to know if the person with whom you're dealing is assertive or not. Fortunately, it's not hard to tell. It is simple as this: An assertive person will greet you with a firm handshake, and get down to business with a minimum of formalities. This person needs enough information to make a decision, but not too much. If you overload them with information, they'll think, "Oh come on! Don't give me all this flimflam! Who are you trying to con? Just give me the facts."

Conversely, an unassertive person will greet you tentatively and want to spend time getting to know you before he or she gets down to business. This person's approach will be more like this: "Oh hi. It's nice to see you again, come on in. Can I get you some coffee? How's the children?"

First, you must analyze if the buyer you're trying to persuade is assertive or unassertive. If the buyer is assertive, go for the close. Give the facts and ask to go for your proposal. If he or she is unassertive, take your time. Give all the information wanted, be sure the buyer feels comfortable with you, and then gently nudge toward a decision.

Emotional Versus Unemotional

The next dimension to consider is whether your buyer is emotional or not. You can tell this by the way you are greeted and the way things are reacted to. The emotional buyer will greet you with either warmth or excitement and react with attentive enthusiasm to your appeal. The unemotional person will greet you in a businesslike manner, which may even appear cold to you. If, for example, you're having breakfast meeting with both an emotional and an unemotional person, you'll easily spot the differences. The emotional person will be friendly toward the waitress, call her by name, and ask how she is and what she recommends. The unemotional person will ignore the waitress unless he needs something and then make brief, businesslike requests. He may not even want to see the menu.

The way a buyer will react to your persuasion proposal depends on the level of emotion, combined with the level of assertiveness. Here's how the four possible combinations of these two factors will react:

- **Emotional/Assertive:** "Let's run with it. Sounds like a terrific idea to me. How fast can we put it into effect?" or "Sounds like a crazy idea to me. Too crazy for us. What else do you have?"

- **Emotional/Unassertive:** "I really appreciate you bringing this to me. I like the idea, but I wouldn't feel comfortable going ahead without talking to the employees about it first. I hope you understand." or "I just don't think this would fit in with what we do here. We don't like to rock the boat with a lot of new ideas."

- **Unemotional/Assertive:** "I'm only going to go with this if it makes us money. Show me it'll do that and I'll give you the go-ahead today." or "We've tried that before. Sounds like a good idea, but it won't work. Trust me."

- **Unemotional/Unassertive:** "I can see you've really done your homework on this. Subject to our verifying the results of your research, I'd like to give you a tentative go-ahead." or "I wouldn't feel comfortable jumping into something like this. We'd have to do some thorough research before we could consider it, and we're so backlogged, I don't know when we'd ever be able to get around to it."

The emotional, assertiveness ratings of the people with whom you're dealing have a lot to do with the way you go about getting a decision. In order to pigeonhole them into the correct one of the four categories, be sure to evaluate their assertiveness rating first, and then their emotional rating. It's much harder to do the other way around.

•••

Now let's move to how the buyer reacts to your proposal. There are basically two steps that the buyer will go through as you try to persuade her. She will listen to what you have to say, and then they will process that information with either conscious or unconscious thought.

Open- or Closed-Minded

Let's consider the first step: listening to what you have to say. People listen with either an open or a closed mind.

Open-minded people evaluate what you have to say based on what they hear or observe. They make up their minds based on what you have to tell or show them.

Closed-minded people evaluate what you have to say as it relates to what they already know. These are the people who believe that Japanese cars are better made and will not listen to any evidence to the contrary. It's the buyer who is happy with his present supplier and won't take the time to listen to your proposal.

Obviously, a closed-minded person is harder to persuade. With open-minded people, you may be able to persuade them by talking about what you or your product can do or by letting them read about it. With a closed-minded person, your persuasion must include letting them see a demonstration or, better yet, getting them to take part in a hands-on demonstration.

Open-minded: Show and tell.

Closed-minded: See and do.

When it's not obvious, how do you tell whether a buyer is open- or closed-minded? For the sake of example, let's say that you sell glass bottles and you're trying to get a spaghetti sauce company to switch to you as its packing supplier. You might say to the buyer, "You tell me that your present supplier is the best in the business, but how do you know that?"

If the buyer says, "I never hear any complaints from our production department," or "I read the quality control reports," you're probably dealing with someone who is open-minded. Lucky you!

However, if this person says, "I personally inspect the rejects every week, and it's never more than one-tenth of one percent," or "I spent five days at their plant in Pacoima. Nobody can touch their quality control," then you've probably got a closed-minded person on your hands. You have to get this person to see what you can do.

Conscious or Unconscious Thought Processors

The first step to their decision-making process is how they listen to your proposal—be it with an open or closed mind. The second step involves how they process the information you give them. Let's say that you've gotten past the resistance of a closed-minded person and been able to lay your story on her. Now you have an additional factor to consider: Does she process the information you've given her consciously or unconsciously?

Conscious thinkers process the information with their five senses. Unconscious thinkers go with their intuitive feel about your presentation.

Let's recap the five senses, so you get an idea of the process that conscious thinkers use:

Sense	Meaning	Example
Visual	Seeing	A painter
Auditory	Hearing	A musician
Tactile	Touch	A potter
Gustatory	Taste	A chef
Olfactory	Smell	A perfumer

You're not likely to run into many people whose primary sense is tactile (touch), gustatory (taste), or olfactory (smell). You will be primarily concerned with distinguishing between auditory and visual people. So, here's a quick test to see which you are: Close your eyes and think of the house in which you lived when you were 10 years old. Hold that thought for 15 seconds, then open your eyes and continue reading.

When you did that exercise, did you primarily *see* the house in your mind, or did you mainly *hear* things (such as the laughter of children or your mother working in the kitchen). As I told you in the earlier chapter on credibility, most people are visual. They believe more what they see than what they hear.

The point I'm making here is not that you should be able to analyze which of their five senses dominates. I want you to realize that some people are persuaded by what their five senses tell them. Some people are dominated by their sixth sense, intuition. However, it is interesting to note that you can tell whether people are visual or auditory by the expressions of speech they use. Here are some comparisons:

Visual	Auditory
I see your point.	I hear you.
Take a look at this.	Listen to this.
Do I have to paint a picture?	Do I have to spell it out?
Did I make myself clear?	Did you hear what I said?
Looks like we should.	Sounds as though we should.

If you determine that the person you're trying to persuade is primarily using his five senses to analyze your presentation (a conscious thinker) you will know that you must be concrete in your appeal. He needs to see it, hear it, touch it, taste it, or smell it in order to be convinced. Do everything you can to let him experience your product or service sensually. For food or drink, tasting and smelling will be important as well.

Conversely, some people don't interpret your presentation with their five senses at all. They react more by gut instinct or intuition. These people are called kinesthetic (feeling) people. When we add kinesthetic language to the chart, we get a new "feel" for what's going on!

Visual	Auditory	Kinesthetic
I see your point.	I hear you.	I feel you're right.
Take a look at this.	Listen to this.	Get a sense of this.
Picture it.	Do I have to spell it out?	Can't you grasp it?
Is it clear now?	Did you hear what I said?	Understand?
Looks like we should.	It sounds good.	Feels good to me.

When dealing with kinesthetic people (unconscious thinkers) it's less important that you let them see, hear, touch, taste, or smell your product or service. The way to persuade them is to paint vivid mental pictures of how it's going to feel to be doing business with you.

(What I've covered in this chapter is based on the work of famed psychologist Carl Jung, and I cover it in more detail in my tape program *Confident Decision Making*, which is available by calling my office at (800)-Y-DAWSON.)

Key Points From This Chapter:

1. Assertive people make decisions quickly. Unassertive people are slow decision-makers.

2. How quickly you push for a decision must be based on their level of assertiveness.

3. Next, determine their emotional level. From this you develop four different persuasion appeals:

    Emotional/Assertive: Razzle-dazzle them with how exciting the project will be, and how they have to jump on the opportunity before it passes them by.

    Emotional/Unassertive: Warm them up slowly to the idea. Tell them how good everybody's going to feel.

    Unemotional/Assertive: Tell them the bottom line benefits, and push for a fast decision.

    Unemotional/Unassertive: Give them lots of precise detail, because they make a decision based on facts, but they need an overload of information.

4. Next, determine if the buyer is open- or closed-minded. You can persuade the open-minded buyer with show and tell, but the closed-minded buyer must see and do.

5. Next, does the buyer process the information you've given her with conscious or unconscious thought? Conscious thinkers process the information with their five senses. Unconscious thinkers go with their intuitive feeling about your persuasion presentation. So with conscious thinkers, you must let them see, hear, and touch your product or service. With unconscious thinkers, it's more important to romance their imaginations.

Part Three

How to Become a Power Persuader

IN PART THREE I'LL TEACH YOU HOW TO DEVELOP THE PERSONAL characteristics of a Power Persuader. Although you may think that some people are naturally persuasive, this just isn't so. There are three learnable skills that will draw other people to you and make them want to please you.

Firstly, we'll cover that hard-to-describe quality we call charisma. We simply like some people so much that if they were to ask us to do anything, we would. This is definitely the case with the fan of a pop music star: Ask any 16-year-old boy how he'd react if Britney Spears asked a favor of him. This is also true for admirers of political leaders and of top people in any profession. It's a subtler motivating factor, but it's so critical to effective persuasion.

Then I'll teach you how to develop a sense of humor. (And yes, you really can learn that.) There are only five things that make people laugh, and everything else is a variation on those five things. What could be simpler?

Finally, I'll teach you the one thing that every salesperson would like to do better: remembering people's names.

Personal charisma, a sense of humor, and the ability to remember anyone's name instantly are the three personal characteristics of a Power Persuader.

17

Developing Charisma:
How to Make Your Buyers Love You!

HAT IS CHARISMA?

It's that rare quality that makes people like you, even when they don't know much about you.

It's that intangible that makes people want to follow you, to be around you, to be influenced by you.

It's that "*je ne sais quoi*" that causes people to see you from across a crowded room and want to be with you.

Salespeople who have it tell me, "Roger, the only reason my people do business with me is because they like me."

Celebrities who have it are at a loss to explain it. Art Linkletter gets a standing ovation whenever he walks onto a stage. "Roger," he told me, "I can tell you when it started, but I can't explain it."

We all know it when we see it, but we all have a difficult time explaining exactly what it is. John F. Kennedy had charisma. Richard Nixon did not, and it surely was the factor that cost him the 1960 presidential election. Ronald Reagan had it, although President Bush the father didn't. Bill Clinton had it like no other president. Even his enemies would give him that. Al Gore does not.

Robert Redford has it oozing out of his ears. You may think that it's good looks. Perhaps charisma is just our way of verbalizing the feeling we get when we meet a good-looking person. No, that's not it. Charles Bronson is as ugly as a fencepost and he has it.

Have you ever met a male model, one of those guys who poses for truck commercials? They're gorgeous, but their personalities are as one-dimensional as the billboards on which their images are splattered.

A Very Special Quality

So, what *is* charisma? We've all heard of charismatic religion. Charisma comes from the ancient Greek for "gift." In that sense, the word *charisma* refers to a gift from God of a special talent, such as the ability to heal or to prophesize.

German sociologist Max Weber was the first person to bring the term into modern-day usage and present it as a learnable skill. Weber referred to it as a form of authority. Until the start of the 20th century, authority was thought of as either law or tradition. Even if current law didn't prescribe a mode of behavior, people would still be persuaded to behave in a certain way because of tradition—a respect for the way things were done in the past. Max Weber introduced the concept of charisma as a third form of authority; one that people could be persuaded simply by the personality of another person.

In popular usage, charisma is defined as *a special quality that gives a person the ability to capture the imagination of another person, inspiring support and devotion.*

Wouldn't it be great to walk into a room and immediately know that everyone there was aware of you? Wouldn't it be great to walk into a buyer's office and know for sure that she will smile with pleasure, then reach out, hit the intercom button, and say, "Hold my calls?"

How about being in a company meeting while a big argument is going on. You quietly say, "This is what I think," and the whole room goes quiet. Wouldn't it be great?

Charisma—The Nonverbal Persuasion Power

Charisma is the nonverbal form of persuasion, and Power Persuaders know that at least 50 percent of the impression they give people is nonverbal. A study done at the University of Southern California attempted to show how people could communicate their emotions in a sales situation. The study showed that only 7 percent of our ability to communicate emotion was through the words used, 37 percent was the emphasis you gave to the words, and 55 percent was entirely nonverbal. (As my friend George Walther pointed out to me, this study is frequently misquoted. It refers only to emotion, not all communication.) Whatever the numbers, it's indisputable that what people see and sense about you is often more important than what you say.

Someone can glare at you and spit out, "You bastard!" and it's an expression of utter contempt. Or he could laugh, punch you gently in the arm, and say, "You bastard," and it would be friendly and even complimentary.

An expression that linguists like to play with is this: "I didn't say that he stole my car." What does that mean? It can mean a lot of things depending on where you put the emphasis on the words.

1. **I** didn't say that he stole my car. (My attorney said it.)
2. I didn't **say** that he stole my car. (I wrote it in a letter to the newspaper.)
3. I didn't say that **he** stole my car. (He told his driver to steal it.)
4. I didn't say that he **stole** my car. (I used the word *purloined*.)
5. I didn't say that he stole **my** car. (It was my wife's car.)
6. I didn't say that he stole my **car**. (I said that he stole my pickup truck.)

From this demonstration you can see why the study showed that 37 percent of your ability to communicate emotion is from the emphasis that you put on the words. That leaves 55 percent that is nonverbal—either your body language or the charisma that you project with the words.

To Understand Charisma, Imagine the Opposite

At my Power Persuasion seminars I ask the people in my audience to define charisma. It's a very interesting exercise, because nobody seems able to define it. They know what it is when they see it, but they don't know how to define it.

When you have trouble defining something, try to imagine the opposite. This makes it a lot easier. So, let's look at the opposite of charisma. Although you may have trouble defining charismatic qualities, you don't have trouble identifying the person you don't like, do you?

You probably don't like people who are self-centered and are only concerned with their own well-being. Take John Paul Getty, for example.

He was the richest man in the world, but nobody would want to change places with him, because he was so self-centered. Aristotle Onassis once said that he could only do business with him, once he understood that Getty had absolutely no sense of what was right or ethical. He would only ever act in his self-interest.

If we accept that the least charismatic person is the one who's most self-centered, we understand that charismatic people are those who have learned to expand their center. Their mental vision of their world has expanded to include all the people with whom they come in contact. Charismatic people are just as sensitive to the emotions of the people around them as they are to their own emotions. That's what makes people so charismatic.

If you had asked Mother Theresa to tell you about herself, she would have had a tough time. She had expanded her center to where she became one with the world in which she lived. Martin Luther King, Jr. had that same quality of being unable to distinguish his plight as a black man from the plight of black people throughout the world. Bill Clinton was a very charismatic politician because he was constantly telling us that he "felt our pain."

To become a truly charismatic Power Persuader, you must learn to expand your center. However, it's not enough just to have wonderful feelings inside of you. To be a Power Persuader, you must learn how to project those feelings to the rest of the world. This is what I'll teach you in the next chapter.

Key Points From This Chapter

1. Charisma is a form of authority. It affects people's behavior as much as respect for the law or respect for tradition.
2. It's a strong non-verbal form of communication.
3. If you have trouble understanding charisma, think of the opposite. With whom would you least like to spend the rest of your life on a desert island?
4. To be more charismatic, work on expanding your caring for other people to a larger circle of influence.

18

12 Ways to Project an Awesome Charisma

O KAY, SO NOW WE KNOW WHAT CHARISMA IS, BUT HOW DO YOU project it, so that people know how lovable we are? In this chapter, I'll teach you 12 ways to project an awesome charisma.

Rule 1: Make everyone you meet feel special.

Treat everyone you meet as if he or she is the most important person you'll meet that day. Now, that's very easy to say and very hard to do. Obviously, the people you meet in any given day have different levels of importance to you. The person who parks your car at a restaurant isn't as important to you as the waiter. Both aren't as important to you as the client with whom you may be dining. However, the important thing is to leave the impression that everyone you met felt that they were important to you.

But isn't this phony? Isn't it manipulative? Won't it come across as such? I don't think so, because what you'll find is that after you've adopted this habit and made it yours, these people will become important to you.

At my seminars and speeches, I make it a habit to stand at the door and shake hands with people coming into the room. With the smaller groups I can shake everyone's hand. If somebody sneaks by me, I even make a mental note of what they're wearing, and before I start I go up to that person and say, "I didn't get a chance to meet you when you came in. I'm Roger Dawson."

With the larger groups I can't get everybody because they're coming in through different doors. However, I can usually meet about 500 in a 15- to 20-minute period. The results of this are amazing.

First, the meeting planners can't believe I'm doing it. Their typical response is: "I've been running these meetings for 10 years, and I've never had a speaker meet the people at the door like that."

Second, it dramatically improves the audience reaction to the talk. Nobody ever heckles a speaker whose hand they've shaken. It would violate the bond we created.

Thirdly, I can really get a fix on the mood and background of the audience when I meet them like that.

However, far more important is the effect it has on me. I really enjoy doing it. After a while the difference between people becomes absolutely fascinating. Most people are comfortable with it. I offer my hand and say, "Hi, I'm Roger Dawson." If they look puzzled, I'll add, "Your speaker," and then they'll tell me their name and move on.

Am I being manipulative? Not at all! I really do enjoy meeting them. How long would you want to live on this planet if you were the only person on it. Not long, right?

It is people who make life worth living. Isn't it sad that we spend so much of our time and effort to accumulate things? We've got to learn to use things and love people, not use people and love things. Don't get me wrong, I've met lots of people I don't like. To this day I'll turn my back and walk away from people who make crude racial remarks or who want to run down our country.

What I'm saying is that when our life's adventure has run its course—when we're making that final review of the way things were—it will be the people we met who will give us pleasure. The things we accumulated don't count.

What we mustn't do, however, is patronize people. If a person's job is to check your coat, let him do his job. Don't slow him down with tedious small talk that's clearly a transparent attempt to show him how humble you can be.

Rule 2: Develop a great handshake.

If we've truly expanded our centers to include all those around us, we can get the right message across in a second or two with the right handshake.

When was the last time you asked someone to evaluate your handshake? Could you be a pumper, a crusher, or a wet fish and not know it? You should ask both a woman and a man for an opinion.

Let me give you a great tip for eliciting responses. Don't ask, "What did you think of my handshake?" Chances are they'll just say, "Great."

Try asking, "On a scale of one to 10, what did you think?"

They might say, "It was great—about an eight."

Then you can say, "Help me out. What would it take to make it a 10?"

This is also a terrific way to probe for information in all kinds of areas. If you're a salesperson and you can't get a fix on whether the buyer is ready to place the order or not, ask "So where are you on investing in this equipment, on a scale of one to 10, 10 meaning you're ready to order right now and one meaning you wouldn't take it if we gave it to you?" I've never had anyone refuse to give me a number.

She might say, "Well, I guess I'm at about a six." You could respond, "Help me out. What would it take to get you to a 10?"

She might respond, "I'll tell you what's bothering me. I see your figures about the projected savings, but I need something stronger than that. For me to go with this, I'd have to be guaranteed that kind of savings."

Bingo! In a few short seconds you've isolated the objection and almost got the buyer's commitment, if you can satisfy that one concern.

You might be a sales manager trying to hire a new salesperson for your company. You need to find out if the money you're offering is going to be enough to get him on board. "How do you feel about coming with us, on a scale of one to 10, 10 meaning you're ready to decide right now and one meaning you've already ruled it out?" You'll get an instant fix on how this person feels, without having to come right out and ask if you're offering enough money.

This is one of the most powerful tools I've ever learned for finding out what's going on in a person's mind, and it seems to work every time.

Get some feedback on your handshake, and practice if you have to, and get feedback on your ideas.

Rule 3: Notice a buyer's eye color.

Remember that you don't just shake hands with your hand, you also do it with your eyes. In the old days when woman expected men to kiss their hands, it was almost a passionate act to place your lips on the back of the hand while gazing up into her eyes. It has just as much impact today. Here's a trick that charismatic people have learned. When you shake people's hands and look into their eyes, make a mental note of the color of their eyes.

Making this a habit not only forces you to look into their eyes, but it also puts a twinkle into your eyes. It creates a special moment of interaction with the buyer.

Rule 4: Push out a positive thought.

The third part of a good handshake is the thought that you project at that moment. Remember that for a second or two, you're physically touching the buyer, and you have strong eye contact. If you believe in auras, they're intertwined. I believe people can unconsciously sense what you're thinking at that point. You need to push out some powerful positive thoughts at that point. If it's a person of the opposite sex, think to yourself, "This is the person I've been looking for all my life." If he or she is of the same sex, think to yourself, "This is a great person. I'd really like to know this person better."

Doesn't that sound silly? It does. Yet, you'll be amazed at the instant bond you create with people when you use this method.

So a charismatic handshake has a one, two, three punch. The right grip, the right eye contact, and the right thought projection.

Let me tell you my favorite story about shaking hands. Teddy Kennedy was campaigning for his Senate seat in 1962. He was shaking hands outside a factory early one morning. "Teddy," said a grimy worker, "I understand that you never worked a day in your life." This was something that his opponent had made a campaign issue, and Kennedy braced himself for an onslaught. "Let me tell you something," the worker continued, still warmly pumping his hand. "You ain't missed a thing."

Rule 5: Give sincere compliments.

Developing the habit of giving sincere compliments is not as difficult as it sounds. Think of it this way: Flattery is telling the buyer *precisely* what he or she wants to hear.

The reason we're reluctant to compliment people directly relates to our self-esteem. We fall into the trap of thinking, "Why would they care what I think? I'm not that important." This isn't exactly a self-image that's likely to draw other people to us, is it?

I remember speaking at a state association meeting of auto parts dealers in Oregon. During the lunch, with about 200 members and their spouses in the room, the activity of the executive director of the association fascinated me. Instead of sitting up at the head table, he spent the entire time walking around the room greeting the members. He seemed to know most of them by name, and he appeared genuinely excited and glad to see them. He looked more like a senator or governor running for reelection, and he was sincere. He really had expanded his center to include *all* the people in his association.

He impressed me so much that I sent him a postcard saying that of all the association meetings I'd attended, I'd never seen anybody do a better job of working the audience. He was so good at what he was doing that he didn't need me to point it out, and I almost didn't send the card because I didn't want him to think I was trying to butter him up.

A couple of months later I happened to be talking to him on the phone, and he immediately mentioned my postcard and told me how good it made him feel. By that time I'd completely forgotten that I'd sent it, and had to scramble to figure out what he was talking about. I was so surprised that he valued my opinion, I vowed I'd never hesitate to compliment someone again.

Rule 6: Catch people doing things right.

If you're a sales manager, you've probably had one of your salespeople say to you, "You never tell me that I'm doing a good job!" We probably all have, and sometimes our reaction is callous. We think, "Oh, come on, this is a business we're running here, not a kindergarten. You're paid to do a job, and I don't have time to run around all day patting you on the back." That's a little like the husband saying to the wife, "Don't keep asking me if I love you. Of course I love you, that's my job."

Let me tell you an experience that caused me to get on the bandwagon of constantly thanking employees. (Perhaps it'll change your thinking as well.) I was sitting in the back of the room at a convention in Las Vegas where I was the concluding speaker. The president of the company was thanking the employees who worked hard to make the convention a success, and he gave special thanks to his assistant for her efforts. All of this is very routine: I'd heard it a 100 times. His assistant was sitting close to me, so I turned around to add my congratulations. Tears were streaming down her face! She was so emotionally overwhelmed by this compliment that she had to get up and leave the room.

Compliments *do* mean a lot to your people. If your salespeople would break into tears if you paid them a compliment, maybe it's time to rethink your policy!

So let's get off this kick that people will think our compliments phony or manipulative and play the One-Minute Manager game: Let's catch somebody doing something right. People really do care what you think, and they really do appreciate your mentioning it.

Rule 7: Looks *do* matter!

Every ugly kid in the world has been told by his or her parents that looks don't matter. You have to tell this to children when they're really young, because when they've been in kindergarten for a week and a half, they'll have figured out that looks do matter, and they matter a great deal.

Because in this chapter we're talking only about non-verbal forms of persuasion, it's important that we talk about this straight from the shoulder. First, don't panic if you don't feel that you got a fair shake in the "looks" department. Charisma depends a lot more on what you do with what you've got than with what nature actually blessed you.

Franklin D. Roosevelt, confined to a wheelchair, was one of the most charismatic personalities that ever graced the Oval Office. Adolph Hitler was an ugly runt of a man, but his magnetic ability to galvanize his audiences into action was legendary. It took the combined might of the world's forces to stop him. Joseph Stalin had absolute control over the Soviet Union for 29 years, and he was borderline ugly.

Remember that 90 percent of your appearance is the way you dress, not your face. If style doesn't come naturally to you, hire an image consultant so that you'll know what colors to wear and what to avoid. Find someone who looks stylish and ask him or her for advice. You'll be amazed how eager that person will be to recommend a new hair-style or new makeup. Above all, don't be one of those people who gives up on his or her appearance. Some people have such low self-esteem that they have labeled themselves as hopeless in the looks de-partment so they have given up on wearing makeup, styling their hair, or wearing fashionable clothes. When your parents told you that looks don't matter, you didn't really believe them, did you?

Rule 8: Take a check up from the neck down.

So let's conduct a ruthless examination of your wardrobe. Spend-ing money on clothes is a cost of doing business, just as your car is, and it's a far better investment. You've got to spend money to make money, and one of the first places to start is at the dry cleaner. If you're still having shirts and blouses laundered at home, quit it right now. For about a dollar or two each you can get them laundered professionally. They look much nicer, and, really, don't you have better things to do with your time?

Start sending your clothes to the dry cleaner regularly. Wear them a couple of times at most and get them on down there. Of course that starts to cost real money, but the charismatic look that makes you a powerful persuader demands that you make the investment. Don't worry about it. You're going to get it back many times over.

Next, go through your wardrobe, and throw out anything you haven't worn in the last year. You'll be amazed how many clothes you have hanging in your closet that you don't like enough to wear but haven't thrown away.

I saw Bill Cosby do a skit on that in Las Vegas. He came on stage wearing an old fishing hat, explaining he didn't really like the hat, but he couldn't bear to throw it away because he had "time in" on it. He went on to point out that many of us are working at jobs that don't give us any satisfaction anymore, but we don't quit because we've got so much "time in." And many of us are in relationships that died years ago, but we hang on because of "time in" on them.

Rule 9: Smile 2 seconds longer than they do.

What's the most important thing we can wear that will improve our appearance and make us more charismatic? Smile. I believe it's the only form of communication that's completely universal. In the 103 countries I've traveled, a smile means just one thing: I like you, I trust you, and I'm glad we're together.

I remember travelling in central China, which was for many years completely isolated from the rest of the world. A generation of people had grown up who'd never seen even a picture of a person from the outside world. However, even in the most remote areas of China, a smile was universal. Even people who had never seen a Western person before would always respond to a warm smile.

You know what I've found about smiling? Many of us think we're smiling when all we're doing is parting our lips a little. So let's get a little feedback on how other people see our smiles.

Let's pick three people who know us well, and ask: "On a scale of one to 10, do you think I'm a person who smiles a lot?" My guess is that the response will surprise you. Although you might think you're a happy-go-lucky person who goes out of your way to be cheerful, others may see you as a very serious person who's seldom in a good mood.

If your friends give you sevens or lower on the scale, you need to force yourself to smile a little wider and a little longer. Look into the buyer's eyes, making a mental note of the color of them, and smile broadly. Wait until he or she smiles back, and hold it for two seconds more. Two seconds is probably longer than you think. To count out two seconds, say slowly, "One hundred and one, one hundred and two."

Rule 10: Work on pushing out empathy.

Don't forget that there's a world of difference between empathy and sympathy. Consciously making an effort to be sympathetic can come across as condescending—like pity. Nobody wants that.

Empathy is letting our feelings and emotions flow with the buyer. To truly identify with their mood and disposition. As the Indians say, "You don't truly know a man until you've walked a mile in his moccasins." (Or as the Indians in Palm Springs say, "Until you've driven a mile in his Cadillac.")

Do you want a simple explanation of the difference between sympathy and empathy? Sympathy is seeing a seasick woman on a boat and going over to put your arm around her. Empathy is going over and throwing up with her.

Take a moment and think of somebody who has that special persuasive charisma that we've been talking about. Can you picture this person in your mind? Okay, now take another moment and try to define what makes you feel comfortable when you're with this person. Don't picture what impresses you about this person, but why it feels good when you're around him or her.

Is it because there is a big smile on his or her face? Is this person happy, cheerful, and enthusiastic—The kind of person who is always up?

No, probably not. Sure, if you're in a bright upbeat mood, it's fun to interact with someone who's in a similar frame of mind. If you're under pressure—perhaps somebody has just chewed you out and you're struggling to meet a deadline, people like that are a pain in the neck.

The secret here is that we're drawn to someone who's in a similar emotional state. The neuro-linguistic experts call this "mirroring." Some go as far as saying that you should mirror the angle of the head, hand gestures, the way that they're standing or sitting. The point is that we feel more comfortable with people whom we feel are like us—and that feeling is what we call empathy.

Let's look at how empathy might work in a business situation. Joe sells office supplies and is calling on Mary Smith, one of his regular accounts. He walks into her office with his usual smile and good cheer. "Hi, Mary. How are you today?" He looks into her eyes and sees the usual sparkle is missing. She replies, "Oh, okay I guess," instead of her usual: "I'm fine, Joe. How are you today?"

If Joe centers on himself and what he wants to get out of this meeting, instead of having true empathy toward the people around him, he'd probably go right ahead and tell her the great joke about the fisherman and the mermaid he was planning to tell her. But because he's a charismatic person and has learned to center on the people around him, he immediately picks up on her flat response and says gently, "Mary, are you feeling all right?" Her answer will give him an indication of where to go from there.

She may say, "Oh yes, I'm fine. I just have a problem with the scheduling and I was trying to figure out how to rearrange it to suit both shifts. I just hate to ask the night shift to come in early; their schedules are hard enough already. I'm glad you're here. It'll give me an excuse to think of something else for a few minutes."

Now Joe can tell his mermaid joke, set the mood, and go on with his presentation.

Still, it might go differently. She might say, "Oh, Joe, I feel awful. I had to have my dog put to sleep this morning, and I just can't put it out of my mind."

Obviously, this is not a good time to tell a joke. Instead, he displays genuine empathy by mirroring Mary's emotions. "Oh, gosh, I know how terrible that can be. We had an old sheepdog for 15 years we loved, and we had to do the same thing just last year. Although you know it's better to put them out of their misery, it just makes you feel terrible, doesn't it?"

Empathy isn't only important in cases of sadness or sorrow. It also can be projected in times of joy and happiness. Let's look at a different view of Joe and Mary. Joe greets Mary with his customary smile and enthusiasm, and this time she responds with a more cheerful and happy attitude than usual. "Boy, do you look happy today! Did you win the lottery?" This shows Mary that Joe centers on her enough to notice that her smile is bigger than ever. She may or may not choose to share her joy, but the fact that Joe was interested in her feelings won't go unnoticed.

Of course the very definition of empathy, as opposed to sympathy, is that it's an involuntary expression of relating to the buyer's emotions. It isn't contrived. However, many of us feel empathy, but haven't learned to express it. The charismatic Power Persuader has learned to center on the buyer, not on himself or herself. Expressing the empathy he feels has become a natural part of who he is.

Rule 11: Respond to people's emotions, not to what they say.

Have you ever wondered why some people have a remarkable ability to relate to the way you're feeling? This person might be your boss. One day the shipping department has messed up another order to your best customer and you lose control. You go storming into your boss's office, and yell, "I've had it up to here with those people in the shipping department. They can't get anything right. Why did you hire such a bunch of imbeciles in the first place?"

A bad boss will respond to what you're *saying*, not what you're *feeling*. He might say, "You can't come in here yelling at me like that!" or "I'm not going to fire the entire shipping department just because you want me to!"

However, a good boss will respond to what you're *feeling*, not to what you're *saying*. This boss might say, "Wow, you're really upset about this, aren't you? Sit down, and tell me why you feel the way you do."

You can almost feel your anger melting away, and you might say, "Well, I don't mean that we have to fire them, but it really makes me mad. What can we do to solve the problem?"

I'm sure you've had a similar experience, haven't you? You may not have known why your anger suddenly melted away, but it was because they responded to what you were feeling, not what you were saying.

Rule 12: Maintain a childlike fascination for your world.

Earlier, I talked about searching for the meaning of charisma by first identifying its opposite and then working back from there. I said that one characteristic of a people lacking charisma is that they are self-centered. Another characteristic of a non-charismatic person would be that he or she is boring.

The opposite of being bored is being fascinated!

Have you ever taken children to Disneyland for the first time? They're full of wide-eyed wonder. Everything is fascinating to them!

This expression of wide-eyed wonder is another aspect of charisma. It's the essence of surprise, delight, and joy that a charismatic person displays when listening to someone who's talking about his or her special interest. Everyone wants to feel they are special in some way, that they do something better than anyone else, and chances are they do. Whether it's their job, their hobby, or being a parent.

Truly charismatic Power Persuaders have expanded their centers to the point where they're just as conscious of other people's talents as they are of their own. They give the buyers the opportunity to talk about their talents. They find that unique part of each person, that special interest that sets them apart from all the others.

I once met a man whose hobby was raising rare orchids. Now that's about as far from my interests as you can get. I want excitement in my life. I want to be on the go all the time. And here was a man who had the patience to work on developing a unique strain of orchid that might take 15 years to come to full bloom! Yet, to me it was absolutely fascinating. Just spending the afternoon with him enriched my life.

In fact, the older I get, the more fascinated I become with life. The world in which we live is so complex and so varied. You could spend 75 years traveling around just this one planet in a vast universe and never know it all. You can live with a person for 25 years and suddenly realize that you never have understood him or her. You could spend an entire lifetime studying any one of a 1,000 subjects and never learn everything there was to be known about it.

Just imagine, if you can, that some vast cosmic force put you in charge of the creation of this planet. Would you have ever, in your wildest dreams, thought to have made it so complex? To give every human a *different* genetic footprint? To make every snowflake different? To make people so different that they're willing to fight wars to impose their views on other people?

Of course it's natural for us to be wide-eyed in wonder at the world in which we live. And we're irresistibly drawn to people who share that wonder. It's a big part of persuasive charisma.

In the next chapter, I'll teach you another aspect of charisma that will draw people to you: developing your sense of humor.

 Key Points From This Chapter:

1. Developing charisma is a powerful part of Power Persuasion. People are drawn to and are receptive to influence by charismatic people.

2. Charisma comes from expanding our centers, so that we are just as conscious of the people around us as we are of ourselves.

3. Be sure to treat everyone you meet as the most important person you'll meet that day.

4. When you shake people's hands, train yourself to look into their eyes and make a mental note of the color of their pupils.

5. Learn the art of giving sincere compliments. People really do care what you think.

6. Take a check-up from the neck down. Conduct a ruthless examination of your wardrobe. Go through and throw out anything you haven't worn in the last year. Then, if you don't already, start sending your clothes to the dry cleaner regularly.

7. Work on your smile and, when someone smiles back, keep smiling for two magic seconds longer.

8. Learn to express the empathy you feel for other people.

9. Retain a wide-eyed wonder for the world in which we live and the unique talents of the people who live in it.

19

How You Can Develop
a Dynamite Sense of Humor

"Analyzing humor is like dissecting a frog.
Few people are interested and the frog dies of it."

—E.B. White

THE CLASSIC GREEK MODEL OF PERSUASION CALLS FOR ETHOS, pathos, logos...and a return to ethos.

In layperson's language, that means starting by getting them to like you (ethos). Then, touch their emotions in your appeal (pathos). Back it up with a little logic (logos) in case they have to justify their decision to someone else. Then use ethos again so they won't change their minds...and they'll be glad to see you the next time.

Nothing—absolutely nothing—will build their liking you better than a great sense of humor. You can say all the right words and do all the right things and still be unable to persuade unless the buyer is receptive and inclined toward being persuaded. Also, as we have seen, people are more easily persuaded when they are mildly distracted. So, nothing positions people as effectively as a sense of humor. Even the most hostile people can be won over with the use of good humor.

Aristotle recognized the use of humor as a persuasion tool in the fourth century B.C. He said that humor is primarily concerned with man as a social being rather than as a private person, and the purpose of humor in our society is to persuade people that their behavior should be changed. Humor holds up a mirror to society to reflect its foibles and failings, in the hope people will see the error of their ways and be persuaded to change.

English essayist William Hazlitt pointed out, in his classic essay On *Wit and Humor* that "man is the only animal that laughs and weeps; for he is the only animal that is struck with the difference between what things are, and what they ought to be." Even today, 180 years later, serious students of humor don't argue with that premise.

If Aristotle could see the nationwide proliferation of comedy clubs, and the incredible amount of humor available to us through cable television, he'd draw a very interesting conclusion: We see more in our society that needs correcting than ever before.

The Power Persuader sees a good sense of humor as having a three-fold purpose. It makes the buyer receptive to persuasion, it provides a mild distraction, and it's also an excellent way to point out to the buyer that he or she is mistaken, without causing offense.

A Good Sense of Humor may Stop You From Going Crazy

There's an important side benefit to your sense of humor: It's going to stop you from having a nervous breakdown one day. "What happened to Harry?" you hear at the office water cooler. "He just couldn't take the pressure. One day he just cracked."

Ever wonder where that expression comes from? What cracks? Things that are hard and brittle. Things that are soft and warm and flexible don't crack—they bend. Many noted psychiatrists go as far as to say that the very definition of good mental health is a flexible, humor-filled attitude.

President Reagan was the only president in modern times who appeared to get younger in office. While other presidents visibly aged on the job, he appeared to thrive on it. How could he handle so much pressure so well? One reason was that he could laugh at himself. An assassination attempt gave him a bullet wound—but he could joke with his wife Nancy about it. He told her, "Honey, I forgot to duck!" as they wheeled him in after the shooting, "I hope the doctor's a Republican."

When everyone was criticizing him for falling asleep during a Cabinet meeting, he deflected it all by declaring, "I have left orders to be awakened at any time in case of national emergency, even if I'm in a Cabinet meeting."

How to Develop a Sense of Humor

The problem with the need for humor as a persuasion tool is that a sense of humor can be likened to a Rolls Royce: Everybody wants one, but very few people know how to get one. Most of us know a funny joke when we hear one, but few of us know what makes it humorous. It either seems funny, or it doesn't.

What I'll do in this chapter is to show you what causes people to laugh. Knowing this will help you to remember jokes, and it will definitely help you to develop your wit—that magical recognition and expression of a humorous thought.

My purpose isn't to turn you into a stand-up comedian. I don't want you to become a person who's known primarily for the jokes you tell. (You know somebody like that, don't you? They're not good persuaders.) As managers, they're not taken seriously. As salespeople, they never develop the credibility of a person who takes things more seriously.

However, when you understand humor better, you'll see laughter in the world around you and you'll be on your way to being seen as a person with a "great sense of humor." You'll appreciate what a great persuasion tool humor can be.

There Are Only 5 Things That Make People Laugh

Did you know that there are only five jokes in the world—that there are only five things that make people laugh?

"That's crazy," you say, "I can turn on cable TV and watch stand-up comedians tell jokes all evening and never hear the same joke twice."

That may be true, but in fact they're all variations on the same five original jokes. To be a Power Persuaders you need to know what they are.

Unless you know why people laugh, you can't use humor as a persuasion tool. If the only way you can use humor is to hope you can remember a joke you heard somewhere else, hope you tell it right, hope the buyers haven't heard it, and hope they find it funny, you'll never graduate to true wit. You'll simply be a poor imitation of a stand-up comedian.

Understanding and being thoroughly familiar with the five things that make people laugh is as fundamental to persuasion as learning the alphabet is to reading.

So let's talk about the five things that make people laugh, and from then on you'll be able to identify every joke you hear with one or another of them.

The First Type of Humor: Exaggeration

Probably the first joke ever told in history was based on exaggeration. Perhaps it was in Central Europe about 40,000 years ago. A group of cavemen were sitting around the fire after a busy day hunting. Thor had just stubbed his toe on a rock and was hopping around cussing up a blue storm. One of the cave-dwellers was searching for a way to describe just how mad Thor was, when a visual image crossed his mind.

"Thor madder than saber-toothed tiger with dinosaur stuck in its throat!" he shouted.

All the others picked up on this visual image and started to laugh because it was so outrageous.

In this way the first joke was created. It was funny because he had created a visual image that vastly exaggerated the situation. When we stretch a thought to a ludicrous point, it triggers something in our mind that makes us laugh.

Today, Jay Leno says, "It was so cold in New York that the Statue of Liberty was holding the torch *under* her skirt." It's the same joke. He's using the same funny idea, only the situation has been changed.

Fred Allen used to talk about the scarecrow that was so scary the crows not only stopped stealing corn, they started bringing back corn that they'd stolen two years before.

Most golfing stories are only funny because of the way players exaggerate their passion for the game.

"Why did it take so long to play? Harry had a heart attack on the seventh fairway. From then on it was: hit the ball, drag Harry...hit the ball, drag Harry!"

I was playing golf on St. Thomas with my friend Irv Clausen. Irv's not that old, perhaps in his late sixties, but he likes to joke about his age. After sinking a 30-foot putt on the first hole, he said "Toss me my ball, would you, Roger? At my age, I don't care to get that close to a hole in the ground."

We were playing five-dollar greenies. When he hit the green on the first par three, I pulled a five-dollar bill out of my pocket. "Why don't we just settle up at the end," he said.

"Okay, but at your age, Irv," I replied, "I thought you'd like to settle hole by hole."

They're all the same joke, it's the same theme of exaggeration that triggers the laugh. Only the words have been changed.

Take a look at these famous people who got their laughs with exaggeration:

- **Richard Nixon:** "It's the responsibility of the media to look at the president with a microscope, but they go too far when they use a proctoscope."
- **Tallulah Bankhead:** "They used to photograph Shirley Temple through gauze. They should photograph me through linoleum."
- **Melvin Belli:** "I'm not an ambulance chaser. I'm usually there before the ambulance."
- **Muhammad Ali:** "My toughest fight was with my first wife."
- **Johnny Carson:** "I know a man who gave up smoking, drinking, sex, and rich food. He was healthy right up to time he killed himself."
- **Dolly Parton:** "You'd be surprised how much it costs to look this cheap."

- **Phyllis Diller:** "I was in a beauty contest once. I not only came in last, I was hit in the mouth by Miss Congeniality."
- **Raymond Chandler:** "It was a blonde, a blonde to make a bishop kick a hole in a stained glass window."

So, a mother is trying to persuade her sleepy child to quit watching television and go to bed. To head off a possible conflict, she uses a little humor. As she puts her arm around the child, she says, "Come on, dear. If you watch any more television tonight, your eyeballs will turn square." The child can't resist smiling.

"Oh, Mommy, you're silly," she says. But she quietly gets up and goes with her to the bedroom.

So if we take a point and stretch it to the ridiculous, it triggers a laugh. But what if we go the other way? What if we compress a point to the ridiculous? We downplay it instead of emphasizing it with exaggeration? Yes, that works as well. The other side of exaggeration is understatement.

If the cave-dweller had watched Thor hopping around and quietly observed "He doesn't seem to like doing that," the other cavemen probably would have laughed. It would've been the same joke, but turned inside out.

One of my favorite John F. Kennedy witticisms took place at a press conference where his support of civil rights legislation was being questioned.

"Do you mean to tell me," the reporter asked, "that if Mrs. Murphy runs a boarding house, the federal government is going to tell her whom she must accept as a guest?"

Kennedy calmly replied, "That would depend on Mrs. Murphy's impact on interstate commerce." A classic piece of understatement!

Here are some other classic examples of understatement:

- **Muhammad Ali:** "I'm retiring because there are more pleasant things to do than beat up people."
- **A theater manager as flames lick up the curtains behind him:** "Please listen carefully to the following announcement."

- **Ronnie Shakes:** "I like life. It's something to do."
- **Woody Allen:** "The universe is merely a fleeting idea in God's mind—a pretty uncomfortable thought, particularly if you've just made a down payment on a house."

So the buyer leans back in his chair and says to the salesman, "Joe, we'd love to buy your product, but your prices are too high!" But Joe's a Power Persuader. Instead of taking offense at that, and creating confrontation, he diffuses the comment by feigning surprise and saying, "Gee, Charlie. You're the first buyer who's ever mentioned price to me. I didn't know price was important to you!" Charlie sees the humor in this understatement and responds with an understatement of his own. "Well, yes Joe, sometimes it makes a difference."

The Second Type of Humor: The Pun

Probably the next most popular form of humor is the pun. A pun describes any time that you use the same word, but out of context, or substitute a word that's so similar in sound that it's almost indistinguishable.

Senator Alan Simpson of Wyoming started his dinner speeches by saying, "I know you all want the latest dope from Washington—well here I am."

The most famous one-liner of all time, Henny Youngman's "Take my wife—please!" is really a pun. Nobody ever stops to analyze it, but the humor really comes from using the word "take" out of context. He leads you to believe that when he says "take," he means "for example." The "please" added to the end of the sentence switches the meaning of the word "take" to that of "remove."

Here are some other examples of jokes that may not appear to be puns, but really are:

- **Robert Byrne:** "Get in good physical condition before submitting to bondage. You should be fit to be tied." (Robert Byrne is the author of my favorite quote book: *637 Best Things Anybody Ever Said.*)
- **David Chambles:** "Better to have loved and lost a short person than never to have loved a tall."

- **Dean Martin:** "If you drink, don't drive. Don't even putt."
- **Henry Morgan:** "A kleptomaniac is a person who helps himself because he can't help himself."
- **Jack Pomeroy:** "A communist is a person who publicly airs his dirty Lenin."
- **Mae West:** "She's the kind of girl who climbed the ladder of success wrong by wrong."
- **Zsa Zsa Gabor:** "I am a marvelous housekeeper. Every time I leave a man I keep his house."
- **Andrew Mellon:** "Gentlemen prefer bonds."
- **Groucho Marx:** "If you're insulted, you can leave in a taxi. If that's not fast enough, you can leave in a huff. If that's too fast, you can leave in a minute and a huff."

Of course the pun purist will take exception to my saying that all twists on words are puns. They're into the more convoluted word construction jokes, such as this one:

Chuck is a salesperson who is so overworked that he decides to have himself cloned. He biologically produces a replica of himself and sends him out to work half his territory. Everything's going fine and nobody notices the difference. But suddenly the clone starts using bad language on his clients. Nothing Chuck can do stops him. In desperation he takes him to the top of the Empire State Building and throws him off. Chuck is arrested for making an "obscene clone fall."

The problem with pure puns is that they tend to get a groan rather than a laugh, because they're cerebral. Although clever, they appeal to the intellect rather than the funny bone.

We can analyze humor to figure out what can trigger a laugh, but nobody knows what really causes humans to laugh. Probably the surprise connection of two illogical thoughts causes a neural misfiring in the higher cortex—the frontal lobes of the brain—creating a unique reaction in the limbic system, resulting in an intense feeling of enjoyment.

The convoluted pun can't do that.

"Take my wife—please!" can do it every time.

So Power Persuaders are always alert to the possibility of the pun to use as a tool to divert attention from a sensitive point. Remember the politician who was determined not to get dragged into the debate over abortion? He deflected attention with a clever pun. A reporter yelled, "And just what do you think that the governor should do about the abortion bill." He replied, "I think he should pay it!"

The Third Type of Humor: The Put-Down

The third form of humor is the put-down. Perhaps the first put-down was when one of the cave-dwellers pulled out a chicken he had killed that day and started to share it. Perhaps someone said, "Good old Og, he never forgets his friends!"

"That's true!" somebody else may have laughed, "But he's only got two."

The cave-dwellers would've looked at each other with apprehension. In the past, whenever somebody had said something unpleasant, it was usually just before a fight, and somebody got killed. However, this seemed different. The caveman who had said it wasn't angry; he was laughing. Suddenly the butt of the joke, Og, started to smile. Then they all started to laugh. For some reason, insulting other people makes us laugh. It's probably relief that we're not the one being put-down.

"Dan Quayle took lessons from Ronald Reagan to try and improve his image. He was always out at Reagan's ranch, chopping horses, riding wood." For many years, nearly all American humor was based on this same joke—the put-down. Here are some examples:

- **David Letterman:** "Fall is my favorite season in Los Angeles, watching the birds change color and fall down."
- **Fred Allen:** "The town was so dull that when the tide went out, it refused to come back."
- **Bob Hope:** "Ronald Reagan was not a typical politician because he didn't know how to lie, cheat, and steal. He'd always had an agent for that."

Comedy teams became popular, with one person always putting down the other. Abbot and Costello, Laurel and Hardy, Dean Martin and Jerry Lewis, Burns and Allen, Rowan and Martin, the Smothers Brothers—the list goes on and on.

Then suddenly "put-down" humor changed. It took a new twist. Comedians changed the butt of the joke from the other person, to themselves. They started putting themselves down, and it was funnier, because nobody could get offended.

Jack Benny's self-imposed reputation for stinginess was legendary. The longest laugh ever recorded on radio occurred when a supposed mugger pointed a gun at Jack, and yelled, "Your money or your life!" Jack didn't say anything for a full 30 seconds. His expression didn't change. "What's the matter with you?" the furious mugger yelled, "I said 'Your money or your life!'"

Finally Jack protested, "I'm thinking, I'm thinking."

The studio audience roared with laughter, stopping the live radio show for many minutes.

Here are some other examples of self deprecating put-downs:

- **Rodney Dangerfield:** "My wife has cut our lovemaking down to once a month. But I know two guys she's cut out entirely."
- **Joan Rivers:** "After we made love he took a piece of chalk and made an outline of my body."
- **Gary Shandling:** "I have such poor vision, I can date anybody."

Of course, all racial humor is put-down humor. It's curious that the same jokes are told around the world, only the nationality is changed. In America, it's the Polish guy who threw himself to the ground and missed. In Canada, it's the Newfy—the person from Newfoundland. In England it's the Irishman, in Ireland it's the Englishman, and in Australia it's the Tassie—someone from Tasmania.

The problem with racial humor is that acceptance of a mild put-down of a national or racial characteristic can become license for vicious slander.

If it's okay for me to tease a Scot for his thriftiness, how can I protest when a white South African pokes fun at a black worker in a diamond mine?

Remember what Aristotle said? That humor is primarily concerned with man as a social person, not as an individual. And that the purpose of humor is to hold a mirror to our foolish actions and hope, that by revealing them, we change peoples' behavior. When we bear that in mind, we can quickly distinguish between the put-down that is designed to reveal a foible and bring about change and a put-down that's merely malicious.

Never was this more clearly illustrated than with the hit television series *All In the Family.* We knew the purpose in Archie Bunker's racial slurs was to hold his foolish actions up to the public—and in doing so change people's behavior, which the program did remarkably well.

Power Persuaders are interested in humor for bringing about change in the buyer's thinking. We're not interested in malicious put-downs.

Even today, a surprising amount of humor is based on the put-down. For example:

A woman real estate agent in New York calls her unemployed husband at home and says, "Honey, you can't believe what just happened! I just sold the Empire State Building. I'm getting a $5 million commission! I'm on my way home—hurry up and get packed!"

So he asks her, "Shall I pack for cold weather or warm weather?"

And she says, "What does it matter? I just want you packed and out of there by the time I get home."

•••

Power Persuaders are always aware that putting themselves down can charm even the most hostile antagonists. Both Presidents Kennedy and Reagan were past masters at this. Remember when Kennedy had the persuasion challenge of getting people to quit focusing on the rumors that his father had bought his Senate seat for him? Kennedy put it to rest and brought the house down at a 1952 Gridiron dinner, when he pulled a telegram out of his pocket and told the audience that it was from his father. "Dear Jack: Don't buy a single vote more than necessary. I'll be damned if I'll pay for a landslide."

The Fourth Type of Humor: Silliness

The fourth thing that makes us laugh is silliness. Groucho Marx said, "Last night I killed a lion in my pajamas. How he got into my pajamas, I'll never know!" The mental image of a lion in his pajamas is silly. It doesn't match our established way of thinking, so it makes us laugh.

Whereas most American humor is based on the put-down, most British humor, even to this day, is based on silliness. Robin Williams says: "British policemen don't wear guns. If they're chasing someone, they yell, 'Stop! Or I'll yell 'stop' again.'"

Probably the British like this kind of humor because it's a complete mirror image of the stuffy English lifestyle.

The Goon Show was immensely popular on British radio in the 1950s. Here's a typical scene from the Goon Show:

Henry and Minnie are recurring characters. They're an elderly couple enjoying a quiet evening at home. Suddenly there's a noise outside like an invasion of savages. Henry softly remarks, "They've come to rape and plunder, Minnie." Minnie quietly replies, "I'd better go upstairs and get ready, Henry."

Peter Sellers was one of the Goons. Even when he became a worldwide superstar, much of his humor, such as Inspector Clouseau in the Pink Panther films, was based on incongruity or silliness. For example: "Are you going to come quietly or do I have to use earplugs?"

Monty Python's Flying Circus was one of the few British shows that became popular in the United States without massive rewrites. Relying heavily on men playing women's roles and totally absurd themes, the entire show is an expansion of Groucho Marx's "lion in my pajamas" comment. It's a glorious salute to silliness. Today, the *Airport* and *Naked Gun* movies have picked up the banner of silliness and lurched forward with it.

It's all the same joke, only the words have been changed. Here are some other examples of silliness:

- **Tallulah Bankhead:** "The less I behave like Whistler's mother the night before, the more I look like her the morning after."
- **Yogi Berra:** "Toots Shor's restaurant is so crowded nobody goes there anymore."
- **Groucho Marx:** "I don't have a photograph to give you, but you can have my footprints. They're upstairs in my socks."

- **Jack Warner** (upon Ronald Reagan becoming president): "It's our fault. We should have given him better parts."

A national newspaper in England did a survey to find out what its readers thought was the funniest joke ever told. The winner, believe it or not, was this little gem:

At the head table at a huge banquet, one man leaned to another and said, "Pardon me old boy, did you realize that you just wiped your face with a piece of cabbage?"

"Did I really? I'm so glad you told me. I thought it was a piece of lettuce."

To illustrate how there are no new jokes, 50 years before, Sigmund Freud had used this story in his book *Jokes and Their Relation to the Unconscious*:

A man in a restaurant dipped his hands into a mayonnaise bowl and ran them through his hair. When the waiter looked surprised, the man said, "Oh, pardon me. I thought it was spinach."

(This may have been the real reason Freud had to leave Vienna so suddenly!)

Incidentally Freud's extensive study of humor led him to believe that laughter was a coping mechanism, a way of dealing with repressed feelings and releasing them. To substantiate this, he pointed to the fact that so much humor is sexual in nature.

Then, many of Freud's theories seem off the wall in today's world. Did you know that for many years Freudian analysts saw deep significance in the fact that the great Sigmund always sat on the right side of the couch when he was treating patients?

He was astonished when he found out that his disciples around the world would only treat patients when seated on their right. "Don't they know that my couch was only arranged like that because I'm hard of hearing in one ear?" he exclaimed.

Power Persuaders know when to use a little bit of silliness to defuse a tense situation. Many years ago I worked for a boss who needed constant reassurance that I was loyal to him, which I was. The problem was that we had different biological clocks. He was always at his desk by six o'clock in the morning and in bed by nine in the evening. I prefer to work late at night and definitely see no point in confusing my day by having two six o'clocks in it.

One morning I wandered into my office at a little after nine and he was waiting for me, so upset that his veins were popping out of his forehead.

"You know, Roger, I don't think that you have any loyalty to me at all."

This wasn't a good way to start the day. I knew that I'd have to find some way to get across how silly this was.

"Of course I'm loyal to you," I reassured him, "Why, I'd come to work in a dress if you wanted me to."

"I don't want you to come to work in a dress," he screamed at me, "I just want you here at the same time I get to work in the morning."

I gave it a long pause, and finally said, "I really had my heart set on the dress!"

He finally burst out laughing, we went off to get some coffee, and he never questioned my work schedule again.

The Fifth Type of Humor: Surprise

One of my favorite jokes relies on surprise:

"Did you hear that Uncle Harry wants to marry a 20-year-old girl? Can you imagine that? And he's 80 years old! I told him he's a fool. It could be fatal. And he said, 'If she dies, she dies!'"

Why is that funny? Because the ending surprises us. One moment we're talking about an old man risking his life, a very serious subject. The next moment we've completely switched gears, and we're portraying him as an adventurous old rascal.

When we're surprised by something, our fight-or-flight syndrome goes into instant action. Our pulse quickens, and adrenaline starts to flow. When we suddenly realize the situation isn't dangerous, laughter results. Joke writers use this to lead us down one path, and then quickly take us 180 degrees in the opposite direction. It makes those neuron explosions in your frontal lobes that much crisper.

"Me worry?" says the wife, "Why, he'd never cheat on me. He's too honest, too pure...too scared."

"You'll be glad to hear that our auditors have come up with a very workable solution to our cashflow problems: bankruptcy."

- **Woody Allen:** "I have an intense desire to return to the womb. Anybody's womb."
- **Tallulah Bankhead:** "If I had to live my life again, I'd make the same mistakes, only sooner."
- **Phyllis Diller:** "Burt Reynolds once asked me out. I was in his room."
- **W.C. Fields:** "Start every day with a smile and get it over with."
- **Will Rogers:** "Diplomacy is the art of saying 'Nice doggie' until you can find a rock."
- **Mark Twain:** "I thoroughly disapprove of duels. If a man should challenge me, I would take him kindly and forgivingly by the hand and lead him to a quiet place and kill him."
- **Mae West:** "Whenever I'm caught between two evils, I take the one I've never tried."
- **Henny Youngman:** "Do you know what it means to come home at night to a woman who'll give you a little love, a little affection, a little tenderness? It means you're in the wrong house, that's what it means."

Note that in each of these jokes, the punch line or word must come as close to the end of the joke as possible. Comedians call this the "train-wreck approach." You get listeners on board the train with your opening line. Then you head them off in a particular direction. Just when they're convinced they know where the train is heading, you wreck the train with the surprise punch line.

Learning What Makes It Funny

You've seen that there are really only five jokes: exaggeration, puns, put-downs, silliness, and surprise. Let's make up a memory hook that will help us remember those. A good memory hook should conjure up a silly visual image, so how about, "Every Pickled Person Sounds Stupid."

At this point you may be thinking, "This is interesting, but so what? What's this got to do with Power Persuasion?"

With a little practice, any time you hear a joke, you'll be quickly able to identify what makes it funny. This will help you remember it, if you should want to repeat it. That's because you've identified the only part of the joke worth remembering—the reason it makes people laugh. If you want to retell it and can't recollect the words, it won't matter because you'll be able to fill in the inconsequential details. The only thing that matters is keeping the point of the joke intact. If you know what makes people laugh, you won't have to rely any more on trying to remember the joke that you heard the other day to inject a light-hearted note in any proceedings.

Secondly, you'll now be able to customize the joke. As you understand what makes it funny, you can change all the characters and circumstances, because the basic humor remains. The joke will be yours, you'll get the credit for it, and you won't have to wonder if they've heard it before.

It's a quirk of human nature that if we're the one telling the joke, it's funny to us however many times we hear ourselves telling it. However, if someone else is telling us a joke we've heard before, it doesn't make us laugh. The surprise is gone. Those neurals in your frontal lobes won't pop because they've built up immunity.

So the key to humor is to sneak up on people, and surprise them with the punch line. Of course they'll have heard the joke before—there are, after all, only five jokes in the world—but when you customize the joke, while maintaining the reason why it's funny, they won't recognize it. So the surprise element is present, and that's what makes those neurals in your frontal lobes pop crisply.

A Practice Session on Identifying the Style of Humor

Let's try this out and see how we do. Let's practice.

I'll tell you a series of old jokes, and you decide whether the joke is exaggeration, a pun, a put-down, silliness, or a surprise. Remember the memory hook: "Every Pickled Person Sounds Stupid."

Let's start with a Henny Youngman classic. "They have a new thing nowadays called Nicotine Anonymous. It's for people who want to stop smoking. When you feel a craving for a cigarette, you simply call up another member and he comes over and you get drunk together." What's the joke? Is it a pun, a put-down, an exaggeration, silliness, or surprise?

This is a good example of surprise. There are 42 words in the joke. Forty of them take you in one direction, and the last two take you in a completely different direction.

Let's try another Henny Youngman story: Despite warnings from his guide, an American skier in Switzerland got separated from his group and fell, uninjured, into a deep crevasse.

Several hours later, a rescue party found the yawning pit and, to reassure the stranded skier, shouted down to him, "We're from the Red Cross!"

"Sorry," the imperturbable American echoed back, "I already gave at the office!"

What's the joke? Well, silliness of course. I'm surprised that Henny didn't make it an Englishman down in that crevasse! Our formula tells us that the perceived pomposity of the English would add to the silliness.

In the presence of a client he wished to impress, a high-powered executive flipped on his intercom switch, and barked to his secretary, "Miss Jones, get my broker!"

The visitor was duly impressed, until the secretary's voice floated back into the room, loud and clear: "Yes, sir, stock or pawn?"

What's the joke? Of course, it's a put-down.

Notice that a put-down is always more effective when the person being put-down is pompous and full of self-importance. When the Marx Brothers threw the cream pie, it was far funnier if it hit the opera singer than if it hit the janitor.

Now let's try a Myron Cohen favorite: Irving made a lot of money one year in the garment business and decided to buy a racehorse. One day he brought all his friends to the stable as the vet was laboriously working on the horse.

"Is my horse sick?" asked Irving.

"She's not the picture of health," said the vet, "but we'll pull her through."

"Will I ever be able to race her?"

"Chances are you will—and you'll probably beat her, too!"

What makes that funny? Is it an exaggeration, a pun, a put-down, silliness, or surprise?

Well, it's a pun isn't it? It's "take my wife—please," with the words changed. The set up was using the word *race* to mean competitively, with another horse. The punchline changed the meaning of the word *race* to mean the owner running with the horse.

This is from comedian Dick Shebelski: Tommy came home from school very dejected.

"I had an awful day," he told his mother. "I couldn't remember an answer and it was embarrassing."

"Forgetting one answer is nothing to be embarrassed about," soothed his mother. And the boy said, "During roll call?"

What's the joke? Exaggeration of course. The thought of someone not able to remember his own name is so absurd that it's funny. Exaggeration is a very popular comedy theme. Probably 30 percent of all the jokes you'll ever hear involve exaggeration.

So by now you should be getting the hang of identifying what makes the joke funny. Continue this exercise the next time you watch a comedy club on television. Wait for the punchlines and determine if each one is an exaggeration, pun, put-down, silliness, or a surprise.

The Sales Persuaders
Best Type of Humor: Witticisms

The most useful form of humor for the persuader is the witticism, that spontaneous cross-connection of two diverse thoughts.

There's no question the level of wit is directly related to a person's level of intelligence. You may have a different definition of intelligence, but mine is very basic: "The ability to research the memory banks and pull together two unconnected concepts."

The ape in the cage sees a banana just beyond its reach. However there is a stick within reach, and it uses the stick to pull the banana to him. That's not intelligence; that's instinct or trial and error. But let's suppose the ape finds the stick too short to reach the banana. However he uses the stick to pull toward him a longer stick that's out of his reach, and uses that stick to reach the banana. That's intelligence.

Here are some examples of pure wit that required intelligent thought:

- **David Brenner:** "A vegetarian is a person who won't eat anything that can have children."
- **Herb Caen:** "The trouble with born-again Christians is that they are an even bigger pain the second time around."
- **Johnny Carson:** "When turkeys mate, they think of swans."
- **Sam Levenson:** "The reason grandparents and grandchildren get along so well is that they have a common enemy."
- **Dorothy Parker:** "One more drink and I'll be under the host."
- **Helen Rowland:** "I takes a woman 20 years to make a man of her son, and another woman 20 minutes to make a complete fool of him."
- **George Bernard Shaw:** "A government which robs Peter to pay Paul can always depend on the support of Paul."
- **Arturo Toscanini:** "I kissed my first girl and smoked my first cigarette on the same day. I haven't had time for tobacco since."

See how each one of these depends on an intelligent mind making a connection between two previously dissimilar thoughts?

All good humor involves some cleverness—some display of intelligence. Let's validate that against each of our five jokes:

Exaggeration is only funny if it's clever. If David Letterman says "It was so cold in New York today, the people were bundled up like

Eskimos," that's exaggeration, but it isn't funny because it isn't clever. If he says "It was so cold in New York today the attorneys on Wall Street had their hands in their own pockets," that's funny because it's a clever exaggeration (plus a put-down).

The classical style pun relies almost exclusively on its cleverness. But also lesser puns require the rapid association of one word with a similar-sounding but illogical second word.

Even the bluntest of humor, the put-down, must be clever to be funny. If Joan Rivers were to say, "I went to a nude beach and a gang of Hell's Angels insulted me," that's not funny. However, "I went to a nude beach and a gang of Hell's Angels viciously gang dressed me," is one of her classic lines.

Silliness also needs to be clever. Take Dudley Moore's classic drunk act in the movie *Arthur*. On the evening he reluctantly proposes to the heiress, played by Jill Eikenberry, he gets smashed at the dinner table. She lovingly says, "A good woman could stop you from drinking, Arthur." Dudley Moore processes this piece of information through the fog of alcohol, and concludes, "It would take an awful big woman."

It's interesting to see how social standards affect our sense of humor. When the first Arthur movie came out in 1981 it was a big hit. Seven years later, *Arthur II* was a flop. What changed was the public's perception of drunkenness. It's no longer seen as silly: It's now seen as tragic. Drunks now conjure up visions of broken homes and mangled bodies on the highway.

Similarly, "crazy" jokes are no longer funny. Our more enlightened society sees mental problems not as an aberration, but as a disease and a potentially curable one, at that.

The fifth joke we talked about, surprise, takes a lot of intelligence to construct.

On the borders of California, we have signs that say, "Leaving California. Please resume normal behavior." Remember that our definition of a surprise joke is one that leads you in one direction, and then quickly diverts you to another train of thought. To think of a line like "resume normal behavior," you'd have to be visualizing a "resume normal speed" sign, and then search through millions of other mental images in your memory banks to come up with the surprise association "behavior."

Witticism takes that kind of mental association. Witticism is the construction of one of the same five jokes, but done instantaneously, as the situation calls for it. But it can be learned.

A 30-Day Program to Improve Your Sense of Humor

So here's a 30-day program to improve your sense of humor and increase your ability to come up with witty comments.

First use the "one to 10 technique" to find out how people you know rate your sense of humor. Because this is a sensitive area, take two off any number they give you. Take five off if you're asking someone who works for you!

Then get one of those joke books or Web sites that lists hundreds of jokes and go through it, quickly identifying whether the joke is exaggeration, pun, a put-down, silliness, or surprise. Some, of course, will be a combination of two or more.

Then get in the habit of analyzing a joke every time you hear one. Once you become thoroughly familiar with identifying the core of every joke, you're ready to start developing your own witticisms. Now you understand that there are really only five jokes in the world, it will be a lot easier for you.

Power Persuaders understand that personal charisma is a key factor in getting the buyer to see it your way. And developing a good sense of humor is a big part of charisma.

If you're not sure how important developing a sense of humor is, remember that the two most popular Presidents of the last five decades have been the two with the best sense of humor: John Kennedy and Ronald Reagan.

In the next chapter, we'll work on another thing that will build your charisma: the ability to remember and use the buyer's name.

Key Points From This Chapter

1. Nothing positions people as effectively as a sense of humor. Even the most hostile people can be won over with the use of good humor.

2. The flexibility that comes with a good sense of humor will stop you from having your nervous breakdown.

3. Don't try to remember jokes. Instead learn what makes people laugh. It's not hard because there are only five things that make people laugh.

   - Exaggeration (and its flip side, understatement).
   - A pun, which describes any time that you use a word out of context, or substitute a word that's so similar in sound that it's almost indistinguishable.
   - Put-downs, which are much funnier when the story-teller is putting him or herself down.
   - Silliness, which can be very effective in defusing a tense situation.
   - Surprise, which leads us down one path, and then quickly takes us 180 degrees in the opposite direction.

4. The punchline or word must come as close to the end of the joke as possible.

5. The memory hook, "Every Pickled Person Sounds Stupid," will remind you of: exaggeration, puns, put-downs, silliness, and surprise.

6. The most useful form of humor for the persuader is the witticism, that spontaneous cross-connection of two diverse thoughts.

7. All good humor involves some cleverness—some display of intelligence.

8. Get one of those joke books that lists hundreds of jokes and go through it, quickly identifying whether the joke is either exaggeration, a pun, a put-down, silliness, or surprise.

20

You Don't Need to Forget Another Name

THIS WILL BE THE FOURTH, AND FINAL, CHAPTER ON DEVELOPING the charisma that can make you a Power Persuader. And I'm sure you would agree with me that remembering people's names would make you able to project your charisma further. It's the top communication skill that every salesperson wishes he or she could perfect. Using a buyer's name, especially when he or she doesn't expect you to remember it, sets people up to be influenced by you.

Don't you just hate it when you're introduced to someone and two minutes later you can't remember his or her name? Or worse yet, you think you can and get it wrong! I'm not trying to make you blush! I've been there. I've done it. I know exactly how humbling that can be. Nobody had a problem remembering names the way I had a problem remembering names. I went to all the seminars and learned all the cute tricks, and I still found myself being introduced to someone, and two minutes later I couldn't remember their name for the life of me. It was as if I'd never heard it in the first place.

The problem with those seminars is that people who are brilliant at remembering names teach them! How about a seminar by someone who's a complete klutz at doing it, like me?

The Magic Secret to Remembering Names

Well, I finally figured out a way that I could become possibly *good* at remembering names.

I can't shake hands with 200 people and then pick them out of a crowd and call them by name. If you come up to me in Dallas, and say, "Remember me? I was in your negotiating seminar in San Francisco two years ago," I'm still going to go draw a blank.

But at least if I were introduced to you at the start of a business meeting, I could say good-bye to you as you leave and call you by name. So, here's the magic secret to remembering names:

There is no magic key to remembering names.
It's hard work!

I think that the bulk of the problem is that everyone's running around looking for a secret trick that will suddenly turn around years of bad habits.

It's akin to dieting. Everybody's looking for the easy way to do it. More than 100 diets are published a year, every one of them promising miraculous results. Yet, the only people who really lose weight and keep it off are the ones who have come to the conclusion that there is no easy way. They know that to lose weight, they have to quit drinking alcohol, exercise more, and eat less.

Similarly, there is no easy way to remember names. As my high school teacher used to say, "Don't waste any time looking for an easier way to do this. If there was an easier way, Roger would've found it years ago."

Selective Memory—How It Works

Your mind is constantly analyzing information input and deciding what to do with it. Think of your mind as having a short-term memory and a long-term memory. The vast majority of input that we receive need not be saved at all. The make and model of the car that you passed on the freeway, the color of the dress on the woman who passes in front of you at the stop light. You have no reason to retain these images or a million other images that flash before you every hour.

Some things you need to retain in your short-term memory: your hotel room number, the directions you were just given to the buyer's office, or where you parked your car.

And some things need to memorized and put permanently into your long-term memory: where you live, your Social Security number, your ATM PIN number, and the password to access your e-mail account.

The problem with remembering names is that we very often don't make the decision to save them to short-term memory, much less make an effort to commit them to long-term memory.

That was my problem. When I was introduced to somebody, I heard the name, but I instantly discarded it. Five seconds later, I couldn't recall it.

The solution was to develop a system that would discipline me to commit these names to short-term memory. The system I stumbled across is remarkably effective.

The Trigger That Makes You Remember

To avoid that unpleasant experience of being introduced to someone, only to realize a few seconds later that his or her name didn't register with us, we first need a trigger signal.

This is a signal that the moment we think of it, triggers our memory to note the person's name. If you've ever seen a hypnotist at work, you know what I'm talking about. He implants a trigger word in the subject's mind that causes that person to react automatically whenever he or she hears the word.

Trigger words or thoughts have been around for a long time, and they're very effective. The trigger thought I stumbled across, and have found so very compelling, is to make the color of a person's eyes the trigger signal that reminds us to take note of their name.

Here's why it's so effective: Names don't register with us, because we've developed a bad habit over the years. We hear a name and our subconscious mind automatically reacts to tell us to ignore it. Because we haven't been trained to notice the color of a person's eyes, we don't have any bad habits about that yet.

As we notice the color of their eyes, our mind is concentrating, focused on observing their eyes. That's the trigger for us also to take note of their name.

Do you recall that when we talked about charisma, I told you how important it is to take note of the color of a person's eyes? It creates a special moment of interaction with that person, that says "I care about you." As your eyes comes into focus with their eyes, there's a special connection that takes place.

What we're doing here is creating an "unthinking response" in your mind. You shake hands; this triggers the thought to notice the color of their eyes. Now add another thing to this automatic reaction: "Shake hands, color of eyes, remember name."

Invariably, whenever you meet someone whose name you need to remember, you'll be shaking hands with him or her. You'll only need to concentrate on this technique for a few days before you'll automatically be associating shaking hands with noticing the color of their eyes. And this will trigger you to pay attention to their names.

How to Transpose From Short-Term to Long-Term Memory

Now the question becomes this: When and how do we switch that name over from short-term memory to long-term memory? Sometimes you don't need to use up your long-term memory storage banks with a person's name. You'll hear their name as you're introduced and the only time you'll need it again is when you say, "Nice to meet you, Bob," as you say good-bye a few minutes, or even seconds, later.

That's the way it is when I meet people in the doorway of my larger seminars. If I can remember their name until the end of a brief conversation, that's all I have to do.

If you decide you must commit this name to long-term memory, there are some memory recall techniques that will be helpful to us. Let's look at some of them.

Initial Steps to Burn a Name Into Your Memory

There are several ways to do this. Use one, or perhaps two, of them every time you're introduced to someone.

First Way: Clarify the Spelling

Is that Kathy with a "C" or a "K"? People ask me a lot "Is that Roger with a 'D'," although I almost never meet anybody who spells it that way. Is that Terry with a "Y" or an "I"? Is that Vivian with an "A" or an "E"?

Second Way: How Do They Like to Be Addressed?

Do you prefer "Dave" or "David"? Should I call you "Julia" or "Julie"? Is it "Frederick" or "Fred"? Do you like "Tom" or "Thomas"?

Third Way: Clarify the Pronunciation

The best way to do this is with Cockney rhyming slang. Cockneys are the Londoners who are born within the sound of Bow Bells, the church in the working class East End of the city. They talk in a weird language that's composed almost entirely of words that rhyme with the word they really mean. For example, a Cockney says, "I'm going up the apples and pears, with a cup of rosy lee, for me trouble and strife." What he really means is, "I'm going upstairs, with a cup of tea, for my wife." In his rhyming slang, stairs became "apples and pears." Tea became "rosy lee," and wife became "trouble and strife." Now aren't you glad you invested in this book?

So verify the pronunciation with a rhyming word. Is that "Chilton," as in "Hilton"? Is that "Sutton" as in "button"? Is that "Blair" like "wear"?

Fourth Way: Relate the Name to Something Famous

Next, relate the name to a famous person or place if that's possible. This is a good technique because it also gives you a good visual image to work with. Is that Parks, as in Yosemite? Perhaps you see a waterfall pouring out of his ear. Washington like the president? Perhaps you see an old-fashioned white wig gradually slipping down over his eyes. Lewis like the boxer? And you see yourself ducking as a big red boxing glove comes swinging from behind his back. Letterman like the comedian? And you see him sitting at his desk throwing a cue card over his shoulder through an imaginary window. Remember that the more ridiculous the image, the more likely to are to recall it.

Fifth Way: Use It Quickly

The next time you talk to the person, you should start your conversation with, "Don't you agree, Anne?" or "Mr. Travis, isn't it true that...." If you find that you've forgotten the name, don't try to bluff your way through. The only way that you'll ever fulfill your potential to remember names is to correct a mistake every time you make it. Force yourself to say, "I'm sorry, but your name slipped my mind.... Oh yes, Anne. Well Anne, don't you agree that...?"

What we're tapping into here is spaced repetition recall, which is magically effective. I use it all the time and it works incredibly well. If you force yourself to remember something three times in a row, you have a very good chance of getting it into your short-term memory so that you'll recall it when you need it.

When I park my car at the airport for example, I need to remember the area in which I parked. I've trained myself to look up at the sign when I lock the car and say to myself, "I parked in 4C." Then I let that out of my consciousness until I'm halfway to the terminal. Then I repeat, "I parked in 4C." Then, once more as I approach the terminal doors, I repeat, "I parked in 4C." Using spaced repetition recall, I find that I'll still be able to remember the parking location when I return five days later. Try that with names and you'll be surprised how well it works. You're introduced to the buyer's assistant. As you shake hands you notice that she has deep brown eyes. That's your trigger hook to remember her name. Let it slip out of your consciousness for a couple of minutes and think of her name again. You recall that it is Juanita. After another two or three minutes look over at her again and think, "Her name is Juanita." After that you'll almost certainly be able to remember her name when you leave the meeting.

At some point schoolchildren reluctantly come to the conclusion that they are not going to be allowed to daydream and that life will be simpler if they simply pay attention. Similarly, it doesn't take long for us to train ourselves to pay attention to names, if we correct ourselves every time we forget.

Remember that you'll have to suffer a few slings and arrows in the process. People say to me, "Roger, you say you're good at remembering names, but you forgot mine and you only heard it five minutes ago!"

That's true, but I care enough to be working on it and correcting myself when I goof. Don't laugh at the fat man jogging down the street. At least he's doing something about it. Save your scorn for the fat man who gave up and is lying on the couch eating French fries.

Sixth Way: Use it Again When They Leave

Finally, be sure to use the name again when they leave. "Joe, it was really good to meet you," or "Karen, be sure to call me if you come to Los Angeles." Again, if you've forgotten by then, you must ask them again. "I want to be sure that I remember your name. Tell me again. That's right, Cathy with a 'C.' Thanks for helping me out."

Please don't turn me off on this last point of asking them again. I realize that you're thinking, "I'm not going to make a fool of myself doing something like that. It would be too embarrassing."

Trust me, it won't take long. If you'll do it every time for three weeks, you'll have broken a bad habit that has been building up for... how long? Ten years, 20, perhaps 30?

Does the name Pavlov ring a bell?

•••

So here again are the six keys to remembering a name:
1. Clarify the spelling.
2. Confirm how they like to be addressed.
3. Use rhyming slang to confirm the pronunciation.
4. Relate the name to a famous place or person if possible and add the visual image.
5. Use the name as quickly as possible, asking them to repeat it if you've forgotten. Using spaced repetition recall the name again at two or three minute intervals.
6. Use the name again when you say good-bye, once more asking for the name if you've forgotten.

Don't Try to Outdo the Experts

Power Persuaders know another major rule to help remember a name is don't try to outdo the experts.

You've probably decided that you can't remember names because you've been to a seminar where the speaker could remember the names of the 200 people he met at the door.

Then, you tried his techniques, couldn't make them work for you, and gave up. You developed a poor self-image of your ability to remember names.

You've overlooked the fact that the speaker probably has a tremendous natural aptitude for remembering names. He has also been working and training with the techniques on a full-time basis for several years. Finally, he probably spent an hour or so before the seminar mentally preparing himself to do a brilliant job.

Now we, as rank amateurs, come along and expect to emulate this professional. It isn't going to happen. If he has this tremendous aptitude, and we don't, we're going to have to work much harder at it to make it happen.

We all fall into this trap. I know I do with playing golf. I'll play once or twice a week at most and then rush out to the course and go straight out to the first tee. I take a couple of practice swings and start flailing away at the ball. No wonder I can't hit the stupid thing!

Meanwhile the professional golfer, who has 10 times the natural aptitude I have, has put himself on a rigid exercise program to develop his or her muscles and mental coordination. Professionals invest a lot of money in exactly the right equipment. They wouldn't dream of teeing off until they've spent an hour on the practice tee, and they take more golf lessons in a month than I've taken in a lifetime.

What's the Lesson to Learn Here?

The lesson is that if you're not brilliant at doing something, such as remembering names, you've got to give yourself every possible advantage, not disadvantage, over the people who are the top experts.

Power Persuaders know that giving yourself an advantage in remembering names means doing the following four things:

One, make a file card on each of your business associates and customers or clients. The card shows the person's secretary's name, and the names of his or her spouse, children, and pets, if you've been told them.

This doesn't have anything to do with remembering names, but while you're at it you might as well make a note of the town she's from and the college she attended. Also her birthday, her hobbies and sports, her political leaning; and her favorite cocktail, cigarettes, food, and restaurant.

Update his or her card with a few brief comments every time you meet with someone. Pay special attention to the personal things. The competition remembers the business stuff, and you will too.

Power Persuaders give themselves the advantage of being different.

How much business could you do if you could do things such as this consistently? "Harry, the last time I was here you mentioned that your son was interested in going backpacking in Montana. Here's an article I clipped from my local paper I thought he might like to see."

Does all this sound excessive? Maybe so, but the objective is to give yourself an advantage that other people don't have. My friend Harvey Mackay, in his fun book *How to Swim with the Sharks*, advocates maintaining a 66-item questionnaire on each of your business contacts. And Harvey Mackay has done very well indeed.

The second way to give yourself an advantage in remembering names is this: Maintain a card on your friends, also. This will be invaluable when you go to a cocktail party and can call their spouses by name.

The third way to give yourself an advantage in remembering names is to maintain an overall list of people and titles for any company with which you do business. This doesn't carry all the detailed information the individual cards hold, but it lists those people you're liable to run into as you walk through the building.

The fourth advantage is to get in the habit of pulling up the company's Web site before you go visit. It will refresh your memory. Also, there's no reason for a buyer to be answering questions that you could have answered by going to the Web site. Thanks to the Internet you can be well informed about the company before you set foot in the door. In addition to a wealth of product knowledge, you'll know the names of all the top personnel, and you'll be able to read last year's annual report and every press release that they have put out for the last six months. My favorite search engine is Google (*www.google.com*). On the homepage type, in your client company's name and hit the "I feel lucky" button. It'll take you right to your client's Web site.

The Key to Remembering Faces

Of course, remembering a name is one thing. However, when you see them again, does their face conjure up the right name from your memory bank?

Remembering the name of your waiter in a restaurant is going to get you better service. He responds to your apparent caring about him, and it's a lot easier to get his attention if you know his name. But you don't need to be able to remember his face for that. Knowing that he's the tall one, short one, or skinny one is enough for that.

However if you meet him at the gym the next day and want to call him by name, you better have done something about remembering his face.

The key to remembering faces is the outrageous visual picture. The mind doesn't think in words; it thinks in pictures. Power Persuaders know how to use this to create pictures in the buyer's mind.

Still, if we can link the person's face to his or her name, and wrap them both up with an outrageous visual picture, it will be memorable.

We already talked about Mr. Parks with the Yosemite Falls pouring out of his ear. It's a good visual picture, but it's probably not going to help you remember his name, unless his ear is the most distinctive feature he has.

If he happens to be the kind of guy about whom people think, "Here comes the guy with the big ears. What on earth is his name?" Then it will help. You'll think "big ears," big enough to pour a waterfall through, Yosemite Falls, Yosemite Park. Bingo!

So be sure that you've linked your OVPA (outrageous visual picture acronym) to the physical feature that you'll notice first.

If you see Mr. Parks's nose coming first, then the falls come out of his nose. If he has eyes that water, then picture them as the source of the river that ends with the falls.

We talked about Mr. Washington, with the colonial white wig that slips over his eyes. That's good if the first thing that you notice about him is his bald head. You think, "I bet he gets cold, he should wear a wig, a colonial wig, like George Washington." Bingo!

However, if Mr. Washington's most prominent feature isn't his bald head, then pick somewhere else to hang his wig.

Remember that the more outrageous your OVPA, the easier it will be for you to remember, but it must be related to the feature that you notice first.

An Exercise in Memory Discipline

Here's an exercise that you can have fun with, and it'll cause you to take a quantum leap in your ability to remember names.

I've been using it for years now, and I've surprised myself at how well I can do it. The exercise is to see how many names you can remember consecutively in any given day.

Here's how it works. Each day you remember the name of the first new person to whom you're introduced. Then when you're introduced to the second new person that day, you add the name to the mental list. Review the entire list each time you add a name.

The objective is to see how many new names you can remember, without missing anybody.

So let's say you start the day, and the first new person you meet is the waitress at the coffee shop. Her name is Sheila. Then somebody comes over to the table, and your breakfast companion introduces him as Harry.

As you move Harry's name into your replay memory, using the techniques we've talked about, you think to yourself, "That's two so far, Sheila the waitress and Harry the attorney."

The receptionist's name on your first call of the day is Patty. You mentally add her name to the list and then review your list of three. Sheila, Harry, and Patty.

Your business appointment is with Fred Thompson, but you've met him before, so he doesn't go on the list. But he has a new secretary, so you add Lillian to the list.

During the appointment, the controller of the company comes in and is briefly introduced. You add Susan to the list, and review the list in your mind. Sheila the waitress, Harry the attorney, Patty the receptionist, Lillian the secretary, and Susan the controller.

Five so far and you're still in the game. By lunchtime, your list might look like this:

1. *Sheila*   Waitress at breakfast.
2. *Harry*   Attorney I met at breakfast.
3. *Patty*   Receptionist.
4. *Lillian*   Fred Thompson's secretary.
5. *Susan*   Controller.
6. *Jackson*   Parking lot attendant.
7. *Mark*   Pumped gas for me.
8. *Carla*   Airline reservation clerk.
9. *Jean*   Rental car reservation clerk.
10. *Harry*   Guard at Jones Computers.
11. *Sarah*   New receptionist at Jones.
12. *Tim*   Software salesman at Jones.
13. *June*   Teller at bank.
14. *Liz*   Hostess at Denny's.
15. *Dorah*   Waitress at Denny's.
16. *Jim*   Introduced to at lunch.

Note that you don't have to meet the person to have them go on the list. On this day, you called to make a plane reservation, and they answered, "United Airlines, this is Carla. How may I help you?"

You were careful to mentally note her name, and when you said you goodbye, you said, "Thank you, Carla."

When you called for the rental car, they answered, "Budget Rental Car. This is Jean. For what city please?"

You responded, "Jean, this is for Boston on October 4th. Do you have a special on a full-sized car?" When you completed the conversation, you were again careful to use Jean's name when saying goodbye.

What does all this accomplish? It forces you to pay attention to names. It may not be important to remember the airline reservation clerk's name and use it when you say goodbye, but it is excellent training.

The way the game is played, if you forget a name, you're out for that day. You still work on your memory skills of course, but the game is over until tomorrow.

The enjoyable part of the game is to play with it, make it fun, and see if you can beat your previous personal best. It's a great way to hone your memory skills and have a little fun while you're doing it.

Why not have a little side bet going with your significant other? The one who has the shortest list at the end of the day has to cook or pay for dinner?

So the next time I meet you, I want to hear you say, "Hi Roger, and you're number 16 for the day." I'll know exactly what you're talking about!

How Important Is It to Remember Names?

Is it really worth all this effort to improve your ability to remember names? Power Persuaders know it is.

During the first six or eight months of our life, we hear our name about 8,000 times before we finally recognize it as our personal identity! In school it's the first word we learn to write. We grow up not wanting our name to be slandered or tarnished. We'll do almost anything to protect our good name. And it's one of our most valuable assets. We can borrow money "against our name." If somebody has the nerve to forge our name, we accuse them of a felony and hope they'll be put in jail, where their name will be taken away and replaced with a number. That's how important our names are to us.

Isn't it obvious that being able to remember a person's name is a major part of Power Persuasion?

And what is your potential for remembering names? How good could you get at it, if you really worked at it? Your full potential is that you'd never forget a name, even if you didn't meet that person for 20 years. That's your potential. That's what your 13 billion brain cells are capable of doing. If we reached 10 percent of our potential, people would call us brilliant at it.

Using these techniques may never make you brilliant with names, but isn't it worth the effort to get close? Power Persuaders know that using a person's name is a key element in personal charisma.

Key Points From This Chapter

1. Remembering names is the number-one communication ability that every salesperson wishes they could perfect. It sets buyers up to be influenced by you.

2. There is no magic key to remembering names. It's just hard work!

3. Remember your mental trigger for remembering names. When you meet someone, observe the color of his or her eyes, and think of his or her name.

4. Work with the six steps to committing a name to long-term memory:

    a. Clarify the spelling.

    b. Confirm how they like to be addressed.

    c. Use rhyming slang to confirm the pronunciation.

    d. Relate the name to a famous place or person if possible, and add the ridiculous visual image.

    e. Use the name as quickly as possible, asking them to repeat it if you've forgotten. Use space repetition recall to bring up the name two more times at two-to-three minute intervals.

    f. Use the name again when you say good-bye, once more asking for the name if you've forgotten.

5. Don't try to emulate or outdo the memory experts, because it will only frustrate you. Give yourself every advantage, such as:

    -   Making a file card on each of your business associates and customers or clients.

- Updating the card with a few brief comments every time you meet with that person.
- Maintaining a card on your friends also, so that you can refer to their spouse and children by names and make reference to their hobbies and interests.
- Research a company's Web site before you make the call. It will refresh your memory.

6. The key to remembering faces is the outrageous visual picture. This of their most prominent facial feature, and invent an OVPA that leads you to their name, such as, watery eyes, waterfall, Yosemite Falls, Mr. Parks.

7. Become aware of everybody's name and use it, even the telephone operator at a company, for example, or the airline reservations clerk.

8. Play the memory discipline exercise game. See how many consecutive names you can remember during the day.

9. Nothing is more important to us than our name. If you only developed 10 percent of your true ability to remember names, people would call you brilliant.

Part Four

Learning Persuasion Techniques

IN PART ONE, YOU LEARNED HOW TO PLAY THE PERSUASION GAME.

In Part Two, you learned how to analyze the buyer.

In Part Three, you read about the personal characteristics of a Power Sales Persuader.

And in Part Four, I'll teach you a magic technique that I learned from a former prisoner-of-war interrogator, which he believed could get anybody to tell him anything he wanted. You'll be amazed at how effective it is.

Then, I'll show you eight ways to persuade the angry buyer.

Finally I'll address the question that salespeople ask me more than any other, which is, "How can I get the buyer to open up and start talking to me?" I'll teach you the eight reasons why buyers won't open up and what you can do about it.

21

A Magic Persuasion Technique

L ET ME TELL YOU ABOUT A PERSUASION TECHNIQUE THAT'S SO SIMPLE, and so effective, that's it's amazing so few people are aware of how powerful it is.

I learned it from Al Tomsik, a friend of mine who used to interrogate Japanese prisoners of war during World War II. He told me that when he used this technique it was certain he would eventually persuade the prisoner to give him the information he wanted. He said it was so powerful that even prisoners who came into the interrogation room willing to die rather than give any information would break down and tell him what he wanted to know without any physical threats at all.

I've used the technique consistently for several years now and found that it has remarkable effects. It will soothe an angry person, draw out a non-communicative person, and measurably increase your percentage of positive responses.

Because it's so simple, I'm concerned that you'll dismiss it without taking the time to see how powerful it can be for you. However, Power Persuaders can develop it as a magical persuasion tool.

This simple technique is to use the person's name, at the start or end of a sentence, and make your request. You must tilt your head a little and smile as you say his or her name.

1. Use the buyer's name at the beginning or the end of a sentence.

2.   Make your request.

3.   Tilt your head and smile as you say it.

Doesn't that sound incredibly simplistic? What on earth is the big deal about that? Try it and you'll see how magical it is. Experiment by leaving out one part of it, and you'll see how important it is to do it just the way I'm telling you.

Let's say that you want to get a refund on something at a store, and you don't have the receipt. You walk up to the clerk and you say, "Please refund this for me. I'm sorry, but I don't have a receipt." You're polite, but unsmiling. The clerk is probably going to hassle you over the refund.

Now try it again. This time, note the clerk's name from his name tag and say, "Good morning, Larry. Would you mind refunding this for me? I'm sorry, but I don't have a receipt." As you finish, you flash Larry your most sincere smile, and tilt your head slightly as you hold his gaze. Larry wonders for a moment if you're honest and sincere, and then quickly grants your request.

Why the Magic Formula Works

What do Power Persuaders find so magical about this? Let's take each element of the technique separately.

First, the use of the buyer's name. Naturally, we know that using a person's name is music to the ears. When greeting people as they come into my seminars, I've learned how to read their name badges with peripheral vision, so they can't tell I'm doing it. When I greet a stranger by name and they've forgotten they're wearing a name badge, the effect startles them. I'm meeting them for the first time, but I say, "Hi, Joe. How's it going?" Joe's not sure if I've met him before, or whether somebody else has pointed him out as an important person for me to meet. Yet, the response is always pleasant surprise and a warm return greeting.

Second, the tilt of the head. Power Persuaders know that the tilt of the head is a basic body-language skill. You can tell whether a person is hearing what you're saying just by watching for this. If the head is straight up, it's almost certain that his or her mind is miles away. A slight tilt of the head means that he or she is paying attention. Unconsciously we know this, even if we're not aware of it. When you use this with people, they sense that you are listening and concerned about them, even if they don't know why they're getting that message. Tilting the head very slightly gives intensity to your persuasion.

Third, the use of a smile. What power there is in a smile! As Laurence Sterne wrote, "I'm firmly persuaded that every time a man smiles, it adds something to this Fragment of Life." You can make the most outrageous requests of people and get away with it, as long as you keep smiling!

Put the three together and it makes a dramatic difference to the way you come across.

Let's say that your name is John. You've just come home from a busy day and you're in your favorite recliner. The *CBS Evening News* is on and you're glancing through the day's mail. Dan Rather is just finishing a story, and you hear him say, "And that's something we all need to be concerned about, wouldn't you agree, John?" At the sound of your name, you look up sharply, and Dan Rather is looking at you expectantly with a big smile on his face. Suddenly you're drawn into the scene, and he's asking for your positive response.

Sure, that's a dramatization, and the impact one on one is subtler than that, but there's no question that this technique will improve your persuasion batting averages.

How to Use the Formula

Here's how you can use this formula: Imagine that you sell office copy machines. You've been faithfully servicing one of your major accounts for years and regularly stopping by to see that everything is running smoothly. You've trained their new operators as the need arose. The company is about to move into a new, larger headquarters, and you're looking forward to writing a big new order for additional machines. Then you find out that they're already considering two proposals from your competitors, and they didn't even ask you to bid!

You make an appointment with the vice president in charge of operations and say, "All that I'm asking is that you listen to my proposal with an open mind. Fair enough, Harry?"

A slight tilt of the head and an open smile. Irresistible, right? Even if his mindset was that he wouldn't even listen to what you had to say, you'll see his resistance melt.

Probably, your problem here is one of credibility. Over the years, he's come to think of you as a repair person, not a salesperson. Your persuasion challenge is to change his perception of you.

Remember that credibility is such an important issue in persuasion that I devoted all of Chapter 3 to that one issue.

Let's say you're a sales manager and you've decided to institute a change in procedure that you know won't be popular. Perhaps the change is that you will no longer reimburse any item on an expense account, regardless of how minor, unless the employee attached a written receipt.

To help persuade your people that this is a needed change, you've selected the three salespeople who have the most influence with the rest of the force. You're going to sell them on the plan before you announce it. Smart thinking, right?

There's a knock on the door, and one of the people with whom you've made an appointment, Joe, is there. "Come in, Joe," you say with a warm grin on your face. "Have a seat. I've got a new policy to implement, and I want to ask for your support."

Does that meet our criteria? No, it doesn't. Although it's true that you used the name and smiled, it wasn't at the end of the key sentence.

Let's try again. Knock, knock. "Come in. Have a seat. I've got a new policy to implement, and I want to ask for your support, Joe." Now whip out a big smile as you begin to say his name.

That little shift in emphasis is what makes the magic formula work. It may be all that you need to get Joe over into your column.

Am I saying that this little technique will get Joe to support you regardless of how badly he thinks of this new policy when you explain it to him? Of course not. However, Power Persuaders know that whether you get support from a person often doesn't depend on the issue at hand. They really don't feel strong enough about it one way or the other. Their support often depends on nothing more than their attitude when you first present the idea to them. The technique is a great one to position them to feel receptive to your proposal.

Key Points From This Chapter

1. Use the buyer's name at the beginning or end of a sentence.
2. Make your request.
3. Tilt your head and smile as you say it.

22

8 Ways to Persuade an Angry Buyer

L
EARNING TO BE A GOOD PERSUADER IS A LITTLE LIKE LEARNING warfare in military school. All the things you learn make perfectly good common sense. They seem logical and you're sure they'll work. Then you get out onto a real battlefield, and the wheels come off! You're shocked into the realization that the other side hasn't gone to the same school. They're not fighting by the same rules with which you were taught to do battle.

What's the similarity between that and learning Power Persuasion? All the things I've taught you will work fine, until you run into someone who's not playing by the same rules. The "rules" in this case being politeness, common courtesy, and acting in their best interests. In other words, the difficult person.

In this chapter I'm going to teach you to deal with the buyer who's so angry with you, or the world, that he or she can't see straight. It's one thing to persuade a calm person who's thinking logically. It's another thing completely to persuade someone who's so angry that they're reacting irrationally.

The thing that separates the ordinary persuader from the Power Persuader is that the later can handle even the difficult person and still come away with two basic requirements: getting what is wanted and getting it by persuading him, not with tricks or manipulation.

Running unexpectedly into a furious person is akin to stepping on a land mine. You're looking forward to a pleasant experience with someone with whom you've dealt in the past, and suddenly *KAPOWEE*!! You're flat on your back wondering what on earth happened.

Even surprise is preferable to dreading a meeting with someone you know is angry. "The vice president wants to see you in his office at three sharp," your secretary says, "and wow, did he sound mad!" That kind of thing is enough to ruin anyone's day, isn't it?

Or how about this one: Your best account faxes you from Atlanta, and says, "Serious problems. Be here at 9 a.m. tomorrow. It's suggested you bring legal counsel."

We've all had to deal with angry buyers, so let's look at how to approach them. What can we do to resolve the problem, and what we can do to persuade them to our points of view?

Technique 1: Are you the target?

The first consideration should be this? Are you the cause of the anger, or is the person upset with someone else, and it's just rubbing off on you?

Laura Huxley, the widow of the great author Aldous Huxley, wrote a book titled *You Are Not The Target* that talks about this syndrome. She holds that when people are rude to you, it's very seldom you with whom they're upset. It's the person they ran into before you. First, decide if you're the target of their anger or if it's really somebody or something else.

Perhaps you selling food products to supermarkets and you're trying to get the buyer to allow you to put demonstrators in their stores to hand out samples of your new passion-fruit piquant sauce. As we discussed in Chapter 13, it's important to exorcise the problem. You might come right out and say, "I can tell that you've had a bad experience with this kind of thing in the past. Why don't you tell me about it?"

My experience is that people are very willing to share their feelings with you. People who "wear their anger on their sleeve," are very often doing so because they want to air their feelings but don't know how.

The response you get in this situation may be, "Sure, I'll tell you why I'm upset with you guys. The last time we let demonstrators in they left a mess all over the floor. A customer slipped in it and we got hit with a law suit."

Psychologists will tell you that almost all depression is caused by internalized anger. It's very therapeutic for you to encourage the buyer to get his anger out. I agree that you're there to sell your piquant sauce, not perform therapy, but if you don't do this, the buyer will internalize his anger even more and become even more resistant to your persuasion attempt.

I once asked a person for a contribution to United Way and he angrily told me that he wouldn't give any money if the Red Cross was going to get a share of it. Of course, a simple response to that would be to isolate the objection. It's easy to do and you avoid any confrontation.

You say, "Is that the only thing that's bothering you? You're telling me that you wouldn't have a problem with contributing to United Way, if you were assured the Red Cross wouldn't get any money from you?"

"No, I don't have a problem with those others. It's only the Red Cross I won't give to."

"Fine," you say, "we can handle that. We'll just exclude Red Cross from any part of your donation. There's a place to specify your charities right here on this pledge form."

However, isolating the objection isn't the best way to handle an angry person. If you've got the time, you're better off to let him get the anger out of his system. He is anxious to do that, and after he has vented his bad feelings, he'll be much more receptive to your persuasion.

In this case, I was curious. You don't often run into somebody who has anything against the Red Cross. What on earth did he have against them?

Apparently, when he was a soldier during World War II he'd pulled into a French railroad station on a troop train and the Red Cross was there selling cigarettes. He felt they should have been giving them away. All those years later, he was still burned up about it. Because he brought it up so eagerly, he clearly wanted to talk about it and get it out of his system. After he'd talked about it for a few minutes, he finally answered his question. "I guess they probably had a problem giving special treatment to smokers." Then he went ahead and made a generous contribution, without asking to exclude Red Cross.

So the first rule for persuading an angry person is to decide whether they're angry with you or with somebody else.

Technique 2: A magic expression.

If it really *is* you with whom they're upset, I've got a solution for you. It's a persuasion technique I learned at The Wilshire Country Club in Los Angeles, and I think it's pure magic. My golfing partner was Maurice, a very charismatic immigrant from Argentina, who'd become successful in the housing development business. One of the other players in our foursome was having a bad day. His game started off well, but then he really started flubbing shots. Maurice and I were off to the side of the fairway waiting for this man to hit. He made the mistake of "looking up" as he hit the ball and topped it, causing it to bounce only a few yards down the fairway. His face turned purple, and he came storming over to Maurice, accusing him at the top of his voice of talking during his backswing.

How did Maurice react? Did he deny it? Did he laugh at his friend for getting so upset? Did he try to put it off by saying, "It's only a game?" Or did he yell back, "Don't take it out on me, just because you're having a bad day!"

These things just would've made the other person angrier, wouldn't they? Instead Maurice, a master Power Persuader, pulled a magic expression out of his persuasion arsenal. He simply said with great sincerity, "David, my friend, I apologize to you, from the bottom of my heart." I watched with amazement as the anger drained out of the other man, like water draining out of a bathtub.

"Oh, that's okay," he mumbled. "It isn't your fault."

I don't know what it is that makes that expression so magical, but I've used it dozens of times since, and I've never seen anyone stay angry under the onslaught of its sincerity.

Try it the next time you're faced with a person who's angry with you. "I apologize from the bottom of my heart." You can never apologize too profusely, because the moment she feels that you've gone far enough, she'll let you know by accepting your apology.

Perhaps you've an appointment with a key buyer. You've eager to get her support for a key advertising program. Despite all the precautions that you take, you end up being 15 minutes late for the meeting. You squeeze his hand warmly, look into his eyes, and lay that magic expression on him.

"I apologize to you from the bottom of my heart." Then watch her anger melt away!

Technique 3: Restating the objection.

Another great technique for handling a person who violently disagrees with you is to restate the objection in a question form, without agreeing.

Let's say you're selling recreational vehicles. Your prospects look at the model, but they're clearly in a rotten mood. The husband pulls out a kitchen drawer, examines it, and says, "Boy, is this thing cheap. I could do a better job than this." If you're brand new in sales, you may take that as a rejection of this model and try to sooth things over by saying, "Let's look at the next one. You may like that better."

If you're a little more experienced, you may have heard that objection before, and you're prepared to counter it. So you say, "But don't forget that weight is very important. If it was made with heavier materials, it would take more gas to run and cost a lot more to operate."

However, if you're a Power Persuader, you simply say, "You feel that you could build better cabinets?" Don't be sarcastic. Simply restate the objection. This will quickly tell you if it's a problem about which the person is really concerned or whether it was just a passing comment.

Often, you'll find out he was just making conversation. When you feed back the objection, "You feel that you could build better cabinets?" he'll often reply, "Yes, I used to be a cabinet worker, and I was good too. Still, it seems like nobody can afford that kind of quality anymore."

Having found out the objection isn't going to be a deal breaker, you can move to isolating the objection. You might say, "Is the quality of the cabinets the only thing that's bothering you?" He responds, "No, the price is ridiculous too." So you counter, "If we made the price right for you, could you live with the cabinets?"

He could say, "You'd practically have to give it to me." Now you can start to close him. "Let's sit down and see how far apart we are. Fair enough?" Notice that you never mention the buyer's bad mood or in any way react to it. If you're not the target, why should it bother you?

Technique 4:
"That hasn't been my experience."

We've seen how we can handle the angry person's objection by restating it, but not agreeing with it.

Another, slightly stronger, way to handle the angry party is to acknowledge her problem, but to disagree gently with her, using the, "that hasn't been my experience," technique. Communications expert Connie Merritt taught me this one.

Let's say your VP of marketing yells at you, "This promotion slogan really stinks, Joe. We'd be a laughing stock if we used it!"

"That hasn't been my experience," you quietly reply.

"We can't tell our customers the competition sells more corn flakes than we do. They'll buy from our competition!"

"That hasn't been my experience."

"And what's this about an 800-hundred number so they can call in and complain? The call would cost more than the corn flakes. We'd go broke."

"That hasn't been my experience."

The boss is finally beginning to run out of steam.

"Well, Joe, since you've got so much experience, why don't you tell us exactly what your experience has been!"

At this point, you've positioned the marketing VP to be receptive to your ability to persuade her. Isn't that a great idea? Be careful you're not combative when you say it. Keep it very low key, almost under your breath: "That hasn't been my experience."

You shouldn't attempt to persuade an angry person before you've prepared the persuasion by smoothing things over, any more than you should start to paint a fence before you've prepared the surface by scraping off the old flakes of paint and sanding the surface smooth.

Technique 5: Handling the showperson.

Some angry people are so insecure that they're heavy-handed in their approach. Even though a simple suggestion would do, they feel it necessary to use threats.

You're manning a booth at an industry convention. Your regional manager storms in one day, in a foul mood.

"Harry," he screams, "this place is a disaster. Get it cleaned up, or I'll get someone in here who can."

If this is out of character for your regional manager, get concerned. However, if he always comes on strong like this, there's no point in aggravating the situation.

"Don't worry, Mr. Jones. I'll get it fixed, and I'll get it fixed right now."

Mature people don't let the screamers of the world get their blood pressure up.

Though this incident happened many years ago, I can remember it clearly. I was the Merchandise Manager of a large department store in Bakersfield, California. My job was to get the sales moving, and I was willing to do what it took to accomplish that. I was in the appliance department when Jimmy Kephart, one of our top salespeople, was caught about to ring up a transaction at a sale price, the day before the event was supposed to start.

The store controller, a classic bean counter, was screaming at him, "I could get you fired for doing that! Don't you dare ring that sale up!"

Jimmy calmly said, "Oops, my mistake." Then he put the salescheck away. The controller stormed off with a look of self-righteous satisfaction on his face. I moved in to salve Jimmy's wounds and give him a little pep talk.

It wasn't necessary.

When I got there, he had calmly retrieved the sales slip and was ringing it up again.

He cheerfully said to me, "Isn't life wonderful? Every day you learn something new."

"Wow, what a positive attitude," I thought.

Jimmy continued. "Today I learned not to ring these up when the controller's around."

What common sense! Why go to war with someone who's going to retreat soon anyway? When faced with a showperson, learn to back off.

Technique 6: Don't exacerbate the situation.

When faced with an angry person, don't make the situation worse. It's amazing how little situations can get completely blown out of proportion. Just because somebody gets on his or her high horse and decides that he's not going to let the buyer get away with something.

It's equally amazing how a little bit of tolerance can make even the thorniest of problems go away. In July 1988, Attorney General Edwin Meese was in trouble. He was under investigation on several charges of impropriety, and the Democrats were holding him up as an example of corruption in the Reagan administration. Although he was never prosecuted, he was forced out of office by the problems.

In Washington, the hottest-selling tee shirt of the summer had Ed Meese's picture on it, with the slogan "Ed Meese is a Pig." A man making a delivery to the Justice Department was wearing one of the tee shirts. They told him he couldn't come into the building wearing a shirt that contained a derogatory comment about their leader.

He said, "This is America. I can wear what I want." Every day he showed up in the shirt, tempers flared. He was clearly baiting the Justice Department. An attorney who worked there, hoping to please the boss, filed a lawsuit and sought an injunction to prevent him from wearing it.

He went to the Civil Liberties Union, and they filed a counter-lawsuit, claiming his protection under the principle of free speech. When it hit the evening news, Ed Meese heard about it for the first time. "I don't care what he wears," he said. "I've got much bigger problems to worry about." And it was all over. The whole problem simply went away, because the attorney general chose not to be concerned by it. The man made deliveries in his T-shirt for a few more days and then quit wearing it because it wasn't fun anymore.

A woman once walked into an Indiana supermarket and took a grocery checker hostage at gunpoint. What did she want? She wanted the local newspaper to print a statement on its front page. I'm sure you've heard of situations such as this ending in disaster. The newspaper refuses to be blackmailed, the politicians get involved, the SWAT team starts shooting, and people get killed. But not in this instance. What happened? The newspaper editor said, "We don't have any problem printing her statement." It printed a rambling statement the woman dictated to them, the content of which didn't make sense to anyone. The woman turned over her gun and went to jail. The whole problem just went away.

How much simpler does it need to be? When faced with angry people, at least consider the possibility of ignoring the problem or simply going with their demands.

Technique 7: First find out what they want.

The first stage of persuasion, establishing objectives, is particularly important when dealing with an angry person. First, get them to tell you what it would take to resolve the problem.

Let's say you're at home one Sunday afternoon, watching a tennis match on TV. In one hand you've got the channel changer for the commercials. In the other you've got a glass of beautifully chilled Chardonnay. You're having a good time! Got the picture?

In the distance you hear a car coming at high speed. It's roaring down the highway. It swerves into your street on two wheels. It comes to a skidding, screeching halt in front of your garage. The car door slams open and shut. The front door of the house is flung open. Your spouse storms into the living room and yells at you, "Well, you've done it to me again!" What do you respond?

You're wrong if your response was, "Done what?" or "What are you upset about?" Power Persuaders know the correct response should be, "I'm sorry you're upset. What is it you want me to do?" First find out what your spouse wants you to do. The request may be so small you're better off to go with it.

Your spouse may say, "I want you to apologize to my mother!"

Then you can respond, "Fine. Hand me the phone." You can resolve this during a commercial break. You don't even have to put your Chardonnay down!

Technique 8: Charm them to death.

For sheer charm in dealing with angry people, you can't beat this story. British film producer and director Sir Alexander Korda once promised a part in his new movie to English actress Ann Todd. However, he reneged at the last moment and gave the part to someone else.

She was furious and let Korda know exactly how she felt about him. "I wouldn't have done it to anyone else," said Korda, "but we're such good friends I knew you'd forgive me."

Key Points From This Chapter

1. Decide if you're the target. Are they angry with you or somebody or something else?

2. Try this magic expression: "I apologize to you from the bottom of my heart."

3. Restate the objection: "You think it's too expensive?" Then, see if they restate it or back off.

4. If this is a person who's habitually angry, consider appeasing, rather than antagonizing him or her.

5. Be careful not to exacerbate the situation by needlessly taking a stand on principles—when the wisest course of action may be to agree to their demands.
6. Be sure you completely understand what it would take to resolve the problem before you make any concessions to them.

23

The 8 Reasons Why
Buyers Won't Open Up

I N THIS CHAPTER, I'LL TEACH YOU HOW TO PERSUADE THE CLAM—THE buyer who just won't talk. He won't respond to any of the suggestions or proposals you make, and you never know where you stand with him. Apart from the angry person, the next most challenging buyer to deal with is the clam.

This especially applies to a salesperson who can't get the customer to raise objections. If you're not in sales, you'd think the last thing a salesperson wants to hear is an objection. But in reality, salespeople *love* objections. Only people who have objections buy. People who just agree with everything, aren't buyers—they're lookers.

My background is as a real-estate broker. In real estate, we knew that if we showed potential buyers a home, they weren't going to buy if they walked through it saying, "Isn't that great, don't you just love the kitchen, isn't the view fantastic?"

It was the people who said, "The kitchen's a bit small. We'd have to knock that wall out. Isn't that wallpaper ugly?" They were the real buyers.

In today's overheated real-estate market, if you've got somebody who doesn't think the price is outrageous, you know you've got a "looky-loo" on your hands.

Figure Out Why Won't They Talk

So we're faced with the challenge of persuading someone who has clammed up. She just won't talk.

Why won't she talk? The first step must be to figure out why the buyer is so unresponsive. There are eight reasons she won't open up. If you guess the wrong one, you're going to make the situation worse. Either she'll become even more determined to be uncommunicative, or she'll do the opposite and you'll have an angry buyer problem on your hands.

Let's run down the eight reasons, with a quick action plan for each.

The First Reason: Obsession

The first reason is "obsession." They can't concentrate on what you're saying because they're obsessed with another issue. Maybe the boss just told him or her they're being transferred to the head office in New York. Or the spouse just called to say they have five numbers correct on the state lottery, and they'll know next week if they've won $50 million. Perhaps his daughter didn't come home last night. Or his or her competitor for that big promotion has just been called to the president's office.

The only way to handle the obsessed is to confront the problem. But do it gently. "What is it that's bothering you, Joe? Perhaps I can help."

In my experience, there are two ways that this thing can go from there. Either Joe will shrug off the problem and start concentrating on your proposal, or he'll say, "It's really tough for me to concentrate right now. Could we talk about this again Monday morning? Would 10 o'clock be good for you?" Clearly this leaves you well positioned for a successful meeting Monday.

Cheerfully agree, and you've built up some obligation power, which I talked about in Chapter 4. However, don't immediately jump on this, because you have another option and it could be valuable.

You could risk going for a fast close. "Joe, I'd be happy to meet with you Monday, but it isn't that big a deal. I've determined we need a distribution center in Seattle to cover our northwest territory. We'll cut our freight costs by 3.2 million dollars a year. All I need is an okay to spend $75,000 on a site-selection study."

Because the human mind is incapable of holding two thoughts at once, Joe's going to have to force his mind off the yacht he'll buy with his $50 million lottery winnings. If your proposal doesn't sound that outrageous to him, he's going to say, "Sure, go ahead."

If the proposal freaks him out, he's going to say, "Fred, you know that kind of thing ought to go to the board. Let's talk about it Monday." Still, in going for the quick close, you usually have everything to gain and very little to lose.

The Second Reason: Inhibition

The second reason for silence may be inhibition. Some people won't talk simply because they're shy. If you know the buyer it's a lot easier to know what's going on. If you don't, this one can really fool you.

Often, I've thought I was dealing with someone who was hostile or aloof. Yet, when I've mentioned it to somebody who knew the person better, he'd say, "Oh, she's just shy when she meets someone for the first time. Once she gets to know you, she's terrific to work with."

Check it out by turning the conversation to something with which the person will be comfortable—maybe the picture of a child on the wall, or the way the office is decorated. If the buyer immediately turns into a chatterbox, you've found the answer.

It may take you longer to build rapport with shy people, but it's worth it. They bond well, and you'll probably have a great business relationship in the future.

Salespeople know how to draw out the inhibited by asking them questions. I go as far as to say that asking questions is the very definition of selling. When you're asking questions, you're selling. When you quit asking questions, you're not selling any more. I don't know what you're doing; maybe you're giving a seminar or something, but you're not selling.

Of course, the way you ask questions makes all the difference in drawing people out. You *must* ask open-ended questions. Questions shouldn't be answered with a yes or a no. Try this game with a friend. Ask a series of questions that start with a what, where, when, how, why, or who. Challenge him to see if he can answer that question with a yes or a no.

Let me illustrate that to you. See if you can answer any of these questions with a yes or a no:

1.   *What* country was host to the 1996 Olympic Games?
2.   *Where* were the Winter Games held in 1998?
3.   *When* were the games held in Helsinki?
4.   *How* much did NBC pay to televise the Sydney Olympics?
5.   *Why* would they pay so much?
6.   *Who* was the president of the network at that time?

It can't be done, can it? Because you're asking questions that invove what, where, when, how, why, or who, he or she has to respond with something more than a yes or no.

If the inhibited person is asked an open-ended question—one that starts with one of the six words—he's forced to elaborate on his answer, and you'll be drawing him out of his shell.

The Third Reason: Apathy

The third reason is apathy. Some people aren't talking because they just don't care. He's just been told he's being transferred to El Paso and intends to quit instead. Or the one true love of his life just left for Buenos Aires with a tango dancer and all he wants to do is survive the day without an emotional collapse. Perhaps the board of directors just laughed at the expansion proposal he's been working on for the last six months. The one that was going to get him a vice presidency.

You're going to have to romance the apathetic for a few minutes, until you can bring him or her back from the brink. Don't talk about business. Talk about snow-capped mountains, alpine meadows in springtime, and the laughter of children at the beach. Slide in a little bit about moonlight cruises to Bora Bora on barefoot windjammers. When the person's eyes begin to focus again, you can get back to business—and how your proposal is going to make all that possible.

The Fourth Reason: Sulking

The fourth reason for silence comes from the sulker. This person won't talk to you, because she's still upset with you for some grievous wound you inflicted upon her. Instead of getting angry, she's going to let you know how they feel by sulking.

Whether you're really guilty of the offense or not doesn't have much meaning for the sulker. One of her best people quit to go to work for your company, and she's convinced that you stole the person. You sold her competitor goods at the same "once-in-a-lifetime" special price at which you sold them. Then the competitor broke an ad on the same day at 99 cents less.

Or, let's say your significant other thought you spent too much time with a co-worker at the office party the other night. It doesn't take much of this to have you praying for sulkers to turn into raving lunatics and start screaming at you.

At least that would get it out of their systems, and that's what you have to do with a sulker. Much like sucking poison out of a wound, you've got to bring that repressed anger to the surface and get it out. The way to handle these people is to tell a secret, make a confession, and ask a favor.

Take the Irangate crisis for example, when members of the Reagan administration were caught selling arms to Iran and using the money to fund the Contras in Nicaragua. President Reagan should have gone on television and said, "I really shouldn't be telling you this, but I'm so concerned about what happened that I think that your right to know is more important than keeping a National Security Council secret. We made a big mistake. We never should have done it, and it will never happen again. Maybe I'm asking too much, but I'm going to ask a big favor of you. I'm not going to ask you to forgive me, but I am going to ask you to trust me that this kind of thing will never happen again."

If he'd have done that, he probably could have saved us $50 million—the cost of the Senate investigation. And he could have had his administration back on track a year sooner than he was able to.

Lee Iacocca learned the same lesson when his executives were caught driving cars with the speedometers disconnected. Even when the cars were wrecked, they were being fixed and sold as new. Iacocca knew you're better off to tell a secret, make a confession, and ask a favor. Within a week he'd done away with a problem that could have done serious damage to the Chrysler Corporation.

Bring the anger out of a sulker, where you can deal with it. If it's been going on for a long time and doesn't look like it's going to get any better, you might risk a humorous approach. I once quit advertising on a radio station over a mistake that they'd made. I guess it says a lot that I can't even remember what the mistake was now. But after the account manager made the mistake, I'd let him call on me but I wouldn't buy.

Finally he said, "Roger, you haven't done any business with me for a year now. I admit I made a mistake, but how long do I have to do penance. There are folks out there who have committed murder and only done nine months!"

I laughed and agreed that maybe this had gone on enough, and I went back to doing business with him.

The Fifth Reason: Evaluation

The fifth type of person who's liable to clam up is the evaluator. This is the person who's not given to quick judgments. He or she needs to think things through before making a decision.

You can spot the evaluators because they've been open and talkative earlier, but now they've clammed up on you. I'm not talking about the "analytical"—the accountant or engineer personality that's so hard to bring to a conclusion. I'm talking about the average person who has some concerns.

Just as a pilot won't fly a plane without going through a formal checklist, the evaluator has a mental checklist he or she needs to run through, such as:

- "Who might criticize me for going ahead?"
- "Have I negotiated the best price I can?"
- "To which account should I charge this?"
- "Is there anyone else who ought to be in on this decision?"
- "Am I convinced that this is the best product or service available to me?"

If the evaluator has reached the point where he's going through his mental checklist, you've probably done everything you can to persuade him. The worst thing that you can do is talk to him, which prevents him from going through this process.

If a question comes up, answer it and shut up again. Salespeople call it the silent close. Make your proposal and *shut up!* The first person to talk loses. I once watched two salespeople do the silent close on each other. There were three of us seated at the table. One salesperson made a proposal to the other, and shut up. The other salesperson realized that he was doing the silent close and decided to teach the first one a lesson. He wouldn't talk either.

Both sat there, staring at each other. Daring each other to talk. I didn't know how it would ever get resolved. It seemed as though half an hour had passed, although it was probably only about five minutes.

Finally the impasse was broken when the second salesperson wrote *"Decizion?"* on a piece of paper and slid it over to the other. But he deliberately misspelled the word *decision*.

The first salesperson spotted the mistake and couldn't stop himself. He gleefully said, "You misspelled 'decision.'" And having started, he couldn't stop. He went on to say "Look, if you won't go with what I proposed, I might be willing to...."

He countered his own proposal before he even found out whether the buyer would accept what he had suggested!

When the evaluator starts talking again, but it isn't a question, it's time to go for the *assume close*: "So let's go ahead and get the paperwork out of the way."

The Sixth Reason: Penuriousness

The sixth kind of clam is the penny pincher. This person is so penurious that he gets nervous about the possibility of having to spend some money. You can spot these people because they're talkative, until the time you start talking about the price. Don't be fooled because you know these people has money in which to slosh around. Some really wealthy people are as tight as a wrestler's leotards.

Would you believe that some affluent people still order food in a restaurant based on the price of the dish? I know it's hard to believe, but some people are like that! They look down the menu and say to themselves, "I'd really prefer the Eggs Benedict, but they're $8.95, and I'm not worth that much. I'll have the bacon and eggs at $6.95."

Reducing the price when you see the penny pincher is getting uptight is very dangerous. If you think they're concerned about spending money, remember that they're usually more concerned you're going to cheat them. Special deals that you haven't told them about before can make them nervous.

Instead, keep on stressing the benefits, and the return on their investment. It's very important to reassure the penny pincher by showing them everything in writing.

The Seventh Reason: Time Pressure

The seventh type of person to clam up is the stopwatch. This person is the master of time management. His entire day is broken down into five-minute segments. He's all business, and he doesn't have time for chitchat. Be sure not to wreck his day by showing up late, and be sure to establish a time frame when you call to make the appointment. "This will take 30 minutes. Which would be better: Monday from 10 to 10:30, or from 11 to 11:30?"

Then when you get there, reconfirm the time frame. "So Joe, you have 30 minutes that you can devote to this, right? May I close the door?"

Sometimes people who aren't necessarily time-management freaks will clam up on you, if they're running behind schedule. Be careful if the appointment is just before lunch or at the end of the day. Many people will avoid Fridays, and I wouldn't dream of trying to sell somebody on the day before someone leaves for his or her vacation.

Also remember that time pressure can work for you. People become more flexible under time pressure. I've had tremendous luck getting banker loan approval on Friday afternoons. Bankers like to get their desks completely cleared off for the weekend and would rather not have any loose ends.

Whether you should avoid time pressure, or try to use it in your favor, depends on how good you think your chances are going in. If your request is within their normal parameters of doing business, go ahead and use time pressure. However, if your request is way out there and will take a lot of persuading, you're better to schedule when the buyer will have more time to work with you.

The Eighth Reason: Fear

The eighth type of person to clam up is the paranoid. Some people get very talkative when they're scared, but most people clam up. If buyers are concerned you're going to take advantage of them, you can almost feel the temperature in the room drop. Look for the pupils of the eyes to get smaller and for "withdrawal" body language, such as folded arms.

Quickly move to reassure the person, by telling her about your money-back guarantee and by going over the testimonial letters in your file. Perhaps you've been too pushy for her taste, so back off a little until she relaxes.

Although the simple answer may be that the way to get people to talk is to ask open-ended questions, you can see that there's much more to it than that. It takes a careful analysis of why the person has clammed up on you.

 ## Key Points From This Chapter

First figure out why they won't talk. There are only eight reasons:

1. The first reason is obsession. They can't concentrate on what you're saying because they're obsessed with another issue. Confront the problem, but do it gently. "What is it that's bothering you, Joe? Perhaps I can help." If they're still too preoccupied to

concentrate, set an appointment to discuss it later, or consider going for a fast close.

2. The second reason for silence may be inhibition. Some people won't talk simply because they're shy. Draw them out by asking open-ended questions.

3. The third reason is apathy. Some people aren't talking because they just don't care. They're probably upset about something else that has happened in their life. Romance them with talk of the good things in life until they come back into focus.

4. The fourth type of clam is the sulker. He won't talk to you, because he's still upset with you about something you did previously. Bring that repressed anger to the surface and get it out.

5. The fifth type of clam is the evaluator. This is the person who needs to think things through before making a decision. Be quiet. Don't distract her by talking while she's thinking it over. When the evaluator starts talking again, but it isn't a question, it's time to go for the "assume close."

6. The sixth kind of clam is the penny pincher. This person is so penurious that he gets nervous about having to spend money. Don't offer to reduce the price. Just keep on stressing the benefits and the return on his investment.

7. The seventh type of clam is the stopwatch. This person has his entire day broken down into five-minute segments. Be sure to establish a time frame when you call to make the appointment. Then when you get there, reconfirm the time frame. "So Joe, you have 30 minutes that you can devote to this, right? May I close the door?"

8. The eighth type of person to clam up is the paranoid. Some people get very talkative when they're scared, but most people clam up. Quickly move to reassure the person by telling her about your money-back guarantee and by going over the testimonial letters in your file.

24

Sales Management and the Power Persuader

IN THIS FINAL CHAPTER, I WANT TO TALK TO YOU SALES MANAGERS. A SALES manager who is a Power Persuader can raise a floundering organization to great heights. A sales manager who doesn't know how to persuade can destroy even the strongest of sales teams.

There's no greater power of persuasion than that exhibited by a great leader, the uncommon being who leads men into battle like Norman Schwarzkoph, inspires a nation like Winston Churchill, dominates an industry like Bill Gates, or builds a great conglomerate like Jack Welch at General Electric. How do these great leaders use Power Persuasion to get people to follow them? And how can you use those techniques to become a world-class sales manager yourself?

The Sales Manager's Doctrine

I believe in a sales manager's doctrine so powerful that, if carried out fully and followed through to completion, is sure to lead to great success.

This is the doctrine that I believe sales managers should support with all their heart:

"I care more about the success of my salespeople than I do my future, but I care more about the organization accomplishing its mission than either one."

Great success in any sales organization comes from a balanced combination of three elements: the mission, the leadership, and the salespeople who make it happen.

By far the most important thing in this trinity is the mission. It's amazing to me how many sales organizations don't have a clear sense of purpose. Their people and assets are strewn around like a pile of iron filings, going in a myriad of different directions. Do you remember that experiment you did with iron filings when you were a kid? Just tossed in a heap on a piece of paper, the iron filings lay in a dozen different jumbled directions. Yet, when you pass a magnet under the paper, the filings are drawn to it and start lining up and moving in the same direction.

The mission is to the sales team, what the magnet is to the iron filings: It draws the team together and gets them moving in the same direction.

How to Develop the Mission

If you were to hire me to come into your company as a consultant, the first thing I'd do is sit with you and review your mission. That would probably tell me all I'd need to know. From that alone, I'd be able to tell you what's wrong with your business. I'd spend more time gathering supporting data to support my conclusion of course, but I could tell you what's wrong from the quality of your mission statement.

Harold Geneen is a legendary leader of American business. In the 18 years that he ran ITT, he took the company from sales of $750 million a year, and struggling to make a profit, to a huge conglomerate with sales of $16.7 billion and annual profits of $562 million. Along the way he acquired 350 different businesses in 80 countries, so it's no exaggeration to say he knew a thing or two about building companies.

Geneen says that you build a company the way that you read a book, except that you read a book from start to finish. You build a company in the opposite direction, from finish to start.

First, decide what the sales team is to become, and then research what's necessary to get them from the start of the story (where you are now) to the conclusion (where you want to be).

You and I would first sit down to discuss your mission statement. The four key elements of your mission are these:

1. Do you know exactly where you want to be five years from now?
2. Is it clearly and definitively expressed in one paragraph or less?
3. Is it in language that a 10th-grader could understand?
4. Is it a goal that will seem believable to everyone in your sales organization?

If your mission statement doesn't have these elements, I'd suggest you go back to the drawing board and work on it more. This one paragraph—your mission—is the key to your success as a sales manager.

The 4 Key Elements of the Mission

Let's look at each of these four elements:

First, do you know exactly where you want your sales organization to be five years from now?

Sometimes it's less important that you make the right decision than that you make a decision—*any* decision. There's a tremendous release of energy that comes from the decision to move in a particular direction.

Have you ever been at a point in your life when you're frustrated and can't decide which way to go? If so, you know what I mean. The longer it takes you to decide, the lower your energy level goes. Once you pick a direction, any direction, a great release of vitality follows. Suddenly you feel better, and you can concentrate more clearly, knowing you're on the move.

Second, is your mission statement clearly and definitively expressed in one paragraph or less?

This is a clearly-defined statement: To get a 60-percent share of the widget market, with a 32 percent gross margin, within a five-year period. This is very good! It's clear, it's specific, and it has a time frame.

A specific mission statement also tends to narrow your focus. In the mid-1980s, United Airlines went into a disastrous diversification program, which included acquiring Hertz rental cars and Westin Hotels. They dumped the name that had served them so well over the years, and United Airlines became Allegis.

The effect on morale at the airline couldn't have been worse. While they were spending billions to acquire other companies, the flight attendants were on strike to protest a cut in wages. For several months it was hard to find a United Airlines employee who had anything good to say about the company. It took a stockholder revolt, the firing of the president, and a well-written mission statement to get them back on track.

Third, is your mission statement in language that a 10th-grader could understand?

Remember: You'll have to persuade your entire sales force to follow you on this mission. Take a lesson from the carpenter from Galilee: Put it in terms everyone can comprehend. When Jesus said to Peter and Simon, "Follow me, and I will make you fishers of men," it was easy for them to understand. Also, he kept bringing them back into focus, with simple statements such as, "What shall it profit a man, if he shall gain the whole world, and lose his own soul?" Thank goodness that Jesus didn't have a Harvard M.B.A.! He'd have had his mission wrapped up in so much high-flying mumbo-jumbo that what he accomplished in a year of preaching would've taken decades.

Fourth, will your mission statement be believable to everyone in the sales organization, not just those on top?

When Lee Iacocca made his mission statement for the salvation of the Chrysler Corporation, he didn't attempt to say they were going to sell more cars than General Motors does. He didn't even say the goal was to be more profitable than General Motors was. The average employee quickly dismisses that kind of hyperbole.

He simply said, "We're going to make the best cars in America." That was something that all but the most pessimistic employee could believe was possible. Also, it was in plain enough language for them to understand.

The Importance of Informing the Troops

Having clarified your mission statement into an easy-to-understand paragraph, your next job is to see that everyone in the team knows what it is.

The problem is that most sales managers feel the salespeople are not sophisticated enough to care about corporate goals. Or that they are too self-serving to care. So they keep the objectives of the sales division privileged information and attempt to get the sales force in line with manipulation.

I believe that all salespeople and sales support people can understand a well-thought-out and clearly written mission.

It's easy to spot the companies that have done this. It's the hotel bellman who says, "If there's anything at all you need, you just call me. Our goal is to have the highest occupancy rate of any hotel in the city, and we can only do it if you're happy."

It's the secretary at the real-estate company that says, "We'll really work hard for you. Our objective is always to have the highest number of sold listings in our multiple listing service."

It's the service manager at the auto dealership saying, "We'll be happy to take care of it for you. We sold more pickup trucks than any other Ford dealer in the state did last month, and we plan to do it again every month this year. We need you out there, telling people how good we are."

As you know, organizations like that are rare.

Using Persuasion Skills to Sell the Mission

Having clearly projected the goal to everyone in the sales team, it's time to put your persuasion skills to work: to convince the sales force that the team is going to accomplish its mission. That's where all the things we've talked about in this book come into play.

The number-one factor in leadership persuasion is the ability to project that you have a consistent set of standards by which you operate. This is the same persuasion factor about which I talked in Chapter 9.

We all admire tough-minded leaders who have the courage to take a stand. However, all too often, we glorify them for all the wrong reasons. We admire Harry Truman because he, "gave 'em hell." It may be true that he "gave 'em hell," but that's not the reason we admire him. We admire him because he believed in something, and he projected the belief in his philosophy with all his heart.

Do we admire Jack Welch because of his tough language and his streetwise willingness to fight? No, we admire him because of his unwavering commitment in his beliefs. We respect conviction, not belligerence.

Ronald Reagan became the most popular president of the 20th century, although the vast majority of Americans didn't believe in many things he did, because we're drawn to people who fervently fight for that in which they believe.

Building Leadership Credibility

The next most important persuasion factor for sales managers is credibility. Be sure you're applying the credibility factors we talked about in Chapter 3. The first rule for credibility is "never tell them more than they'll believe." I hope you've built that into your mission statement. If you have any doubts about the credibility of your mission to the average salesperson, tone it down a bit. You might want to run it by a few people in the field, to test their reaction. A mission should be grand enough to be inspiring, but don't lose your credibility by stepping over the line into "never, never happen" land.

We talked about using precise numbers when quoting statistics. "Ivory Soap is 99 and 44/100s pure," seems very believable, when we might not believe 100-percent pure. That's why Taster's Choice decaffeinated coffee is 99.7-percent caffeine-free. If your expressed goal is a 20-percent increase in productivity, it may sound as if it's a figure dreamed up in a committee meeting. A 21.6-percent increase looks as though somebody really made an effort to come up with an accurate figure.

Minimizing the perception of personal gain was the next factor we discussed. Lee Iacocca made a brilliant move when he agreed to work for a dollar a year as he was asking the unions to roll back pay. Because of the stock options he had, it wasn't a huge concession to make, but the symbolism of it was enormous. Later, when he started making $20 million a year, he could make a case it was justified because of the sacrifices he'd made earlier.

Also, don't forget the power of the printed word. People believe much more what they see in writing than they do when they only hear it. Don't make the plant look as if Nazi propagandist Paul Goebbels runs your PR department, but putting posters of your mission statement up around the plant is a powerful force. It makes the doubters believe the goal is achievable, and they love the fact that you've stuck your neck out.

As you move toward your goal, you'll want to give recognition to the top producers in your newsletters and promotional pieces. However, be aware that many people react to this with a shrug of the shoulders. They can't relate to the superstars in your business. Power Persuaders know to include some "if they can do it, I can do it" stories. Tell the story of the person who moved off the assembly line into sales and sold $10 thousand the first month. It'll have a lot more impact than a piece about the superstar who sold $10 million worth.

Building Credibility When You're New on the Job

If you're new on the job, there may be some additional things you need to do to build credibility. I've been giving this advice to new managers for 20 years: Don't try to set the world on fire in the first 30 days. Unless you've been sent in to save a dying organization, you're better off to lay low during the first month. You won't be able to do much good in the first 30 days, and you could harm your credibility.

It's better to go to your office, put your feet up on the desk, and sit around for awhile. Let the sales force get used to the idea of a new leader. In 30 days they'll have forgotten that there was somebody else before you, and you can start to make your moves. You might want to let your boss know what you're up to, so that he or she is not wondering what's going on.

This first month doesn't need be unproductive. You can do a lot of getting to know people. Reread Chapter 20 on remembering names and see how many of your salespeople's names you can learn. Do some management by walking around. Hold meetings with the different districts and do more listening than you do talking.

When meeting with your people, try this approach: "I'm new here and I don't know enough yet to help you with the big problems. But maybe I can help you with the little problems. Who's got a little problem that's been bugging them?" You'll be surprised at the little things the employees have given up trying to get done.

You'll hear things such as, "I'd like to be able to e-mail the entire sales force when I need an answer to a problem," or "Why does it takes two weeks to get my expense account approved?"

It's a chance to be a real hero to your people, without having to play fast and loose with the company till. Be careful they don't bring up something that previous management has consistently rejected for good reason. It's important to follow through on every commitment you make, however small it may be. It's a good idea to have a knowledgeable assistant with you who can signal you if you're about to get into trouble.

Also be aware that, if you're new, you may not be as well known as you think. Your boss team may know that you've earned this promotion because of the brilliant job that you did in Cincinnati, but does your sales force know?

Michael Crichton, the brilliant author of *The Andromeda Strain, Jurassic Park,* and *Sphere,* tells a story about this in his autobiographical book *Travels.* He had just completed directing the movie *Coma* and it was being released in the United States with great success. He had been hired to direct *The Great Train Robbery* starring Sean Connery, to be filmed in Ireland. When he showed up on location, he began to feel frustrated because he wasn't getting full cooperation from the British crew. When he came up with an idea, they'd want to discuss alternatives rather than enthusiastically carrying out the suggestion.

In the understated style of the English, one of his assistants casually said, "I think the crew would enjoy seeing one of your films." However, Michael didn't pick up on it. A few days later, the problems had worsened, and the assistant said, "I wish we could see one of your films." Michael thought about it, and then didn't do anything. *Coma* was just being released in the States, and it wouldn't be easy for him to get a copy.

Finally, the assistant said firmly, "I really do think it would be nice if the crew had a chance to view one of your films." Suddenly, Michael realized what the assistant had been trying to tell him, but had been too reserved to come out and state in plain language: that the crew only knew him as an author. They lacked respect for his abilities as a director. He called Hollywood and had a copy of *Coma* airfreighted to him, and they screened it for the entire crew. Overnight the problem went away. The crew had loved the film, gained new respect for his abilities, and never questioned his decisions again.

Be sure everyone is told about your background and experience. Obviously, you can't do this yourself, because they will see you as egotistical. However, your company can handle it subtly for you or your assistant can see that the right things get said in the company newsletter.

Leadership and the Art of Consistency

The next factor that's critical to your leadership persuasion ability is consistency. Is the mission consistent with all they know about you? People can spot a phony a mile off. You're going to have a tough time if the mission comes down, and the people are saying, "Uh, oh! The boss must have been to another one of those seminars!" Top leaders are successful in large part because their actions are consistent with what people know about them.

A business value blueprint is essential to your success as a leader. This is a set of standards by which you run your operation. If the decision you're about to make doesn't conform to your blueprint, don't do it, despite the potential gain. Your people are much more concerned about what you stand for than they are about what you're claiming you can do. When they perceive that you've a set of standards by which you operate, it makes them feel more secure. They know that you won't act erratically by acting outside the perimeters of your values. What you are overrides what you do, every time.

Caring More About the Success of Your People

Now let's review our leadership doctrine again: "I care more about the success of my salespeople than I do my future, but I care more about the organization accomplishing its mission than either one."

Nothing will stop a sales manager faster than his sales force being convinced that the sales manager is pursuing the mission for personal gain—whether that gain be making money, getting promoted, or becoming famous. They can live with their leader getting those things, but it must be as a byproduct of the mission. It cannot be the purpose of the mission.

The accomplished sales manager is skilled in projecting that he cares more about his salespeople's success than he does about his own. If you do it well, you can get away with making your fortune and still not have the peasants storming the palace gates.

The Mission Is the Most Important Thing

Next, you must persuade your salespeople that the sales team making its mission is more important than the individual success of any one person—including you. This is what separates the superstar leader from the merely great. That takes real Power Persuasion skills, but it can be done. It's possible to get your people so worked up about a mission that even if they personally fall by the wayside, they'll still cheer the organization on.

Nowhere is this more clearly illustrated than in the sport of mountaineering. When I was young, I loved to climb mountains. At the 13,000-foot level of Mount Rainier in Washington, I ran into Phil Ershler, who has climbed Mount Rainier more times than any other man alive—more than 200 times. Phil was the central character in one of the most exciting annals of mountain-climbing history. He was a member of the 1984 team that attempted to climb Everest from the north side, from China, rather than the more popular route through Nepal. Only 16 people have ever done this before, and 10 died attempting it.

They were lead by Lou Whittaker, whose brother Jim was the first American on the summit of Everest, back in 1963. Also in the team was Lou's son, Peter, who had become an accomplished mountaineer in his own right. It was clearly Lou's dream that his son reach the top, but the team had enough confidence in Lou's leadership abilities to know that his son wouldn't get preferential treatment.

They'd attempted this climb two years before, with disastrous results. Marty Hoey and Chris Kerrebrock had fallen to their death in separate incidents.

This climb wasn't going well either. Bad weather pinned them down for weeks. Lou Whittaker's sun goggles failed him, and he had to retreat to base camp with snow blindness. Refusing help from his team members, who were needed to continue carrying supplies up the mountain, he descended blind and alone. It was almost a week before he would see again.

With their supplies almost exhausted, they made a last-ditch effort and sent a team of three climbers, Phil Ershler, John Roskelley, and Jim Wickwire, to the summit. Bad weather forced them to bivouac on the mountain overnight. Phil Ershler and Jim Wickwire were using oxygen, but John Roskelley didn't believe in using it. It was against his ethical principles to climb with the aid of oxygen, and Whittaker had reluctantly accepted this. However, now only one bottle of oxygen remained. Wickwire felt that Ershler was in better condition, and unselfishly told him to take the oxygen and go for the summit with Roskelley.

The two men got within a thousand feet of the summit and Roskelley could go no further. Without oxygen, his body was beginning to freeze from the inside. He insisted that Ershler unrope and go on alone.

They were not in visual or radio contact with Whittaker at Camp Four. But miles away, expedition photographer Steve Marts, with a high-powered telephoto lens, could see the two men separate, as Ershler start moving almost imperceptibly toward the 29,035-foot summit.

Even with oxygen, it's very hard to move at that altitude, and every step takes incredible effort: Raise the boot and kick the spiked crampons into the snow to form a foothold. Lock the other leg into place and rest for a second or two, allowing the oxygen in the bloodstream to reach the muscles, and then go for that next step upward. Concentrate, because it's all too easy to hallucinate when you're that high and forget where you are.

Hours later, he reached the summit ridge and crossed from China into Nepal. Inch by inch, profiled against the midnight blue sky, he moved upward until he stood on the summit. "We made it!" shouted Marts into the radio, relaying the success to the climbers down at the lower camp, who couldn't see the summit. "We made it!" Whittaker yelled at base camp. "We made it!"

The fascinating thing about all this, from a management point of view, is that the leader, Lou Whittaker, didn't make it to the summit. His son didn't make it. Every person except Phil Ershler failed in what they had personally set out to do. Yet, they all felt a tremendous sense of personal pride, because the team had completed the mission. They didn't say that Phil Ershler made it; they said, "We made it." When I talked to Phil about it, not once did he say, "I climbed Mount Everest." He simply said, "I was on the team that climbed Mount Everest."

This is a case study in brilliant leadership. Let's examine the two key components of it:

1. In terms of who would make it to the summit, Lou Whittaker had put himself and his son behind the others in importance. It's the first part of the leader's doctrine: "I care more about the success of my people than I do my future."

2. He had projected to the team that the mission was more important than the personal goals of any one person on the team. That's the second part of the leader's doctrine: "I care more about the organization accomplishing its mission than either one."

With the sales manager's doctrine, you can build that kind of dedication and esprit de corp into your sales organization. Then, you will be able to reach all your goals and be a hero to your people.

Painting the Picture of the Mission

Mountain climbing isn't the only area where the mission becomes more important than either the leader or the followers. Look at the story of Moses leading the Israelites out of Egypt. His mission was clear: to lead them to the Promised Land. However, he had a unique leadership problem. His followers knew he'd never seen the Promised Land—no one had ever seen the Promised Land. His ability to sell his followers on the mission depended largely on his skill at painting pictures in the minds of his followers.

Moses never reached the Promised Land, and many of his followers didn't get there. However, the mission was accomplished. Moses had given more value to the accomplishment of the mission than he did to either himself, or any other member of the team, making the goal.

The Essence of Persuasive Leadership

This, then, is the essence of persuasive leadership: the sales manager's doctrine:

> *"I care more about the success of my salespeople than I do my future, but I care more about the organization accomplishing its mission than either one."*

 # Key Points From This Chapter

1. Great success in any sales team comes from a balanced combination of three elements: the mission, the leadership, and the people who make it happen. The most important of these is the mission.

2. First you decide what the company is to become, and then you find out what's necessary to get the company to that goal.

3. The four key elements of your mission are:
    a. Know exactly where you want to be five years from now.
    b. Clearly and definitively expressing the mission in one paragraph or less.

      c.   Use language that a 10th grader could understand.

      d.   Make the goal believable to everyone in the sales organization.

4.   Don't hide your mission in the executive suite! All sales and sales support people can understand a well-thought-out and clearly written mission.

5.   Project that you have a consistent set of standards by which you operate.

6.   Build credibility with the tools I gave you in Chapter 3.

7.   Unless you've been sent in to save a dying organization, don't try to set the world on fire in the first 30 days. Build support by offering to solve the little problems.

8.   If your reputation got you the job, be sure your salespeople know about your reputation.

9.   Your people are much more concerned about what you stand for than they are about what you're claiming you can do. Be consistent in your actions.

10.   Believe in and live by the sales manager's doctrine: "I care more about the success of my people than I do my future, but I care more about the sales team accomplishing its mission than either one."

Postscript

The Secret of Power Persuasion

So what is persuasion? It's the ability to get someone else to do what you want him or her to do, whether by reasoning, urging, or inducement. This translates into the ability to make something happen. Sales persuaders are the motivating force in our society. Nothing happens until somebody sells something.

I've tried to show that Power Sales Persuasion is a combination of factors, among them personal charisma, the ability to project personal standards that are inspiring. A deep understanding that the essence of Power Persuasion is this: that others will only move in a given direction when they feel it's in their best interest to make that move.

So the key to effective persuasion isn't to concentrate on what you want to get from the buyer. Power Persuaders know the secret of Power Persuasion is to focus on what you can give to the buyer. When you give the buyers what they want, they'll give you want you want.

Index

About the Author

ROGER DAWSON WAS BORN IN ENGLAND, IMMIGRATED TO CALIFORNIA in 1962, and became a United States citizen 10 years later. Formerly the president of one of California's largest real-estate companies, he became a full-time author and professional speaker in 1982.

His Nightingale-Conant cassette program *Secrets of Power Negotiating* is the largest-selling business-cassette program ever published. Four of his books have been main selections of major book clubs.

Roger Dawson is the founder of The Power Negotiating Institute, a California-based organization.

Companies and associations throughout North America (and throughout the world) call on him for his expertise in negotiation, persuasion, and decision-making, and for motivational keynote speeches. His seminar company The Power Negotiating Institute, P.O. Box 2040, La Habra, California 90631 ([800]Y-DAWSON [932-9766]), conducts seminars on Power Negotiating, Power Persuasion, Confident Decision Making, and High Achievement throughout North America and around the world. Roger was inducted into the Speakers Hall of Fame in 1992.

Please contact Roger Dawson with any suggestions, criticisms, or questions by e-mailing him at *RogDawson@aol.com.*

Products and Services
by Roger Dawson

Speeches and Seminars by Roger Dawson

If you hire speakers for your company or influence the selection of speakers at your association, you should learn more about Roger Dawson's speeches and seminars. He will customize his presentation to your company or industry so that you get a unique presentation tailored to your needs.

Roger Dawson's presentations include:

- Secrets of Power Negotiating.
- Secrets of Power Persuasion.
- Confident Decision Making.
- The 13 Secrets of Power Performance.

To get more information and receive a complimentary press kit, please call, write, e-mail, or fax to:

Address:
The Power Negotiating Institute
P.O. Box 2040
La Habra, CA 90632

Phone: (800) YDAWSON (932-9766)
Fax: (562) 697-1397
E-mail: *Dawsonprod@aol.com*
Web site: *rdawson.com*

Roger Dawson's audio and videocassette albums are available from The Power Negotiating Institute. You can reach them at:

The Power Negotiating Institute,
P.O. Box 2040
La Habra, CA
90632

You can order by calling (800)YDAWSON (932-9766), faxing (562) 697-1397, or e-mailing *DawsonProd@aol.com*. All major credit cards are accepted.

Audio-Cassette Programs

Secrets of Power Negotiating
Six cassette audio album with workbook and 24 flash cards. *$65*

This is one of the best-selling business cassette albums ever published, with sales of over $28 million. You'll learn 20 powerful negotiating gambits that are sure-fire winners. Then, going beyond the mere mechanics of the negotiating process, Roger Dawson helps you learn what influences people, and how to recognize and adjust to different negotiating styles, so you can get what you want regardless of the situation.

You'll learn: A new way of pressuring people without confrontation. • The one unconscious decision you must never make in a negotiation. • The five standards by which every negotiation should be judged. • Why saying *yes* too soon is always a mistake. • How to gather the information you need without the other side knowing. • The three stages that terrorist negotiators use to defuse crisis situations. • And much, much more.

Secrets of Power Negotiating for Salespeople
Six cassette audio album. $65

This program which supplements and enhances Roger Dawson's famous generic negotiating program *The Secrets of Power Negotiating*, teaches salespeople how to negotiate with buyers and get higher prices without having to give away freight and terms. It's the most in-depth program ever created for selling at higher prices than your competition and still maintaining long-term relationships with your customers. It's guaranteed to dramatically improve your profit margins, or we'll give your money back.

Special Offer:

Invest in both **Secrets of Power Negotiating** and **Secrets of Power Negotiating for Salespeople** and save $20. You can buy both for only $110!

Secrets of Power Persuasion
Six cassette audio album. $65

In this remarkable program, Roger Dawson shows you the strategies and tactics that will enable you to persuade people in virtually any situation. Not by using threats or phony promises, but because they perceive that it's in their best interest to do what you say.

You'll discover why *credibility* and above all *consistency* are the cornerstones of getting what you want. • You'll learn verbal persuasion techniques that defuse resistance and demonstrate the validity of your thinking. • Step by step, you'll learn to develop an overwhelming aura of personal *charisma* that will naturally cause people to like you, respect you, and to gladly agree with you. • It's just a matter of mastering the specific, practical behavioral techniques that Roger Dawson presents in a highly entertaining manner.

Secrets of Power Performance
Six cassette audio album. $65

With this program, you'll learn how to get the best from yourself—and those around you! Roger Dawson firmly believes that we are all capable of doing so much more than we think we're capable of. Isn't that true for you? Aren't you doing far more now than you thought you could do five years ago? With the life-changing secrets revealed in this best-selling program, you'll be able to transform your world in the next five years!

Confident Decision Making
Six cassette audio album, with 36-page workbook. $65

Decisions are the building blocks of your life. The decisions you've made have given you everything you now have. The decisions you'll make from this point on will be responsible for everything that happens to you for the rest of your life. Wouldn't it be wonderful to know that, from this point on, you'll always be making the right choice? All you have to do is listen to this landmark program.

You'll learn: How to quickly and accurately categorize your decision • How to expand your options with a 10-step creative thinking process • How to find the right answer with reaction tables and determination trees • How to harness the power of synergism with the principle of Huddling • How to know exactly what and how your boss, customer, or employee will decide, and dozens more powerful techniques.

Beyond Goals — The Personality of Achievers
Six cassette audio album. $65

You can learn how to go beyond your most ambitious goals with this breakthrough program. Life's high achievers know that there is no substitute for action—the positive, disciplined transformations of thoughts into deeds. This program identifies what makes people high achievers and shows you what—and how—these super-successful people think, how they act, and how they inspire others to help them succeed. It contains fascinating studies of personalities and behavior and transforms them into practical, common sense strategies that will lead you to uncommon success.

Video Training Programs

Guide to Business Negotiations
One hour VHS video. $55

Guide to Everyday Negotiations
One hour VHS video. $55

Guide to Advance Negotiations
One hour VHS video. $55

If you're in any way responsible for training or supervising other people, these videos will liven up your staff meetings and turn your people into master negotiators. Your sales and profits will soar as you build new win-win relationships with your customers and clients. Then use these programs to develop a training library for your employees' review and for training new hires.

12-Part Sales Negotiating Video Series
Only $59.95 per month.

Think how your sales and your profit margins would soar if you could have Roger Dawson speak at your sales meetings once a month! Now you can, with this new series of 12 30-minute videotapes designed just for this purpose. Dawson goes one on one with your salespeople to show them how to out-negotiate your buyers. Play one a month at your sales meetings and watch your people become masterful negotiators!